"Pratt's second book featuring bad-girl sorcerer Marla Mason is just as awesome as the first volume, if not better. Marla's a fascinating protagonist with conflicting motivations, a truly awe-inspiring proclivity for violence and (finally!) sensible clothing.... Superbly written."   —*Romantic Times* (4.5 out of 5 stars)

"Pratt keeps the action lively in this wonderfully whimsical urban fantasy as the adventure of Genevieve takes some wonderfully imaginative twists and turns."   —*Publishers Weekly*

"*Poison Sleep* blends elements of fantasy, mystery, and horror, plus bits of our modern world, to create something more than a facile hybrid or even a page-turner."   —*Locus*

BLOOD ENGINES

"A fast-paced, thoroughly fun, satisfying read."
     —Kelley Armstrong, author of *No Humans Involved*

"*Blood Engines* wastes no time: by page three I knew I was reading an urban fantasy unlike any I'd previously encountered—the characters and world are real, immediate, and unapologetically in-your-face, throwing you into a story that trusts you'll keep up with the fast pace without flinching. It charges along with crisp pacing, a fascinating range of secondary characters, and a highly compelling lead in Marla Mason—her ruthless pragmatism gives her a completely different feel from her fictional contemporaries. I genuinely look forward to the next book!"
     —C. E. Murphy, author of *Coyote Dreams*

SPELL GAMES

T. A. PRATT

BANTAM SPECTRA

SPELL GAMES

A Bantam Spectra Book / March 2009

Published by Bantam Dell
A Division of Random House, Inc.
New York, New York

This is a work of fiction. Names, characters, places, and incidents either are the product of the author's imagination or are used fictitiously. Any resemblance to actual persons, living or dead, events, or locales is entirely coincidental.

ISBN 978-0-553-59136-1

Printed in the United States of America
Published simultaneously in Canada

www.bantamdell.com

OPM 10 9 8 7 6 5 4 3 2 1

For Susan,
part of the family I made

"*Everything that deceives may be said to enchant.*"
—Plato

"*There's a sucker born every minute . . . and two to take 'em.*"
—"Paper Collar Joe" Bessimer
or Michael Cassius McDonald
or David Hannum.
But definitely not P. T. Barnum.
If you thought Barnum said it, you were deceived.

SPELL
GAMES

1

arlita," the man said again, standing just inside the door to her office. He regarded Marla
with an expression of mingled admiration and delight,
extending his arms for a hug.

Marla Mason—ruthlessly pragmatic chief sorcerer of
Felport, a woman who'd recently outwitted the avatar of
Death, who'd once kicked a hellhound across a room,
who'd thwarted the king of nightmares, and who had
even killed a god (admittedly a very implausible one)—
stood behind her desk and stared at him. She'd already
said his name once. She didn't think she could bring herself to say it again just yet. There was a dagger in her
hand—when had she picked that up?—and she gently
put it down. "You. Here. Why?"

"Eloquent as always, little sis." He came around the
desk and swept her into his arms.

"Jason." She spoke into his shoulder, almost breathing out the word. Even his smell was familiar, the

smoke-and-whiskey scent of a bar's back room. She hadn't seen him in almost eighteen years. The time she'd spent without her brother in her life was, by now, years longer than the time they'd been close. Marla pulled away. "How did you find me?"

"You look beautiful, Marlita." He swept a stray strand of hair out of her eyes, and Marla froze. How long had it been since anyone had touched her so familiarly, so easily? Even her occasional lovers were tentative; they knew her well enough to be afraid a little, even in their intimacy. Jason wasn't tentative at all. He was family.

She grabbed his wrist, hard. "I asked you a question."

Marla was tall for a woman, but Jason had a couple of inches on her. He didn't fight, though. "A man can't visit his sister?" His voice was a perfect blend of surprise, concern, and just a hint of wounded feelings. Finely honed. She felt instantly guilty. Jason still had the knack of manipulation. No surprise there.

Marla let go of his wrist. She took a step back and frowned, looking him up and down. He was past thirty-five now, and his lean good looks were touched with something harder, something that hollowed his cheeks and bagged his eyes. Even the marks of wear and tear weren't ugly, though. They gave his face more character, made him seem like a guy who'd seen hard times, and could sympathize with your own suffering. His dark suit fit his frame perfectly, and his eyes twinkled, bags or not. Jason could have been a politician. He wasn't.

"You still on the grift?" Marla asked.

He raised one eyebrow. "Me? A grifter? Heavens, no.

I'm a legitimate businessperson now. Just like you. Nice nightclub, by the way." He sat down in one of the guest chairs before her desk.

She glanced at her friend and associate Rondeau, who had opened the door for Jason and now watched them with undisguised fascination. "It's his club, not mine."

Jason raised his hands and smiled, a smile that said, "We're all in this together," a smile that had emptied many a wallet and opened many a bedroom door. "No need to be coy with me, sis. I'm not from the IRS."

Marla rubbed her eyes. She'd had a long day—actually, a long summer—and this was too much. She'd rather face the literal vengeful ghosts of her enemies again than confront this haunt from her past. "I know it's not in your nature to cut the bullshit, Jason, but, really, why are you here? Do you need money or something?"

"Money's always welcome, of course, but I'm not interested in charity. I heard you were here in Felport, doing well for yourself, and . . . I actually have a business proposition for you." He glanced at Rondeau. "One best discussed in private."

"It's a bad idea to do business with family," Marla said. "It's a sure path to heartbreak. If that's all you wanted, I'll pass."

"Now, that's not the Marla I know and love. You were always curious, sis. Don't you want to know what I have to offer? It'll tempt and tantalize, I promise."

"I'm not sure what you know—what you *think* you know—about my business, but my situation here is complex, and I've got a full plate already. I said I'll pass."

"Marla—"

She held up her hand. "Jason, you're my brother, and that gets you a lot of slack, but keep pushing, and I'll have to push back."

Jason sighed. "I can respect that. You always did know your own mind, so I won't try to change it. I've got a hotel room, and I'm here for a few days at least, depending on how my business goes. Don't suppose you could spare an hour for dinner tomorrow? Or lunch, if being your long-lost brother doesn't entitle me to a whole dinner?"

"Fine. Dinner. Come by tomorrow around six, we'll figure something out."

He stood up, started to go, paused, turned back to her. "Hey. Sister. I didn't come to make trouble for you, I promise."

"Yeah?" She wanted to believe him, but Jason...she hadn't seen him since she was a teenager, and it was hard to forget those old bad memories. Hard to believe he'd changed. On the other hand, *she'd* changed, rather a lot, so maybe she was being unfair.

"Really. I just heard you were here and figured I'd look you up, see if I could interest you in a certain opportunity that's come my way. Sometimes I think back.... Remember when it was you and me against the world?"

Marla felt her throat begin to close. "That was a long time ago, Jason."

"Formative years." He nodded farewell.

Marla dropped into her chair.

"That's your *brother*?" Rondeau handed her a glass

of water. Sometimes it was good to have a friend who knew you that well.

She took a long drink, glad for the excuse it gave her to delay answering. When she spoke, she felt more in control. "Yes, he is. What tipped you off? The bit where he called me his sister?"

Rondeau sat down across from her, in the chair Jason had recently vacated, and whistled. "Damn. I knew you had a brother, but I guess I figured he was dead or in prison or something."

"I kind of figured he was one or the other of those myself."

"You seem a little shaken up. You all right?"

"Sure. My brother the con man shows up unannounced after nearly twenty years, talking about a 'business proposition'? I'm great. If it were anybody else coming at me with this crap, I'd just throw them out, but he's family. What am I supposed to do?"

"Don't ask me," Rondeau said. "I'm an orphan. This shit is a mystery to me." He paused. "It's not like you don't have any choice, though. If you really want to get rid of him, you are a sorcerer. You can make him forget he even saw you today."

Marla fiddled with the scythe-shaped letter opener on her desk and sighed. "Maybe it'll come to that. But I owe him a lot, from when we were kids, when it was just him and me and Mom and whatever asshole guy followed Mom home from the bar on any given night. Jason kept a lot of bad things from happening to me."

"He's a scam artist, huh?"

"Just small-time stuff when we were younger. Hustling pool, short counting, three card monte, convincing drunks to make unwinnable bar bets, selling fake football picks, shit like that. By his freshman year in high school he was so well known in the county that nobody would even play rock-paper-scissors with him, and he'd take weekend trips to Indianapolis to make money. But that was ages ago. Maybe he's reformed."

"Or maybe he's moved on to bigger and better scams. Did you see his suit? It was a nice suit. I know from nice suits." Rondeau plucked the lapels of his vintage green tuxedo jacket, worn over a T-shirt depicting a skeletal rib cage. "He didn't buy a suit like that with three card monte money."

"Wouldn't surprise me. He was always ambitious." *Among other things.*

"So . . . is there a reason you haven't talked to him in all these years, or do you just object to his moral flexibility?" Rondeau didn't even bother to make the last bit sound sarcastic. Marla was a sorcerer. Sorcerers were the very *definition* of moral flexibility.

"We had a . . . falling out. Or more like the scales falling from my eyes, and my seeing Jason for what he is. Or was. I don't want to talk about it."

"Sometimes people do change, Marla. You're not the person you were even ten years ago." He rubbed his jaw absently, and Marla felt the old twinge of guilt—years ago she'd ripped Rondeau's jaw off to use as an oracle, and though he'd been healed by magic and she'd made amends countless times, she still hated thinking about it.

"Does Jason, ah, know about you? What you really do? With the sorcery and so forth?"

"I certainly hope not. I'd rather keep it that way."

"So no telling him you're the witch queen of Felport? Or that I'm not so much a human as a psychic parasite squatting in a human body? Or that—"

"Correct, nix on *all* that, Rondeau. Ideally you'll never see him again, so you won't even be tempted to blather things you shouldn't."

"Another Mason." Rondeau shook his head. "Damn. That's something."

"I don't even want to think about Jason right now. I'm going to go home and crawl under the covers and grind my teeth."

"Still want me to pick you up tomorrow morning so we can go to the airport?"

"Sure. But no staying up all night gambling on the Internet tonight, all right? I don't want to be late tomorrow, and we're going to have a busy-ass day, so you'll need to be well rested."

He said, "You're the boss," but Marla could tell he was already playing Texas hold 'em in his mind. She'd have to make sure Rondeau didn't spend too much time around her brother, or Jason would eventually invite him to a card game and end up owning all Rondeau's worldly possessions.

Unless, of course, her brother had changed—or, rather, changed *back*—into the brother she'd once loved and trusted. It was a tempting thought, and because she found it so tempting, she did her best to doubt it.

* * *

Marla watched the thin trickle of exhausted business-
men and bereaved relatives emerge from the jetway of
the red-eye from San Francisco, dragging their rolling
suitcases behind them like Jacob Marley's chains. When
Bradley Bowman emerged toting a duffel bag, he was so
wide-eyed and awake he seemed scarcely the same
species as the other passengers. "Marla!" He bounded
toward her, dropping his bag at her feet and giving her
a hug.

"Hey, B." She couldn't get over it—this scruffily cute,
charismatic ex–movie star had flown across the conti-
nent to work for *her*. She was supposed to teach him how
to use his peculiar magics, even though his natural gifts
were as a seer and a psychic, while Marla herself was
about as psychic as an axe handle and specialized in
kicking the shit out of people, things, and ideas. But B
was good people. They'd find a way to make it work.
Her operation could use some charm and diplomacy to
go along with the scorched earth and hurt feelings.

B let go of her, but kept beaming. "How'd you get in
here? I thought security stopped people from meeting
their friends at the gate these days."

"B, please. This is me. Airport security is something
that happens to other people."

"I should've known. Where's Rondeau?"

"Waiting with the car. Last time I let him sneak in
here, he made his way to the baggage-loading area and
started rifling through suitcases. After that, I revoked his
conditional invisibility privileges. Come on, we'd better
go to the car before he gets bored and wanders off."

"God, it's great to be here." He followed Marla through the terminal. "Don't get me wrong, being Sanford Cole's apprentice was an honor, and he taught me a lot, but these past few months..."

"Eh, he's an old guy. He can't help it if he has magical narcolepsy. Besides, after a week of working for me, you'll *wish* I dropped off to sleep at random intervals every once in a while, just so you could get some rest." They left the secure area, Marla giving a little wave to the security agent, who still couldn't see her.

"I've done enough sleeping," B said. "I'm here to learn, and I don't mind cutting wood and carrying water."

"Better than Rondeau." Marla passed through the automatic doors, out to the summer morning, which was already heating up. "He just cuts farts and carries debt."

"Movie star!" Rondeau crowed, popping upright from his lean against the Bentley's fender. "Welcome to Felport, where we hardly ever get earthquakes, mud slides, and wildfires!"

"Blizzards and ice storms will be a nice change," B said.

Marla let them hug their hellos—the two of them had become *quite* close during a trip to San Francisco a few months back. She waited for Rondeau to toss B's bag into the car's cavernous trunk before saying, "I'll ride in back with you, B. I need to ask you something, and I don't want to have to twist around to see you."

"I thought apprentices were supposed to get chauffeur duty," Rondeau grumbled, and they all climbed into the car. As Rondeau navigated around dawdling shuttle buses, suicidal cabs, and bleary pedestrians, Marla said, "So are you wiped out? Need to grab some sack time?"

"No, I'm totally wired, and anyway, the plane was nearly empty, I had a whole row to myself, so I slept plenty. Don't worry about me."

"Good. We've got a busy schedule ahead of us. You're no good to me if you don't know the major players in the local scene, so in the next few days, we're going to be visiting a lot of scary, dangerous weirdos and making nice with them."

"Sounds good. But what do you really want to talk to me about?"

Marla grunted. "You being psychic now?"

"Not at the moment. You know I'm lousy at straight thought reading—it gives me headaches. I can just tell there's something else on your mind."

"Well, I was just wondering.... Have you had any dreams lately? About me? Any of *those* dreams?"

B shook his head. "Nope, no prophetic dreams about you, not since your last trip to California. Why?"

"I had...an unexpected visitor last night. I'm wondering if he's going to make trouble."

"What kind of visitor? Demon king? Dark sorcerer? Eldritch being from beyond the back of the stars?"

"Close," Rondeau chimed in from the front. "It was her brother." He paused, and added, "Her *ne'er-do-well* brother," sounding pleased with himself.

Marla smacked him on the back of the head, but lightly; he was driving, after all. "You're going to make me install one of those sound-proof privacy barriers like they have in stretch limos, aren't you?"

"Huh," B said. "I didn't know you had a brother. No, no dreams."

Marla sighed. "I was hoping for some insight, but I guess no news is good news. If you do have any noteworthy nocturnal transmissions, let me know, all right?"

"Sure thing. So do I get to meet this brother?"

"Doubtful," Marla said, but she had a feeling Jason wouldn't cooperate. He was the inquisitive type, and if he hung around town long, he'd doubtless pry into all corners of her life. That kind of curiosity was a family trait.

"You're going to be staying here," Marla said when Rondeau pulled up in front of the club.

"Oh?" B said. "Huh." He didn't sound disappointed, exactly, but she could tell he was trying *not* to.

"You don't want to be roomies?" Rondeau said. "I cleaned out my media room for you!"

Marla snorted. "Media room? You didn't have anything in there but a laptop and an external hard drive full of porn, plus that ancient boom box, which doesn't even work."

"No, it's cool," B said. "I just expected...don't worry about it."

"Ah, I see." Rondeau shut off the car and turned around in the seat. "B wants to know why he has to live with me in my apartment over a nightclub when *you* live in palatial splendor all alone in an old hotel. That, movie star, is a fair question."

"It's hardly palatial splendor." Marla rolled her eyes.

"It's an old flophouse, and only one floor is even suitable for human habitation. Anyway, there's a good reason. When I was out of town this last time to visit you, some bastards broke into my place, kicked the crap out of my mystical security system, and stole some *very* valuable items. I had to beef up security in the place a lot, and now nothing bigger than an inchworm can even walk onto the fifth floor, except for me. Now, I *could* build some exceptions into the spell, to make it possible for you to enter safely, but that shit is all DNA-based, and what if somebody killed you and wore your skin and did some sympathetic magic to trick the system and get at me? That's no good for either of us."

"Since it's only keyed to Marla's DNA, the only way anybody can get in there now is to kill Marla and wear her skin," Rondeau said, "and once she's dead and flayed, she probably won't be so paranoid about people stealing her stuff."

"Forgive me, B?" Marla said. "We'll get you set up in a decent apartment of your own soon, but I want to keep you close at first. Just not so close that you melt into a puddle when you get off the elevator. My office is in Rondeau's *other* spare bedroom, so I'm over at the club most of the time anyway. Go grab a shower and change into some fresh clothes, and meet me after. Then we'll start the Felport magical mystery tour."

"You're not missing much anyway," Rondeau said. "Marla's place is kind of a shithole, and the water pressure sucks."

"He's used your shower?" B said, raising an eyebrow.

"It's not what you think." Marla shook her head vigorously. "We'd just limped home from a fight and he was covered in slime-demon ichor. I got tired of him dripping on the carpet."

"Good times," Rondeau said. "We hardly ever go out together like that anymore."

Half an hour later, B knocked on Marla's office door, wearing jeans and a T-shirt and good walking shoes. He looked well scrubbed and was, amazingly, clean-shaven; she wasn't sure she'd ever seen him with less than a day's stubble. "You look like a ten-year-old when you shave."

"My boyish charm has taken me a long way. Is this the part where I start learning the ropes? Should I prepare myself for some supernatural initiation? Am I gonna get jumped in?"

"Not exactly, though meeting the other sorcerers in Felport can be worse than getting beaten up by gang members."

"That's comforting. Are we taking the Bentley? I've never been a car fanatic, but that's a beautiful machine. I wouldn't mind driving it."

"Nah, we're taking the bus. First rule of being my apprentice, Bradley—don't drive when you can take a bus, and don't take a bus when you can walk. You get a totally different view of the city when you're on mass transit or pounding the pavement. I only drove to the airport because it's so far out, and because I wanted us to be able to talk privately, and you never know where the other sorcerers have spies. There are eyes and ears everywhere. So while we *are* on the bus, keep the conversation away from matters magical, you hear?"

"I am the soul of discretion."

Marla and B walked the few blocks from the bus stop to Hamil's penthouse, strolling on a sidewalk strewn with blossoms from flowering trees. Marla considered their situation. She was not a teacher by nature, and having an apprentice was going to be an adjustment. She'd just have to wing it, like she did most things, and hope for the best. "When I started out in this business," she said, "I had a magical cloak and a reputation as a crazy bitch who was willing to do anything, and those were basically my only assets. My days as an apprentice weren't that productive in terms of practical magic. My mentor, Artie Mann, introduced me to the right people, but he was a pornomancer, specializing in sex magic, and I had no particular affinity for that kind of work. It's all about repression and release, and I'm lousy at the first part."

"So how did you become the well-rounded sorcerer I see before me today?"

"I've always been a magpie. I figured out early on that I didn't want to be a specialist, because I knew I'd get bored if I didn't study anything but divination or illusions or necromancy or whatever. When I was just starting out, I refused to take money in exchange for my services—I'd only work for knowledge. Any sorcerer who wanted me to kick down doors or bust heads or loom around looking threatening or steal back property they'd stolen from someone else in the first place had to pay me with esoteric secrets. At first, when I didn't know much, they pawned low-grade stuff off on me, but as I got more experienced, I was able to strike better deals, and learn serious shit."

"Such as?"

"How to fly. How to avoid being seen, and how to become invisible—and those aren't exactly the same thing, by the way. How to teleport, though I don't recommend it, since there's a double-digit percentage chance you'll be eaten by multilimbed things that dwell in the interstices between universes every time you try. At first I was fanatic about learning powers, you know? Things I could *do,* which made me even more valuable to potential employers, which enabled me to demand bigger and better things in compensation. After a few years I started trading my services for knowledge instead, and I learned a lot of things that conventional wisdom says man was not meant to know."

B nodded. "I get occasional glimpses into that sort of thing myself, in my dreams. Human brains haven't evolved to even *perceive* some things in the universe."

"Oh, yes. I learned stuff I wouldn't have believed, stuff I still find hard to believe. . . . I found out what really killed the dinosaurs—not the asteroid, but the entities that *sent* the asteroid, and why. You know that giant enormous hole of nothing that scientists discovered in the constellation Eridanus a while back, a space a billion light-years across with no matter inside? Some sorcerers have known about that hole for a long time, and there are two or three guys on Earth who don't do anything all day and night but astrally project themselves out into the universe to keep an eye on that hole, and on whatever might someday come out of it. Less cosmic stuff, too. I learned things like who Kaspar Hauser really was. The real facts about the chupacabra."

"The true meaning of Christmas?" B grinned.

"The sinister origins of Secretary's Day, at least. I don't like to let people in on my weaknesses, B, but I might as well tell you—knowledge is my *drug*. I want to know everything, and I want to know it *right now*. To succeed as a sorcerer, you gotta be voracious. Are you voracious?"

"I'm starving. In the metaphorical way we're talking about. Though I could also go for a Danish."

"Good. Because I've pulled some strings. All the sorcerers in the city pay me tribute, you know, just a little slice of their action kicked up to me, since I'm first among equals and all that. But I've made a deal with them to forgo the usual cash payment this month in exchange for, well, magic lessons. For you. You're going to learn six or seven impossible things before a week is out."

B whooped. "Marla, I love you! That's fabulous. Cole was so cautious, he always wanted me to learn all the background before he let me try anything practical— he's the kind of guy who'd make you take four years of music theory before letting you put your grubby untutored hands on the keys of a piano. I had a feeling you'd be more of a hands-on teacher."

"You gotta learn by doing," Marla said. "At least, I did, so that's the way I'm going to teach you. You probably won't kill yourself in the process, and if you do, hell, then it just wasn't meant to be, B." She felt a little bad, since she wasn't being entirely straight with B—she had an ulterior motive for sending him to meet all the major sorcerers in Felport, and she'd tell him about it soon, but she didn't want to put a damper on his enthusiasm just now. "Here's Hamil's place. Get ready for some tea and sympathy."

"The art of sympathetic magic is the art of deception." Hamil held up a bagel. "You create an association be-tween two objects, so they become magically indistin-guishable, and whatever you do to one, also happens to the other." He rolled the bagel back and forth on the table, from one huge hand to the other. B had heard a lot about Hamil—he was Marla's consigliere and close advisor—and had even talked to him on the phone once or twice, but his rather dry and calm voice hadn't prepared B for the enormous bald black physical reality of him.

"Like voodoo dolls?" B said.

"Generally speaking." Hamil's voice held just a hint of disapproval. "But there's so much more to my craft than sticking pins in a poppet to harm your enemies. With the right training, and practice, and luck, you can create a sympathetic link between all sorts of unlikely things. It's all about deceiving the universe, convincing reality that two unrelated things are the same, and when you've been at this for as long as I have, you'll be able to pull off some *very* big lies."

"Hamil says he can create a sympathetic association

so strong he could throw a rock out a window and make the moon come crashing into the Earth," Marla said from the couch. "But he's never proven that boast to my satisfaction."

"For obvious reasons." Hamil held up the bagel. "This is round. It is a wheel."

"I can see how it's like a wheel—" B began.

"*No*," Hamil said. "It *is* a wheel. Go to the window and look down."

B did, and Hamil joined him. The big man held the bagel edge-wise on the windowsill. "It *is* a wheel," he said, softly, as if speaking to himself, and then rolled the bagel along the windowsill.

The right rear tire of an SUV parked at the curb popped off its axle and went rolling down the sidewalk, falling over at the precise moment the bagel did.

B whistled. "Wow. Impressive. Tough on the guy who owns the SUV, though."

"How right you are. Good thing I have this." Hamil went to a bookshelf, took down a hand-sized plastic model of a car, and pulled off the right rear wheel. He went back to the window, humming, and handed B the model. "Why don't you fix it? Admittedly, *adding* complexity to a situation is harder than increasing entropy, but the fundamentals are the same."

"Um . . . what do I do?"

"Convince the universe that this toy is exactly the same as the car below. That by changing one you change the other."

"Okay. But, practically speaking . . ."

"Do you know how sorcery works?" Hamil asked.

"Here we go," Marla muttered from the couch.

"Quiet, you," Hamil said. "Do you want me to teach him, or not?"

"I guess he'll be exposed to a variety of viewpoints, so knock yourself out," Marla said. "I just think you anthropomorphize the universe too much."

"And I think you underestimate the potential sentience of all things. As I was saying, Bradley: do you know how sorcery works?"

"There are lots of different theories. . . ."

"True, but most agree on one point—sorcerers impose their will on the workings of the universe. They change the world just by *wanting* the world to be changed. And that, Bradley, is a power rooted in deception. You must convince the universe that your will is a force of nature, that your desire can no more be ignored than can the forces of gravity or the strong nuclear force. The first step in convincing the universe is to convince yourself. You must be supremely confident and certain of your power."

"Okay." B stared down at the SUV below, and at the toy in his hand, and tried to *will* them to be the same. He stuck the wheel back on the toy, and absolutely nothing at all happened to the car below. "Well, that didn't work."

"And it probably won't, not the first hundred times you try. But the trick is, even when you fail, don't let yourself *believe* you're a failure. Try again, visualizing your success. The ability to hold contradictory thoughts simultaneously is crucial for a sorcerer."

"Okay." Some of this was familiar from B's work with

Cole. He went through the meditation exercises he'd learned, clearing his mind, narrowing the world to the toy in his hands and the car below, trying to make himself a conduit, popping off the wheel and putting it back on, again, and again, and again, and again—

"There!" he said. "The tire moved! I didn't get it all the way on, but it *moved*."

"Really?" Hamil and Marla rose from the couch and came to the window. The tire had risen, wobbled, rolled a few feet back toward the SUV, and then fallen over again.

"Good job, B," Marla said. "And now you're even *more* confident in your abilities, so it'll work better next time."

"That's...that's...well done," Hamil said. His voice sounded oddly shaky. "Keep practicing on your own. Tonight try to, ah, create an affinity between the contents of a glass of water and the contents of a bathtub. Slosh one, and see if you can make the other slosh. Water is one of the easiest things to manipulate, because all water remembers mingling with other water in the past, and the sympathetic association comes naturally. Marla, could I speak to you before you go?"

Hamil shut his office door. "What's up?" Marla said.

"The task I gave Bradley was meant to be impossible. Impossible for *him* anyway. I was going to let him bang his head against the wall for an hour or so, then teach him ways to enhance the sympathetic association between two objects. That toy car didn't really look much like the real one, so I was going to show him how to paint it to match, and to scrape a little paint off the *real* car downstairs to rub on the model, to further enhance the connection between the two. I thought maybe then he'd be able to make the tire twitch, but he got that far just on sheer force of will. He actually has potential, Marla. You chose your apprentice well. I've met more promising prospects, but not often."

Marla grinned. "Good to hear, because I'd be stuck with him at this point even if you thought he sucked. And thanks for not saying that in front of him. You know movie stars and their egos."

"With training, he could be a very valuable addition to the city. I know you don't like to discuss matters of succession, but you'll almost certainly . . . retire someday, and Felport will need—"

"I'm way ahead of you," she interrupted. "You think it hasn't crossed my mind?"

"I think you have a tendency to assume your own indestructibility."

"Haven't met anything that can destroy me yet. Let's not borrow trouble, fat man, or get years and years ahead of ourselves, okay?"

"Yes, all right, fair enough. But try not to scare him off, hmm?"

"Tomorrow I'm taking him to meet Viscarro. If *that* doesn't scare him off, I doubt anything else will. You mind hanging out with B for a while longer? It's his first night in town, and I don't want to leave him alone with Rondeau's corrupting influence yet—I need him sober and not apocalyptically hungover in the morning."

"Certainly. He can keep practicing here. You have plans?"

"I gotta meet a guy."

"This guy wouldn't happen to be your brother?"

"You and your spies." Marla sighed. "I need to see if I can get rid of him."

"Don't underestimate the importance of family, Marla. My own relationship with my brothers is a source of great comfort to me."

"But they live four states away and you only see them on occasional holidays. My brother's right *here*. Besides, you're my family, and so's Rondeau, and so's B. But my brother? Maybe once, but at this point, our relationship is just an accident of blood."

2

Jason came strolling around the corner right on time, which was the first surprise. He'd never been especially punctual when it came to family matters, though he was meticulous when dealing with people he planned to fleece. *Now I'm suspicious.* She stuck out her hand before Jason could hug her again.

If Jason was offended by the preemptive handshake, he didn't show it, taking her hand in both of his warmly for a moment. "Come on, Marlita. I got us a reservation at Étienne's. I'll drive."

"I'm not dressed for a place that fancy." She scowled, gesturing at her cotton pants and rumpled button-down. Jason shrugged. He was immaculate in a gray suit, every stitch the successful businessman, though that old twinkle in his eye suggested it might be a slightly disreputable business. "I think you look fine, but we can stop by your place and you can change, if you're uncomfortable about it."

"Look, I know this great diner south of the park—"

"Please, let your big brother treat you to a nice dinner, would you? In honor of our heartfelt reunion?"

Marla didn't want to get off on the wrong foot—she was hoping to keep this pleasant, shallow, and brief—but she could have told him going to her apartment wouldn't help. The closest thing to formal-wear she owned was the costume she'd worn to the Founders' Day masquerade, and that made her look like a prosperous pirate queen. "Fuck it. My shirt's clean. Let's go."

Her brother offered her his arm in a gesture of exaggerated courtliness, and she took it, shaking her head a little. Ah, Jason. Once upon a time it had been them against the world, when the scope of the world had been limited to a little town in Indiana and the assholes who dwelt therein. It would be so easy to fall back into the old pattern, when he was the all-knowing savvy sophisticate of sixteen and she was a gawky, worshipful fourteen-year-old. But that was half a lifetime ago, and their dynamic had started to sour even before she'd run away from home, when she got a glimpse of what her brother was truly capable of.

But then, she was capable of some pretty awful stuff herself, so who was she to judge?

Jason's car was a brand-new Mercedes, a sleek black piece of precision machinery that seemed sent back in time from a classier future. Her Bentley made it look like a rent-a-wreck, of course, but if Jason wanted to play the big rich man with his rented car, she wouldn't piss all over him. He opened the door for her and she slid in, the leather seat more luxurious than any of the furniture she owned. She popped open the glove compartment and started rifling through the papers inside. By the time Jason got into the driver's seat, she had the registration in her hand. "Shit, bro, you *own* this car? You must have plucked some big pigeons lately."

"I'm doing all right." To his credit, he didn't sound a bit smug. "And while I won't lie and tell you no pigeons were plucked in the making of this fortune, the grift is all about acquiring capital these days. Once I get a nice chunk of ill-gotten gain, I *invest,* and that's where the real money comes from. Hell, at this point I could probably retire, but what would I do with myself? Take up golf?" He navigated out of the seedy quarter of nightclubs and strip joints and bail-bonds offices and quickie check-cashing centers, driving east toward a trendy area near the financial district. Marla didn't come over here often, except when she needed to meet with Nicolette, the chaos magician, who had her headquarters in a skyscraper nearby.

"So you're just in it for the thrill of the con?" Marla fiddled with the climate controls. They made the console of a space shuttle seem intuitive.

"It was ever thus, sis. Money's just a way of keeping score, isn't that what they say?"

Marla hesitated, but screw that—she wasn't the girl who hesitated anymore, hadn't been for a long time. "And the heavy shit? Can I assume that's a thing of the past, too?"

Jason went stiff and still, then let out a long hiss of a sigh between clenched teeth. "One time, Marla." His voice was low. "One time, things got out of control, I admit that, and you'll hold it against me forever? It's not like *your* hands never got dirty, and when they did, I stood by you—"

"Truce." Marla held up her hands. "Ancient history. I'm sorry."

"You're not sorry. You wanted to *know*."

"Okay. You got me there."

"Fair enough. But no, no heavy shit, not since that one time. That was never the way I preferred to play it anyway, but I was a dumb kid, and things just happened. I've come a long way. We both have. Look at you. I hear you're doing pretty well for yourself, running a thriving business."

Marla grunted. She did have business interests, legal and otherwise, but they were basically a side effect of her real job—it was hard to be chief sorcerer and *not* make money. Hamil and, to a lesser extent, Rondeau looked after her affairs for her, and made sure she could concentrate on killing monsters and not on signing payroll checks. "What exactly is it you think I do, Jason?"

"The word is you're a crime boss with a great line of bullshit about all your scary magical powers, which keeps the peons in line and potential enemies scared shitless. I must say, I'm impressed. I knew a guy in New York, he ran a little immigrant neighborhood, and he had everyone convinced he was a badass voodoo priest. The guy would kill a goat or a chicken in an alley every once in a while and people would just crap themselves with fear. It was a good scam, but your operation, it's on a whole higher level."

"What's the guy's name?"

"Hmm? He calls himself Papa Legbone."

"Never heard of him." Which meant he probably *was* a liar, whereas Marla was the real thing. But she was more than pleased to let Jason go on believing magic was a fake bullshit moneymaking stratagem. He might be her brother, but he was still an ordinary, and ignorance was safer for him. "Anyway, I can't confirm or deny any rumors you might have heard, but you know how important it is to have a reputation."

"Oh, I certainly do. In fact, the whole I'm-a-mystical-wizard shtick looks like it could make me some serious money. I was hoping I could pick your brain tonight, see if you can help me make my story a little more plausible."

"And here we go." Marla slapped the dashboard. "I knew you had an ulterior motive."

"You're so dramatic. You think I wouldn't have looked you up anyway, once I found out this was your town? It's just a coincidence I've got a beautiful mark dangling on a string. He's rich, he's credulous, and he's totally obsessed with this occult bullshit. It's all Aleister Crowley this and Hermes Trismegistus that and ancient mystical order of the transcendental whatever the fuck with this guy. I've read up, but I'm hoping you can give me some nice juicy buzzwords to really knock his socks off."

"The new mark's a wannabe, huh?" All sorcerers encountered such people from time to time, ordinaries who were convinced there was magic in the world, and who wanted more than anything to become part of that magic themselves. Clueless people who thought magic— real magic—would make their lives better, when what magic really did was make your life profoundly more complicated. They also tended to think magic was like a wish-dispensing never-ending cash-and-sex machine, without any understanding of the dangers or precarious balance such endeavors entailed and required. The ones who actually did stumble into real magic wound up nervous wrecks more often than not, when they didn't get used up completely in some dark ritual by practitioners even less moral than Marla was. Some thought they were angels or dragons trapped in human bodies, or changelings from the faery realm, or that their mutant powers would kick in any day now. "What, some trust fund kid who hangs out at goth clubs and pretends to be a vampire, like that?"

"I'm not in the business of taking surly teens for their allowance money, Marlita. Nah, this guy's in his forties, and he's stone cold serious, a real obsessive case, just perfect—he's desperate to believe, and I can be very convincing. But it's okay if you don't want to talk about my job. We're here, so let's have a nice dinner, catch up on the past too many years. That valet parking guy look trustworthy to you? I think he's got shifty eyes."

"What, you think he might be *pretending* to be a valet, looking for cars to steal? Like a certain someone I could name did once at a country club back home? I wouldn't worry about it."

"I guess you're right. Sometimes you have to trust people, or you can't get anything done at all."

They gave up the car and went into the glossy darkness of Étienne's, which occupied the first floor of a venerable historic building with dignified points of architectural interest, most of which Marla considered baroquely hideous. Jason gave his name and flashed his grin at the graying maître d', who looked Marla up and down with frank disapproval. She returned his gaze with the kind of stare that made even Rondeau quit fucking around and take her seriously, and the host bowed his head to the reservation book. He escorted them to a secluded table in a dark corner, surely less out of a desire to give them privacy and more from a wish to hide Marla and her workaday wardrobe from casual view.

They were barely seated when their waiter appeared, a middle-aged career type who brought a gravity and willingness to serve that would have done a good undertaker proud. After he introduced himself and told them the specials—including a loin of veal with truffle sauce that sparked Marla's interest despite herself—he asked if they had any questions.

"Yeah, Michael," Marla said. "How much can you pull down in a year waiting tables in a joint like this?"

If he found the question crass or inappropriate he didn't show it. "I am adequately compensated, ma'am."

"No, seriously, I don't need hard numbers, I'm just trying to figure out which ballpark we're in. Come on, I'm a good tipper when my whims are gratified."

Michael looked briefly skyward, then allowed himself the faintest smile. "My sister is a doctor with a healthy private practice. When one takes into account the amount she pays each month for insurance, and the cost of paying off her student loans from medical school, I generally have an income somewhat in excess of hers." He paused. "It is a subject we often laugh about."

"Ha! I figured as much. Rich people are cheap, but even a lousy tip on a bill as big as the one we're going to run up would be a pretty good size. Thanks. We'll be ready for you in a few minutes." She shooed him away.

Jason burst out laughing. "Ah, sis, you haven't changed a bit."

"You never learn things if you don't ask." She perused the menu, amazed, as always, that people voluntarily ate rabbits, which she considered essentially photogenic rodents.

"So what do you recommend?"

Marla looked at him over the top of her menu. He appeared to be sincere, but with Jason, it was tricky to tell. "Why ask me? I've never eaten here before. This isn't my kind of place."

"Marlita! You shouldn't deny yourself the finer things in life. I know you can afford to eat well. Or do you spend all your money on monocle polish and big sacks with dollar signs printed on the sides?"

"I do whatever I want, Jason. Don't worry about me. I've just never seen the thrill of eating in a place where the waiter puts your napkin in your lap and has a special tool just for scraping up stray breadcrumbs."

"I'd heard you were into the whole ascetic thing, but I figured that was just good PR on your part. I also heard you drive a vintage Rolls-Royce, so who knows what to believe?"

"You heard, you heard—who are you hearing all this shit from?" Being even slightly famous, even in very specific circles, was more annoying than gratifying.

"Oh, you know. People like us."

"Criminals, scoundrels, and rogues, you mean?"

Jason winced theatrically. "People of mercurial morality, let's say. I heard your name a few times here and there before I even entertained the possibility that people were talking about my sister. You might've looked me up, you know, when you got into the business. I could've given you some advice. Not that you seem to need any."

"We didn't part on such good terms." She suppressed the urge to touch the daggers hidden up her sleeves. "I wasn't sure you'd want to hear from me."

He grunted. "About that. Our parting. I just want to say—and you know I almost never say this—I'm sorry. I was a stupid kid, and I made an even stupider mistake, and then I compounded the stupidity by trying to drag you into my problems. Looking back, I don't know what the hell I was thinking. Putting that kind of burden on my little sister . . . it's no wonder you got upset and took off. If it's possible, if you can take it as a compliment, I want you to know . . . when that bad shit went down, you were the only one I felt I could reach out to. The only one I really trusted. My *family*. You know?"

Marla shifted in her seat, unable to hide her discomfort. "You asked me for help, and I . . . didn't help you. I figured you'd been holding that against me all these years." *Just like I've been holding the fact that you even asked against you.*

He shook his head. "No. I've just been pissed off at myself for screwing up the one nonpoisonous family relationship I ever had. I thought I'd lost you forever, Marlita." He reached across the table and, lightly, touched her hand. She didn't pull back. "Finding you again, sitting here across a table from you ... it feels like magic." He sat back and grinned. "You know. *Real* magic. Not like the bullshit you peddle."

They could have probed the old wound of their separation more thoroughly, and Marla was tempted to do so, but Jason had apologized—never easy for the men in her family—and some of the tension was broken, so she decided to let it lie, for now. If she kept seeing him (which seemed likelier than it had ten minutes ago) she might revisit the subject, try to explain her own motivations, but for now, she decided to accept this strange situation for what it was: she was having dinner with her brother, and it was pretty nice. "That bullshit magic has done all right by me, Jason."

"Yeah, I can see that. How the hell did you end up in Felport anyway, much less running the place?"

"It just worked out that way. I took the right buses and hitched the right rides, and here I am. I was aiming for New York, because I was a fifteen-year-old runaway, and what the hell did I know? Missed my destination by a few degrees of latitude, but it worked out okay."

The waiter returned, and after they ordered and Jason finished consulting with the sommelier, they fell into a silence that was not so much awkward as inevitable. Having dinner with a friend you hadn't seen in a few weeks was easy—you could talk for an hour just catching up on things that had happened since you last met. But talking to someone you hadn't seen in almost twenty years was, paradoxically, far more difficult. It was impossible to know where to start, and with so much time to cover, it was hard to find common ground.

Jason had already confronted the elephant in the room, and what else did they have to discuss?

Finally, tired of seeing Jason fiddle with his flatware, Marla sighed. "All right, out with it. Tell me about your latest operation."

"Oh, I'd hate to bore you—"

"Don't bullshit me, I'm immune to you. You want to pick my brain, so lay the groundwork already."

Jason leaned across the table. "I've got a big fish on the line. His name is Campbell Campion."

Marla groaned. "Cam-Cam? You're going to rip *him* off? Join the club."

"You've heard of him?"

"Sure. Rich as hell, old family money, lives in a big house out by the beaches. He's king of the wannabes, Jason. Every small-time operator around has taken him for a little dough. Fake psychics, fake séances, fake occult rituals, the whole deal. He's an idiot."

"He's no idiot. He's just so rich he doesn't think twice about throwing away a few grand on the outside chance he'll find somebody who really knows magic. So what if he pays a hundred fakes, if he manages to find just one who's genuine? I could scam him out of a couple thousand before breakfast, but I want to take him for more. A *lot* more. And that means I need more than a crystal ball and a fake Transylvanian accent."

"Ambitious. But even Cam-Cam must be suspicious of more impressive claims at this point. If you're going to clean him out, you'll need a pretty powerful convincer. What's your play? How can you get to him?"

"Oh, well." Jason examined his manicured finger-nails. "As far as that goes, I *am* your brother."

Marla closed her eyes. She counted to ten. It didn't help. She still wanted to leap across the table and assault Jason vigorously with her butter knife. Before she could give in to temptation, Michael returned with their soup course, and by the time he'd peppered the dish to Jason's liking, Marla had squeezed her rage down to a manage-able little ball. "You traded on *my name*?"

"It's my name, too." Jason sipped his soup. "Better to say I traded on your *reputation*. Listen, I couldn't even get in to *see* the guy, he's been burned too many times, but once I let word slip that I was the famous Marla Mason's brother, well . . . What could I do? I saw my in, and I took it."

"I'm not going to meet with him, if that's what you're driving at. I'm not even going to *talk* to him. Don't try to drag me into this." Cam-Cam was the worst of the wan-nabes. Every once in a while some hard-luck alley wizard or ex-apprentice gave him some genuine intel about the magical world, and he came blustering and bribing his way into things he couldn't begin to understand. Trying to buy transcendence, trying to boss people who were used to bossing around the *natural world*. He was insuf-ferable, boorish, and stank of desperation. Once or twice he'd been in the right place at the right time and seen seemingly impossible things, and had his memory erased as a consequence. Most sorcerers had a little forget-me-lots potion on hand for just such situations. Eventually somebody would probably get irritated with Cam-Cam and kill him.

"Don't worry, Campion knows you're a busy lady. I'm pretty sure he's having me followed, though, and his spies will report that I was here with you, and he'll be totally convinced I'm on the level." He shrugged. "That's all I really needed."

She threw her napkin down in her soup, splashing a little onto the clean white tablecloth. "Fuck you very much, Jason. I actually thought you *wanted* to see me, out of good old-fashioned brotherly love."

He wiped his mouth. "I could have hired a woman to pretend to be you, Marla. Hell, I would have dressed her in that white-and-purple cloak people say you used to wear, that would have been nice and recognizable. Come on, I *did* want to see you. But you blame me for multitasking? You've never sacrificed sentimentality for efficiency?"

She sighed, then gestured for the waiter. "Can I get a new napkin? Mine committed suicide." Marla laced her fingers together and rested her hands on the tabletop, hoping that would suppress her desire to wring Jason's neck, because godsdamnit, he was right. She would have done pretty much exactly what he'd done, in his position. "All right, fine. So what's the scam?"

"Oh, that *would* be boring, all those details. Let's just say I'm going to make him think he's neck-deep in a plot involving various powerful sorcerers, warring factions, yadda yadda. It'll be a big production, lots of extras, lots of juggling, but if it works out, he'll beg to keep writing me checks."

"I wish you well. Maybe you can retire to an island in

the South Pacific and send me Christmas cards on odd-numbered years?"

"I *was* hoping for a little advice. You know, some ideas to lend the operation some verisimilitude, since this magic stuff is your line of patter, not mine."

"Hell, Jason. I don't know if I want to help you. Not to be a bitch or anything, but I kind of disapprove of what you do."

"You disapprove? Marla, you're not exactly running a nonprofit yourself. I don't claim to be privy to details, but I definitely have a sense of what kind of pies your fingers are stuck in. They are dirty, dirty pies."

"Sure, I make money from gratifying people's desires. It's not my fault if some of those desires are stupidly illegal. My word is actually good for something, though, and I stand by my deals. You just plain lie to people."

"It's not like I don't have a code, Marlita. I don't rip off old people on fixed incomes, you know? I take money from people who have too much of it. I just redistribute wealth from rich stupid people to less rich smart people. And this guy Cam-Cam, there's nothing in the *world* he wants more than proof that magic exists, and to have some kind of big crazy adventure, and that's exactly what I'm going to give him. If this goes right, he'll never even realize he's been duped, and he'll have the time of his life."

"So what you're doing isn't really wrong, and anyway, he'll enjoy it? That's seriously your argument?"

"It's what I do, Marla. If you don't want to help me, don't help me. Nobody's forcing you."

"Damn right." The next course arrived, delicate bits

of duck wrapped in phyllo dough. She tried to concentrate on eating, but she'd never been any good at suppressing her curiosity. She put down her fork. "What kind of details were you looking for anyway?"

Jason swallowed and said, "I need to offer Cam-Cam something. It needs to be magical, naturally, but it also has to be unspeakably dangerous, so dangerous I can justify keeping it sealed up in a very heavy box all wrapped with chains."

Marla laughed. "Because there's not going to be anything *in* the box, right?"

"Oh, there'll be something. Sand. Rocks. Whatever."

"How will you convince him the mystery box contains whatever you're *telling* him it contains?"

He waved the objection away. "That kind of stuff's easy. Convincing's what I do. I'm just not sure what to convince him *of*. Any ideas?"

"Give me a minute." She pondered. There were artifacts, horrible things in Viscarro's bank of the catacombs, that might fit the bill, but something so deadly it couldn't be looked upon, something so dangerous its existence had to be taken on faith...

She snapped her fingers. "Tell him you've got a vial of the Borrichius spores."

"What are those?"

"They're—" The waiter returned to check on them, and Marla impatiently waved him off. "They're unspeakably dangerous, incalculably valuable, endlessly sought-after, and very probably imaginary."

"That could work." Jason picked up the wine list.

"Let's get something nice and raise a glass to all things dangerous and imaginary."

They settled into the meal, and into each other's company, bouncing around ideas for embellishments to Jason's basic scam, and Marla was surprised to realize she was enjoying herself. Her brother had a quick wit and a mind that twisted like a labyrinth, quite unlike her own ruthlessly linear approach to problem-solving, but she had to admit, his way sounded like more fun. Before long they fell into the inevitable game of "remember when," dredging up names Marla had forgotten years ago, reminding each other of funny and formative moments from childhood—the boy Marla beat up in kindergarten for pulling her hair, the doe-eyed neighbor girl even younger than Marla who'd been hopelessly infatuated with Jason for so many years—and carefully avoiding the emotional minefields in the family plot.

Their final words to each other all those years ago had been so harsh, they'd come to overshadow all Marla's memories . . . but there were other memories underneath, good ones, funny ones, fond ones. She was beginning to remember what it meant to have a brother. She was beginning to think it might not be so bad.

"Hey, Jason." She raised her second glass of wine, which was an extravagance for her. "Thanks for looking me up. This is nice."

"As far as reunions with long-lost siblings go, this is the best one I've ever had. Here's to water under the bridge." He clinked his glass against hers.

* * *

Nicolette was tweaking the drug mix she used for her divining spiders—the one on crystal meth was weaving webs that seemed way too orderly for a proper baseline, so she had to up the dosage—when her snitch phone rang. It was the only phone she kept in her chaos room, because it was the only phone that ever had calls she couldn't afford to miss. She put down the syringe and removed her goggles before answering. "Speak."

"This is Michael. Marla Mason just left the restaurant."

"No way. She only eats at places where the food comes in a greasy sack and you gobble it standing at a counter. I think you've got a mistaken identity thing going on. Recalibrate your instruments, busboy."

"It was *her*. I was her waiter, and the reservation was under her brother's name, Jason Mason."

"A brother, huh? That's interesting. But not interesting enough to warrant a phone call. You're supposed to spy for me, Michael. That means actionable intelligence. Telling me the dessert orders of Felport's ruling elite doesn't count."

A hint of desperation crept into his voice. "I think it was a business dinner. She kept hushing up every time I got close, but I heard her say something about giving her brother some spores."

"Spores? Like anthrax spores? What kind?" Nicolette picked up a steel meat-tenderizer and used it to smash a four-inch-high, badly painted porcelain unicorn to pieces.

"Buh-something . . . Baphomet spores?"

"*Borrichius* spores?" Nicolette dumped the fragments

of unicorn in a mortar and began grinding them to powder with a pestle.

"Yes, that's it."

"Huh. Where, when, how, for what purpose?"

"I don't know. I'm sorry, I only heard a little. I didn't
want to make her suspicious."

"This isn't perfect, Mikey boy, but I guess a dribble is
better than a drought." She checked the pestle. The unicorn hadn't quite been reduced to its component mole-
cules, but it was as close as she could come with hand
tools, and looked like a handful of mostly white sand.

"So it's a good tip? Good enough?"

"Sure, sure. Remind me, what are the terms of our
agreement? I've got dozens of you guys on the payroll
and a lousy memory for names." Nicolette remembered
their agreement perfectly well. She was just fucking with
him. She drew her power from disorder and confusion,
and fucking with people was practically a habit.

"*Cancer.* My sister's cancer."

"Oh, right, the doctor. Sure, I'll keep her renegade
cells in line for a while longer, don't fret. Just keep your
eyes and ears open. Is Ernesto still a regular at the restaurant?"

"He was in last night, but he ate alone. He was reading a book about steam engines or something."

"Dullsville." Nicolette hung up. She considered her
wall of drug-addled spiders. Methed-up spiders aside,
they'd been spinning messier webs than usual, which
probably meant there was potential for extra tasty chaos
in the coming weeks, but who the hell knew? She was
still fine-tuning the whole arachnid divination system.

Fortune-telling had never been her strong point. She had a crazy seer locked up in the basement, giggling to himself and drawing pictures in his own poop, but she was trying to reduce her dependence on outside contractors. Besides, she liked having the webs. They made her penthouse apartment—inherited from her old boss and mentor, a neat freak she'd betrayed and murdered—feel more like her own.

She dumped the pestle of unicorn dust into a glass-walled terrarium filled with similar sand, then washed her hands at the industrial sink she'd had installed in the corner. She was trying not to overthink. Chaos flourished best when impulses were indulged, but what *was* her impulse here? The Borrichius spores were supposed to be serious stuff, created by a mad—or arguably visionary—biomancer back in the '50s, and long since lost or locked up or destroyed, if they'd ever even existed. If Marla was able to get her hands on something that powerful, though . . . how could Nicolette turn that knowledge to her benefit? How could she fuck with Marla and increase disorder in the city, conjure up a big old clusterfuck so she could grow fat on the ensuing disaster?

She left the chaos room, following all the appropriate safety protocols, and went into her office. Turning on her computer, she pulled up the latest edition of *Dee's Peerage,* the encyclopedic list of active sorcerers compiled by persons or entities unknown, which appeared mysteriously on every sorcerer's doorstep once a year or so. *Dee's Peerage* didn't have any juicy secrets—it was kind of the *Who's Who* of the magical underworld—but it was handy for getting the basics. She clicked through the "B"s, chasing a half-remembered entry she'd skimmed while looking for info on Marla's new apprentice, Bradley Bowman, who it turned out didn't rate so much as a line in the current edition.

There it was. "Bulliard." He was a long way from local, being a solo sorcerer up in the Pacific Northwest, but based on his biography the spores would probably pique his interest enough to bring him running to Felport. Nicolette especially liked the bit of his C.V. that mentioned the allegations of persistent fixed delusions and borderline personality disorder. Bringing a guy like that to Felport could only stir up trouble. Getting a message to him would be tricky, but she knew a guy in Seattle who owed her the kind of favor you can't refuse on pain of painful death, so after fifteen minutes on the phone and some threatful cajoling, she'd set things in motion.

Nicolette settled down with a beer and a warm feeling of accomplishment. She felt sort of bad, in the abstract, for the shitstorm she was maybe going to bring down on Marla. Nicolette admired the woman's resourcefulness and willingness to do her own dirty work. But Nicolette was only loyal to disaster, and messing with the chief sorcerer of Felport had the potential to wreck all sorts of things.

3

Marla crept into the spare room where B was bunked down and knelt beside his sleeping head. "Good MORNING!"

She was hoping for a nice startle, maybe an amusing tumble out of bed in a tangle of sheets, but B just opened his tropical blue eyes, yawned, and said, "Good morning to you, too."

"You're no fun. You could have at least acted like it was a rude awakening."

"Not even an actor of my abilities could do that convincingly. I'm psychic. I felt your *mind*. Also, I've met you before." He sat up and rubbed his eyes. "I'm still beat from yesterday. I'm not sure I've ever been this tired before, and that includes fifteen-hour days on movie sets followed by way too much clubbing. Who knew *thinking* could be so hard?"

"Using your thoughts to boss reality is tough, B. You have to be careful not to overstrain yourself. You're still learning your limits. Come on. I'll give you ten minutes to shower, then we need to head for the bank of the cat-acombs."

B crawled out of bed, wearing only a pair of boxer briefs, and Marla took a moment to admire the view. B was gay, so she couldn't *do* anything about it, even putting aside issues of inappropriate behavior between apprentice and master. Still, he *had* been a movie star, and he had the local market on cute cornered, so she looked. He didn't care. He'd made his living being looked at, once upon a time.

"Bank of the catacombs, huh? Sounds ominous."

"Sounds *pretentious*. We're going to see a sorcerer named Viscarro. He's the materialistic type."

Marla went in search of Rondeau while B got ready, and found him drinking a Bloody Mary at the battered kitchen table, wearing a hideous green bathrobe with gold trim. "A little early for boozing, isn't it?"

"Only if you've been to bed, which I haven't."

"You sober enough to deal with that thing this morning?"

"Am I sober enough to carry an envelope full of cash to a guy in a bar? Yes. Going to a bar is high on my list of priorities anyway."

Marla dragged over a chair and sat with him. "Why the slow-motion bender?"

He swirled his drink with a stalk of celery. "Lorelei broke up with me."

"Again? Why this time?"

"You wouldn't believe it."

"You know *that's* not true."

"She cheated on me with some guy last week. She did the whole tearful confession thing. Then, when I didn't get mad—when she realized it didn't bother me—she kicked me out of bed! Said if I didn't care enough to get jealous and possessive, she didn't want me in her life." He shook his head. "You humans are crazy." Rondeau occasionally played the species card when he was feeling persecuted.

Marla snorted. "You don't act the way you do because you're not human, Rondeau. You act that way because you're an ass."

"Bitch," he said, but amiably.

B came in, still damp, but dressed. "If the ladies aren't doing it for you, Rondeau, you can come play for my team."

"Eh, sure, for an inning here and there, but it wouldn't last. Men just don't have the same capacity to drive me bugfuck insane that women do. It's a chemical thing, I guess."

"Sorry you got dumped," Marla said. "Want to get some dinner tonight and listen to me go on and on about how I never liked her anyway?"

"I might take you up on that, if I'm not in a drunken stupor already." He checked his watch. "I'd better get ready to see that guy."

"Finish your drinking *after* the business is done." Marla beckoned for B. She turned to him with a grin when they were in the elevator headed down to the basement garage. "You get to drive the Bentley today. Viscarro's catacombs have entrances all over, but I don't feel like walking down five miles of slimy tunnels, so we're driving closer to the hub."

The car purred to life under B's hand. "This makes the Batmobile look like a go-kart."

B drove a lot less recklessly than Rondeau usually did—Rondeau knew the Bentley was magically crash-proof, and drove like a man with nothing to fear, while B treated her property with appropriate respect. Well, not *her* property—the car, like nearly all her assets, belonged not to Marla personally but to the office of chief sorcerer. Thinking of which...

"Hey, B. How do you feel about taking over my job? Eventually, that is, once I get eaten by dire wolves or turned into bloody jelly by a monster from the center of the Earth?"

B glanced at her, then back at the road. He couldn't have looked more stunned if she'd smacked him in the face with a dead fish. "I would feel...um...I don't think there's a word for the combination of abject fear and confusion I need to describe. Maybe 'terrorfucked.'"

"Huh," Marla said. "See, I agreed to take you on as my apprentice with the idea that I could groom you to take over my job. The only other sorcerer in town I'd halfway trust to do it is Hamil, and he's too smart to accept such a thankless position."

"And...you think I'm less smart?"

"Now, now. *Differently* smart."

B shook his head. "That's heavy stuff to drop on me, Marla. I'm not anywhere even remotely close to ready to contemplate something like that. I'm so underqualified I wouldn't even *comprehend* the entire job description."

"Don't fret yet. Consider this the world's longest interview. I intend to be around for a while, and you're going to be my apprentice for a significant percentage of my remaining time on this planet, but eventually an apprentice has to become a master, or quit the profession. If I'm the one training you, and you don't break or wash out or go crazy, you'll be uniquely suited to run the city when I'm gone." *Assuming he comes to love this place as I do.* That was one thing she couldn't teach, and it was absolutely necessary in her successor. "Have I just totally freaked you out? I figured, between us, honesty is better." She'd also wanted to see which way he'd jump if she sprang something like this on him, of course.

"It's . . . a lot of pressure."

"Good. My job is all about being under ridiculous quantities of pressure. So consider this practice."

"Marla, I'm honored you would even think of me. I'll try not to disappoint you."

"Oh, I'm sure you'll disappoint me at some point. Just don't ever disappoint me the same way twice and we'll be okay."

He grinned. "I'll do my best. I can't tell you how much it—"

"Shush, before this turns into a tender moment. I don't do those." Marla fiddled with the radio, but found nothing but static—until a sepulchral voice said, ". . . darkness, emptiness, everything everything stolen away . . ."

"That is not the Hot 97.9 FM," Marla said.

"Have to pull over." B lurched the Bentley into an empty space in front of a hair salon. "Head hurts. It's an oracle."

Marla grunted and turned up the radio. B was an oracle generator, a supernatural catalyst, and weird entities sometimes precipitated out of potentiality when he was around.

"All-swallowing darkness. And things that grow in darkness. Oblivious, before oblivion. The snuffling of oncoming death."

"I don't understand." B pressed his hands to his temples. "You aren't making sense."

"All is darkness," the voice intoned. "Darkness and darkness and partly cloudy skies today, clearing off by late afternoon, and in our five-day forecast—"

Marla switched off the radio, which had transitioned smoothly from the eldritch to the everyday. "As far as vague threatening voices go, that was one of the vaguest and most threatening I've ever encountered."

"The oracle didn't ask for payment." B frowned at the radio. "They always ask for payment, even if it's just a song, or a kiss, or a cup of coffee, or an old newspaper. *Something* to balance the equation." He lifted his eyes to Marla. "What does it mean, that the oracle doesn't want payment?"

"Maybe it wasn't meant for us." She chewed her lip, troubled. "Maybe it's a case of some celestial wires getting crossed?"

"Maybe." B sounded as uncertain as Marla felt, and they drove on in silence.

* * *

"Seriously," B said. "We're going into the sewers? This is a joke, right? A hazing ritual?"

"Nope." Marla levered the pry bar into one of the slots around the metal disc covering the manhole. "The hazing ritual's not until tonight, after the kegger, and before the circle jerk. You should've read your program." She muscled the cover out of the way and glanced around. They were on a backstreet, and nobody was currently loading or unloading at any of the businesses, so they had the place to themselves. "Lucky there's nobody around," she said. "I can cast a spell and make any cops or nosy neighbors think we're from the sanitation department, but I'm always happier to avoid conflict."

"Right. That sounds like you." B looked down the shaft, at a metal ladder and darkness beyond. "Me first?"

"Of course. You're the apprentice, so you always go first into the unknown. If anyone's going to be eaten by a grue, it should be you."

"Tough job. But at least the hours are terrible." He descended the ladder, Marla following close after him, until they both stood in the low-ceilinged space below. B glanced upward. "Shouldn't we have put out some orange cones or something? What if someone falls down?"

Marla whistled, and the manhole rolled smartly back into place, covering them with darkness. "How's that?"

"If you could just whistle it around with magic, why did you lever it up with a pry bar?"

"I'm missing a lot of my regular workouts, what with dragging you around town. Why miss a chance at a little exercise?" Marla snapped her fingers and a ball of float-ing light appeared over their heads, illuminating a brick-lined tunnel.

"I thought you disdained the whole fairy-lights thing."

Marla shrugged. "I could just give us night-eyes, so we could see in the dark, but Viscarro is a paranoid fuck. I don't want him to think I'm sneaking up on him with murder in mind."

"I thought he was your ally?"

"He is."

"But he's afraid you'll try to kill him?"

"Sure. He's been a sorcerer for a long time. Sorcerers kill one another, even when they're friends."

"Ah, so it's a generalized, healthy sort of paranoia."

Marla seesawed her hand in a so-so gesture. "No, to be fair, he's got specific reasons to worry about me. I've threatened to kill him before."

"Why's that? Is he dangerous?"

"Of course. He's a sorcerer. As to why I've considered offing him . . . you'll see. I think you'll see. We'll see if you see."

"Okay. That's fine. Don't tell me. I'm good with the suspense." Marla set off down the corridor, taking the light with her, and B followed. After a moment he heard a disheartening squishing noise under her boots, and then under his own sneakers. "If I'd known we were go-ing spelunking for poop, I would have worn my *nice* shoes."

"It's okay, Hollywood. A little crap on your shoes will improve your street cred."

"This reminds me of a low-budget horror movie I did when I was first starting out as an actor. We filmed in some sewers without a permit. It was almost enough to make me want to give up movies for the stage, where I was told you never had to deliver lines while standing in feces." He considered. "Unless it was some avant-garde experimental show."

"I wonder how much of the poop down here comes from Viscarro's other visitors shitting themselves with fear? This beautiful stretch of squish leads to a secret access tunnel to his underground lair."

"Cool! Why don't you have a secret underground lair?"

"Like I need that kind of vitamin D deficiency. Come on, through here." She pushed open a distinctly medieval-looking iron grate and led B down a brick hallway that was only a few inches wider than his shoulders—a bigger man, like Hamil, would have been unable to come this way. They arrived at a featureless steel door with a cracked white plastic intercom set into the wall beside it, and Marla reached toward the buzzer, then paused. "Oh, B, there's one more thing."

"What's that?"

"On all these little visits I'm arranging for you . . . keep your eyes open. And keep your *third* eye open." She tapped the center of her forehead. "I pretty much always assume everybody else in town is plotting against me—it's safer to expect the worst—and this is an unprecedented opportunity for me to gain some valuable intel."

"So . . . you want me to spy on the other sorcerers?"

"Well. *Passively.* Don't go unlocking any locked

doors. Just see if you get any psychic twinges. If any of these folks start popping up in your dreams. You know what I mean?"

"I think so. Any particular reason? Do you suspect something?"

"Maybe yes, maybe no. It's a gut thing, and I have to trust my gut. In the past six months, I've had one leading sorcerer try to erase me from existence, and another hire an assassin to kill me the old-fashioned way. I'm supposed to protect the city from outside threats, but it seems like most of my biggest problems have been inside jobs. My entirely irrational and superstitious feeling is that shit like this comes in threes, which means I've got one more betrayal to look out for. I could be wrong. I hope I'm wrong. You can convince me I'm wrong."

B mulled that over. Marla's instincts were probably not to be dismissed. "Do you have any particular people in mind for the role of betrayer of the week?"

"Sure, there are guys I trust more or less than others. But I don't want to prejudice your observations. You're going to meet every sorcerer who matters in town over the next couple of weeks, and I look forward to hearing your judgments."

"Couldn't I just scare up an oracle and ask it... well... whatever?"

"Nah, my concerns are too vague. You know how oracles are. If you don't have exactly the right question, they'll go all cryptic on you."

"True. But if I find something out, sense anything suspicious..."

"Then we might know enough to ask the right questions. Now you get it." She pushed the buzzer.

"Yes?" a tinny voice replied.

"The woods are lovely, dark, and deep." Marla rolled her eyes. The door buzzed open.

"What, is that like a spy code phrase?" B said.

"Yep. Viscarro says it's one he used during the '50s when he was involved with international espionage, but I looked it up, and it's from a spy *novel*. This guy is more full of crap than your sneakers. He knows his artifacts, though."

The door swung open with a click, and Marla led Rondeau into Viscarro's high-ceilinged lair, which seemed like a three-way collision of a bank vault, a library, and a museum of historical oddities. A bleary-eyed guy in office-drone-wear hurried forward to meet them. "The master will see you," he said, and led them past dozens of people scurrying purposefully around, arms loaded with files and boxes, or else pushing shopping carts heaped with the contents of every rummage and white elephant sale held in the past decade.

"These are Viscarro's apprentices," Marla said.

"*All* of them?"

"Sure. You know how most mammals have only a small number of offspring, but nurture them very carefully to adulthood? Whereas spiders have a crapload of babies and don't pay any attention to whether their offspring live or die? My approach to having an apprentice is more mammalian. But Viscarro is definitely a spider."

Finally they were ushered into an office, which was messy and paper-filled and reminded B of the domain of a daily city paper's editor-in-chief, as seen in a '40s screwball comedy. Viscarro himself, seated behind the desk, was not at all what B had expected. He wasn't surprised by the gold-rimmed monocle, or the beaklike nose, or the baldness, or the body, which was like something made of white leather stretched over a framework of coat hangers. B was surprised by the sudden and unmistakable knowledge that the subterranean sorcerer was *dead*.

He sidled over to Marla's side, half hiding behind her, and said, "Nosferatu." His head was full of black-and-white images, a bald pointy-eared creature with clawlike fingernails that seemed, in and of themselves, utterly psychotic. When Marla didn't reply right away, he tugged her sleeve. "Marla. *Nosferatu*."

"Technically, I am a lich." Viscarro didn't look pissed-off or amused or anything else B could easily name. He looked like a corpse with indigestion. "Your apprentice is perceptive, Marla. It took you years to realize my true nature."

"Perceptive is what B does." Marla gestured for B to sit in one of the chairs on the visitors' side of the desk, and he did. He couldn't take his eyes off Viscarro, captivated by the novel vision of an animate corpse. Marla dropped into a chair and propped her feet on Viscarro's desk, her boots shoving aside the wired-together skeleton of some enormous rodent. To B she said, "Viscarro here voluntarily killed himself, then arranged to have his own ghost haunt his earthly remains. His life-force is hidden in some pretty jewel, and as long as that object is safe, he's immortal." She shook her head. "He's an abomination and an unclean thing and all that, but he's *our* abomination, so I try not to let my personal feelings get in the way. He's no vampire, B, and for the moment anyway we're allies. No leading a band of merry monster-hunters down here with torches and stuff, okay?"

"So this is what I've always heard about politics and strange bedfellows," B said.

Viscarro turned to him. "Don't judge me. I was, for genetic reasons, unable to extend my life by the usual magical means—I would have been dead in the early years of this century had I not chosen this . . . venerable, if unorthodox, form of immortality. I'm sad to see you share your master's prejudice. I've always found Marla's hatred for the undead unfair and unreasoning. She despises me because I am a spirit possessing a body through magical means. Yet her dearest friend, Rondeau, is himself a strange psychic entity, also possessing a body through supernatural means we do not fully understand. Why hate me and embrace him?"

"Because you're *dead*," Marla said. "Rondeau's heart pumps, his lungs inflate, his synapses snap and crackle. If the body he's wearing dies, his essential nature will jump ship and find a new, living host. Like every other sensible semisentient creature, he finds dead things abhorrent. But *you,* you're a ghost haunting a corpse, and that's just nasty."

"A body is a body." Viscarro shrugged his bony shoulders. "Dead, alive, alive, dead. I fail to see the importance of the distinction."

"Yeah? So you'd just as soon fuck a living person as a

dead one? What's the point of the *distinction*? Oh, right—one's normal, and one's called necrophilia."

Viscarro sighed. "Touché, I suppose. We shall, as always, agree to disagree. As to your point, sex has not held interest for me in some time."

"Thank the gods for small favors. This is a teachable moment here, B. Sometimes, as chief sorcerer, you have to work with people that, in normal circumstances, you'd set on fire. Viscarro has put his ass on the line—or anyway, his *property,* which is more important to Viscarro than his ass, frankly—to protect the city, and he's been down here longer than anybody, so I don't have a quarrel with him. But dead things have a tendency to find their hold on humanity *slippery,* and if I ever get the feeling he's become more monster than man, well ... Pitchforks. Torches. The whole deal."

B nodded, not sure how to react to this. He knew sorcerers were a morally relativistic bunch, and Viscarro certainly seemed like a textbook definition of that-which-should-not-be, but who was B to judge? Maybe assuming Viscarro was one step away from a flesh-eating night-monster was pure prejudice, the magical equivalent of thinking women belonged in the kitchen or that all gay men liked show tunes. He'd try to judge the guy on his own merits, though Viscarro's whole nature screamed wrongness at B's psychic receivers. How was he supposed to give Marla useful intel when he couldn't even sort out his psychic twinges from his personal squick-triggers? He'd just have to try harder.

Viscarro rose from his place behind the desk. He was shrunken, like a drying husk, barely any taller upright than he'd been seated. "Now that the usual threats of murder and theft are out of the way, Marla, perhaps we can get on with this? I'm a busy man, and I'd just as soon discharge my obligation now."

"Sure thing. B, go with Viscarro. He's going to take you to the antique roadshow, underground sorcerer style."

Rondeau sat in a neighborhood dive bar a few miles away from his neighborhood, a smoky joint occupied at the moment by tired-looking old men and three idle youths lounging around the cluster of pool tables at the back, looking for suckers. He drank a gin and tonic slowly, trying to maintain the cloak of gently buzzing numbness that isolated him from the sour feelings about Lorelei. Why did he keep drifting in and out of that woman's orbit? It never worked out, and he wasn't even sure he *wanted* it to work out, if "worked out" meant getting into a serious relationship. That way lurked madness. He'd only tried to be *honest* with her, but apparently, there was a time and a place for that, and he'd misjudged both.

A guy slid onto the bar stool next to his, though there were empty ones all along the rail, and Rondeau wondered if he was about to get cruised. It was noon on a weekday, and this was a far cry from a gay bar, but stranger things had happened. Maybe if the guy was cute, Rondeau would cruise *him,* for the distraction of the sex or an offended fistfight, both of which usually went well with being drunk. He glanced over.

The guy was Marla's brother, Jason. "Whoa," Rondeau said. "Small world."

"Hey, you're Randy, right?" Jason slapped him companionably on the shoulder.

"Rondeau, actually."

"What's that, French?"

Rondeau shrugged, his brain churning sluggishly through the lower gears. Jason was here. Was that coincidence? Marla didn't believe in coincidence. She believed in the mindless clattering of a blindly mechanistic universe, or, alternately, in conspiracies. She always said he wasn't paranoid enough. "French, yeah. I saw it in a book when I was a kid and kind of liked the sound of it, thought it would be a good name. It's a kind of poem."

"A self-made man, and a self-named one. I like that. And don't get me started on poetry. My mom stuck me with 'Jason Mason.' She was the kind of trailer park poet who dreamed of writing for Hallmark someday. Marla got the alliteration, but me, I'm a walking talking couplet here."

"My sympathies." Rondeau peered into his inexplicably empty glass.

"So, out of all the bars in all the world, why walk into this one?" Jason asked. "Don't you have a nightclub full of booze you could be drinking for free?"

"Had to run an errand for Marla, stayed to have a drink. No. Four drinks."

"That's a hell of a lunch. What kind of errand was it?"

Rondeau made a throat-cutting gesture. "If I told you that, she'd take my head off." In truth, he'd just been dropping off a bribe for the leader of the Honeyed

Knots, a gang that did some occasional work for Marla, but Rondeau was feeling buzzed and overdramatic.

"My sister's one tough lady, huh?"

"I never met tougher, and I grew up around people who'd steal your shoes with the feet still inside if you gave 'em a hacksaw and half a chance." Rondeau straightened, squinted at Jason, and poked him in the arm. "Why are *you* here? You following me?"

"No. You're not my type." Jason grinned. "I'm staying a couple of blocks away. This was the first bar I passed. Just trying to kill some time." He lowered his voice. "And maybe make a few bucks. You want to help me run a little game on those would-be hustlers back by the pool tables?"

"I'm not much of a player, even when I haven't had four drinks. Since I got here. Forty minutes ago."

"Nah, I don't mean shooting pool. First rule of dealing with a grifter, you *never* let them pick the game. But guys like that can't resist easy money, especially when they think it's a sure thing. Want to play along? If we get some dough, I'll kick some back to you for being a good sport."

Jason's proposal spoke to the native larceny in Rondeau's heart. "Why not?" A vestigial sense of self-preservation stirred in him. "I'm not putting up any of my own money, though. Marla said I shouldn't gamble with you."

"Now, that's just unkind. I bet if you think back, you'll realize she probably said you shouldn't gamble *against* me. If you gamble *with* me, Ronnie, you can't

lose. I'm going into the bathroom. Wait a couple minutes, then come in, and I'll tell you what to do."

"Got it?" Jason said.

"I think so," Rondeau said.

"Good. Remember, don't try to convince them. You
let *them* convince *you,* and only reluctantly. Okay. I'm
on. Wait about five minutes, then come out. I should be
gone by then, but if I'm still around, just keep yourself
busy by the jukebox or something until I'm out the
door."

After Jason left the bathroom, Rondeau leaned
against the wall of the toilet stall, took a compact
makeup case from his inner jacket pocket, and flipped
open the lid. He wasn't much of a sorcerer, but his friend
Langford—who was kind of a mad scientist type—had
enchanted the little mirror with a short-range clairvoy-
ance spell. He and Rondeau shared a love of spying on
people. Rondeau muttered the words of activation, and
the round mirror became a tiny viewscreen, albeit more
like a window than a television in terms of resolution.

Jason left the bathroom, walked toward the bar, then
paused halfway, frowning and looking at his hands. He
patted his jacket, reached into all his pockets, and muttered a bit. Cursing—but not loudly—he knelt and began looking underneath tables, crawling around on all
fours like a man who'd lost a contact lens, finally moving
toward the pool tables, where a couple of the twenty-
somethings smoking and holding pool cues finally
deigned to notice him. "Lose something?"

"Ah, just—it's nothing." Jason looked up at them, smiled weakly, and went back to his search.

"Come on. Maybe we've seen it."

Jason paused and rose to his knees, looking oddly penitent. "It's just my wedding ring. It slipped off somewhere, I think, maybe it wasn't even here, I don't know. . . . It's been loose ever since I went on a low-carb diet last year, supposedly it's hard to resize because of all the diamonds—shit, my wife is going to kill me."

"Tough break, pal." One of the guys lined up a shot and cracked his stick against the cue ball.

Jason rose to his feet. "I should retrace my steps, back to the hotel—I'm in town for a convention. Do you think, if you guys happen to find it . . . ?"

One of the pool players laughed. "A ring with diamonds all over it, you said? Just come back later and check the lost-and-found."

Jason sighed. "Okay, I see how it is. Look, you could pawn the ring for a few hundred bucks, probably, but it means more to me—more importantly, to my wife—than that. So if you find it, call me, all right?" He produced a business card and handed it to one of the pool players. "Here's my cell number. I'll give you a reward." He paused. "A thousand dollars. That's more than you'd get at any pawnshop."

Now the men looked interested. "You got a grand on you?"

Jason backed away, holding up his hands. "No, no, I'd have to go to the bank, but if you find the ring . . ."

The men shrugged and circled one of the pool tables. "Sure, mister. If we see your ring we'll give you a call."

"Thank you." Jason sounded miserable, and he kept touching his ring finger, seemingly unconsciously. Rondeau was impressed. "I'd better walk back the way I came."

The men ignored him, and Jason bowed his head and went out of the bar, staring at the floor all the while.

"Poor bastard," one of the pool players said, and the others nodded in solemn agreement.

After a couple of minutes, Rondeau came out of the bathroom, whistling and holding up the gold-and-diamond (or diamondlike anyway) ring to what little light there was in the bar. He went past the pool players, careful not to even look in their direction—Jason had been firm on that point—and one of the men said, "Hey, what's that? A ring?"

"Yup." Rondeau slipped it into his pocket. "Just found it in the john, saw it glittering back behind the toilet when I took a piss, you believe that? My lucky day."

The players exchanged glances. The one Jason had given his card to said, "Let me see it."

"No way. Finders keepers."

"I think it's my ring." The guy stepped around the table, holding the cue with casual menace.

Rondeau snorted, trying to remember his lines. It was mostly improv, but there were some salient points he was supposed to hit. "Oh, yeah? If it's yours, then what's the inscription?"

"Fine. It's *not* mine. But what do you say you give it to me anyway?" He took a step forward.

Jason had said it might go this way, but Rondeau had assured him not to worry about it. He took his butterfly knife from his inner jacket pocket and flipped it open and closed a few times with well-practiced ease. "What say I *don't*?"

The guy laughed. "All right, fair's fair. How about I buy it off you?"

"Why you got such a hard-on for this ring?"

"It's got diamonds on it, right?" He paused. "I saw, when you were holding it. I like stuff like that."

Rondeau shrugged. "I don't know, it doesn't fit my finger, but I figure I can pawn it...."

"Pawnshop might want to see some proof of ownership," the guy said. "Me, I'm a no-questions-asked kind of man." He took a large wad of small bills from his pocket—his stake for hustling—and began counting. "What would you say to a hundred?"

Rondeau snorted. "I'd say 'That's funny.' Then I'd say something you'd probably find offensive."

The guy sighed. "You're gonna make me haggle? Fine. *Two* hundred."

"Make it three, and settle my bar bill for me, and you've got a deal."

"Hey Pete!" the guy yelled, and the bartender looked up. "What's this guy been drinking?"

"Cheap gin, and lots of it."

"All right." The guy counted out the money. "Let's see the ring."

Rondeau fished it from his pocket, gave it an ostentatious little shine against his sleeve, then exchanged it for the cash. He counted the money quickly, then grinned. "Nice doing business with you. That's the most profitable piss I've ever taken. Afternoon, gentlemen."

Rondeau managed to stay calm as he walked out of the bar, but by the time he got to the sidewalk he could barely contain himself—he wanted to skip and cackle. He felt like he'd just fucked a fetish model and then gone hang gliding. He'd engaged in plenty of petty larceny over the years, at least when he was a kid, but he'd never really *conned* anyone, and it was a thrill.

Two blocks away from the bar, Jason sauntered along as promised to meet Rondeau on the corner. He held a cheap disposable cell phone to his ear, and said, "You found it? That's wonderful! Stay there, I'll be back as soon as I can. I just need to go to the bank to pick up the reward money for you." He hung up, then tossed the phone underhand into a garbage can. "How'd we make out?"

Rondeau wordlessly handed over the folded wad of bills. Jason flipped through them with professional precision, separated half the bills, and tucked them into Rondeau's breast pocket.

"Fun, huh?" Jason said. "And we're only out a twenty-five-dollar piece of costume jewelry and a disposable cell. Not a bad take for ten minutes of effort."

"I can't believe that worked!" Rondeau shook his head. He'd seen magic on a regular basis for years, but Jason was a different kind of sorcerer.

"Conning a con man is supposed to be the greatest challenge, but sometimes it's not that hard. Guys like that think they can't be taken, and overconfidence is one of my favorite qualities in a mark. Hey, listen. You were pretty good in there. I've got a little something in the works, and I could use another guy on my team. You interested? It's more involved than that business was, but it won't interfere with your job working for my sister. Hell, you could learn a few things to help *her* make money in the future, right?"

Rondeau considered. Jason thought Marla was a crime boss—which she was, kind of, though not mostly—and thus reasonably assumed Rondeau was some kind of criminal, too, which he was, he supposed, but only technically. He'd had fun running that little scam in the bar, but he wasn't *that* drunk. "I'd have to check with Marla. She can get touchy about moonlighting."

He figured Jason would drop the subject then. Instead, Jason said, "Oh, absolutely. I'll come with you to talk to her about it. What do you say we go grab some burgers to soak up all that liquor, then pay Marlita a visit?"

Rondeau just nodded, already walking along with Jason, giving in to the momentum of events. The Masons were maelstroms, and if you got too close, they'd suck you in. But, Rondeau reflected, it was usually a hell of a ride, and going with the current had seldom steered him wrong. At the very least it would take his mind off Lorelei, and in a healthier way than booze did. He couldn't stand the hangovers anyway.

Viscarro scuttled jaggedly along like a dead leaf blowing down a sidewalk, and soon B lost track of the turns they'd taken through twisting low-ceilinged corridors. Marla was gone, off to tend other business, and B was a little afraid Viscarro was going to turn ghoul and eat him or something, though he was trying to keep an open mind. This had been a rather overwhelming morning. How was he supposed to concentrate on learning magic from a dead man when Marla had dropped this bomb about him becoming her successor? Ever since he'd discovered magic was real, he'd been trying to figure out his place in that world—but he'd never imagined himself at the *top* of it, even on a local basis. If he wasn't up for the job, he probably shouldn't waste Marla's time.

Maybe by the time she needs me to take over, I'll be ready. Maybe she'll make *me be ready.*

"I'm taking you to the limbo room." Viscarro's voice was dry, maybe amused—even with his vaunted perceptiveness, B found it hard to be sure.

"That's where you keep your unbaptized stuff?" B said, and immediately regretted it. This didn't seem like a place for jokes.

"You'll see." They rounded a corner curved like a fishhook, which dead-ended into a shining steel vault door guarded by a wheezingly asthmatic man clutching a rusty halberd in ink-stained hands. "Open the door," Viscarro said, and the guard spun dials and twisted knobs, then shoved hard on a lever, putting the whole weight of his body into it. The door, which was at least two feet thick in cross-section, swung open with silent ease. B wondered if the exquisite balance could be credited to magic or to engineering.

Harsh white lights on the vault's ceiling illuminated when the door opened, revealing shelves of jumbled crap and a long low table with a couple of rolling stools beneath it and a giant magnifying glass on a swing arm fixed to the tabletop.

"This is the land of uncataloged acquisitions. Hence, limbo. I'm going to teach you to establish *provenance*." Viscarro rubbed his hands together in anticipatory glee.

Then followed the most excruciatingly dull three hours of B's life. Viscarro reverently took objects from the shelves and made B examine them, pointing out salient details. The stone pot with the leering monkey face might *look* pre-Columbian, Viscarro explained, but the dirt in the crevices suggested it was fake—genuine artifacts from that era tended to be cleaner, preserved in sealed chambers and thus not especially dirty. This tapestry appeared handmade in the 12th century, but this color of dye was unavailable in Italy at that time, so it was clearly from a later era. This painting might seem a genuine Van Gogh, but careful attention to the aggregate directionality of the brushstrokes revealed it was more likely a forgery. And so on and on and on and on. The guard sat in the corner, furiously marking down Viscarro's pronouncements in a ledger the size of an extra-large pizza box.

B finally croaked, "Could I get some water?"

Viscarro paused in his discourse on noteworthy potter's marks, which was itself merely a long digression from his original point about identifying anachronistic tool marks on purportedly ancient arts and crafts. "Ah, yes, bodily functions." He sent the guard away for refreshments, and, now derailed, squinted at B through his monocle. "I suppose you'd like to get to the magic, hmm?"

"Magic? There's magic? Magic would be nice."

Viscarro tapped his creepily long fingernails on the table. *Nosferatu,* B thought again, but beyond the fact of the guy being *dead* he wasn't picking up any especially treacherous vibes.

"I make my apprentices study conventional methods for years before I teach them more *direct* routes of appraisal, but if I don't show you something beyond the limits of ordinary human knowledge and intellect, Marla will just bring you back. Neither of us want that. She's so damned impatient."

"People who aren't going to live forever sometimes feel the need to rush," B said. The guard set a glass of water before him. B gulped it, even though it seemed to have been drawn from a dying well, complete with specks of yellow sediment settling at the bottom.

"Aren't you impudent? That makes you a good fit for Marla, at least. All right, then." Viscarro went to a shelf and took down a dented gauntlet from a suit of plate mail. "This item, then. It appears genuine, and so it's worth further investigation. Like most of the items here, it was acquired in a bulk estate sale. I buy via the dragnet method, sweeping up loads of offal in hopes of finding a few gems amid the shit. If I didn't have my large staff—and all the time in the world—it would be a disheartening enterprise, but as I have the proper resources, it suits me perfectly."

"So you fish for treasure. Fair enough. What do you do with all the rejects?" B gestured at the jumbled pile of frauds and commonplaces heaped at the far end of the table.

"The *good* forgeries I sell at auction, with fake letters of provenance. I am a highly respected expert in many branches of antiquity, you know, and my word is trusted. Those things that are merely *ordinary* go to...what is it?"

"eBay," the guard said.

"Yes." Viscarro sounded deeply satisfied. "The eBay has proven most lucrative."

"Okay. So this gauntlet. How do you tell...whatever it is you're trying to find out about it? Besides using your encyclopedic knowledge regarding stuff dead soldiers wore on their hands?"

"Objects have memories. The art of accessing those memories is known as psychometry. An object possessed by an individual or kept in one place for a long time carries associations, images, and aftertastes of that contact. I'm told you are psychic, so you should have the necessary perceptiveness. I will merely teach you how to prepare your mind."

Viscarro described meditation exercises and incantations used to focus attention, lecturing with the same tedious thoroughness he'd used when discussing ancient printmaking techniques or the hallmarks of early glassblowing. B did his best to soak it in, finally saying, "So all this works like magical Ritalin?"

Viscarro looked at his guard, who shrugged and said, "Sure, why not?"

"The living are so tiresome." Viscarro sighed, and went on to explain how objects sometimes projected information on slightly out-of-phase wavelengths, so even a sensitive psychic might smell an image, hear a taste, or feel an odor. Viscarro went over some methods for recalibrating one's sensitivities, and finally, when B was ready to bang his head against the table until he blacked out just to make the talking stop, Viscarro laid his hands on the gauntlet, inhaled deeply, and said, "A heavy cavalry knight. Well, of course. Of a good family, but landless, ashamed of his wastrel father, desperate for glory and reward..." He opened his peculiarly colorless eyes. "The associations are strong here. The owner was wearing this when he died, and that tends to make a deep impression. You try. Tell me *how* he died."

B cleared his mind, muttered the right words, felt all his senses turn themselves up to eleven, and laid hands on the gauntlet.

The shimmering gray-white ghost of a bearded middle-aged man in a battered suit of armor appeared, his insubstantial body cut off at the waist by the table. Viscarro scuttled backward, stool toppling. The man said something—it sounded like French, only not quite—and touched the caved-in side of his skull. He held up the shattered remains of his helm, made a disgusted noise, and tossed the broken armor aside, where it vanished in mid-fall.

B let go of the gauntlet, and the ghost promptly vanished. "Cause of death was blunt force trauma to the head. Maybe a war hammer?"

"Show-off." Viscarro scrambled up from the floor and brushed off his clothes. "But it appears you've gotten the hang of it. I'm sure Marla will be pleased with your progress, and release me from my obligation. I'll be glad to see the back of you." He paused. "But while you're here, would you mind looking at this old brass oil lamp? It's defied the analysis of my best technicians."

B laughed. "You want my help? What's in it for me?"

"An infinitesimal reduction in the amount of ill will I bear you," Viscarro said magnanimously.

"Works for me." Who wanted to be on a not-exactly-Nosferatu's bad side?

Nicolette's messenger stopped beneath a tree, sucked down the last drops from his water bottle, and surveyed the forest before him with a sinking heart. What a shitty gig. He ran errands for sorcerers for a living, but he would've turned down this job . . . if he'd been allowed. He owed Nicolette too much to say no to any request, no matter how unreasonable, so here he was, deep in eastern Oregon's Malheur National Forest. One-point-seven million acres of the place, and he had nothing to guide him but a 'chanted compass festooned with dried mushrooms he'd had a local alley witch whip up for him. "Local" meaning "in Seattle"—Nicolette was so firmly a creature of the East Coast that she thought Washington State and Oregon were basically the same place, so why *couldn't* he run this little errand for her? Of course, it was a ten- or eleven-hour drive in his van—this place was practically in *Idaho*—plus the time it took him to find a charm capable of tracking his quarry, plus hours spent literally wandering in the wilderness. The chaos witch had given him a bout of good luck a few years back when he'd needed it most, but on the whole she'd been more bad news than not. He was exhausted, down to running on fumes and magically augmented adrenaline. It wasn't even noon yet.

This forest was a pretty place, no doubt—he smelled sage and juniper and pine, he'd passed two gorgeous lakes, and there was enough mountain scenery for a hundred bottled-water commercials—but tracking down a sorcerer who was, by all accounts, insane and anti-social didn't put him in the mood to appreciate nature. Especially since he'd recently passed a trailhead sign for a spot called Murderer's Creek. He wished he didn't believe in omens. Even the name of the forest, "Malheur," what was that, corrupted French for "Bad Hour"? That was just great.

The compass began to shudder in his hands, the seedpods and dried shrooms swinging away from gravity's pull and pointing up a hill, so he kept clumping through the forest. He reached a dense stand of trees, their trunks ringed with fat clusters of yellow-brown mushrooms. The profusion of fungus sparked a vague memory. Hadn't he read something about this park, about some kind of mushrooms? How they were all linked underground, actually one giant organism, maybe the biggest single living thing on the planet, stretching beneath the earth for miles and miles?

"The Mycelium said you would come," rasped a voice from the thick underbrush among the trees.

The messenger stiffened. "Are you . . ." He consulted the scrap of paper in his pocket. "Bull-yard?"

"Bulliard. The name I took for myself. In honor of the great botanist Jean Baptiste François Pierre Bulliard, who wrote the *Dictionnaire Elémentaire de Botanique.* Do you know it?"

"Can't say that I do."

"A great work for identifying mushrooms. It is important, being able to identify mushrooms. For instance, many cannot tell the straw mushroom from the death cap, and in those cases, tragedy may result. Do you know the death cap? *Amanita phalloides.* My brothers. We killed Charles VI. We killed Emperor Claudius. We attack the liver and kidneys. We have no antidote." The underbrush rustled.

"Listen, I'm here with a message. From an, ah, anonymous benefactor."

"The Mycelium said. The Mycelium said I should *listen.*" The voice had moved—it was off to the left now, and seemed to be coming from a place relatively clear of underbrush, where there was nothing but those honey-colored mushrooms. Was Bulliard invisible? Or was he—somehow this was more horrible—was he *underground*?

"The message is this: the Borrichius spores are in Felport."

Silence. Then a sound like chewing, perhaps like laughter *through* chewing. "That is all? That is the whole of the message?"

"That's it."

"Then we are done. The Mycelium says not to kill you. The Mycelium says, spare your liver and kidneys. I am sad. I have alpha-amanitin. I have bolesatine. I have coprine—for the drinkers, the campers, with their beer cans and their stink. I have orellanin, gyromitrin, mus-carine. I have the hands of a destroying angel, the breath of an ivory funnel. I wear my autumn skullcap, I hold my deadly parasol, I am the deadly dapperling. But for you, not death."

"Good to know." The messenger had been a courier for sorcerers for years, and he'd thought himself pretty well hardened against weirdness and threats, but his business seldom took him to places as remote as this. Being at the mercy of this man's nature *in* nature un-nerved him. He wondered if he could run, wondered if this guy would just pop out of the ground and *grab* him.

"For you, only madness. For you, psilocybin."

Something huge loomed out of the trees to the left, a blur of vegetable coloration, something that might have been a face under a veil of heavy mosses, arms that could have been stout tree branches. The messenger stumbled back, dropping the compass—which was buzzing like an agitated beehive now—and tried to run, tripping on a half-hidden log and falling to the ground. Something fell upon his back, pinning him down with his nose pressed into a cluster of ugly brown mushrooms. He thrashed, and a thick choking dust filled his nostrils and mouth, worming down his throat and airways. He began to gasp.

The thing on his back rose up. "You can run. Try to run. You will not reach the edge of the forest before you begin to see visions. Psilocybin. We were there for St. John the Divine. We will be there for you. The Mycelium may have a message for you. Or you may be given to the forest."

Dosed, the messenger thought, scrambling to his feet and half running, half stumbling down the hill. He'd done acid before, even mescaline, but never shrooms. It wouldn't be so bad, would it? As far as hallucinogens went, shrooms were natural, crunchy; hippies did them. If worst came to worst he could just hunker down and wait out the trip—find a pretty spot by a lake and soak in the view. Besides, it would take a little while for the effects to hit him, and before then—

The trip hit him like he'd run into a wall. The sky opened. The earth opened. The sun melted and dripped down the sky. The light vibrated. The ground laughed.

The messenger saw god. A god. Bulliard's god.

And Bulliard's god saw him.

4

Marla went back to her office after leaving B in the catacombs, and found Jason and Rondeau lounging at the table off the kitchen, drinks in hand, a couple of decks of cards scattered before them. Without a word Marla picked up Rondeau's tumbler and sniffed it, frowning. "This is either plain tonic water with lemon or you got some nice vodka that doesn't smell."

"I'm on the wagon, for the moment." Rondeau held out his hand, palm down. "See how steady I am? Jason dragged me out of a bar before I got so drunk I slid underneath one of the tables."

"My brother, savior of man." Marla consented to be briefly embraced when Jason stood up. Dinner the night before had been ... nice. She wouldn't go so far as to say there were no illusions between Jason and herself—for one thing, he thought her entire *lifestyle* was a sham—but the lies they told each other were different from the lies she told most people, and that was refreshing. Even after all those years apart, there was the unspoken bond of shared experience between them. They weren't so different. Smart, ambitious, ruthless, desperate to leave behind their roots and find new life and purpose elsewhere. She'd found magic. He'd found the grift.

"Marlita." Jason sat down, leaning back in the beat-up old kitchen chair and lacing his hands over his belly. "I've got a proposition for you. I'd like to take on your man Rondeau as a subcontractor."

Marla looked at Rondeau, who looked down into his glass, which he was probably wishing contained something stronger than tonic water. "Oh, really. Do tell."

"Like I told you last night, I've got an operation under way, and I can use another pair of hands and eyes. His brain will come in handy, too. He helped me run a sweet little lost-ring scam at a bar earlier, and he did good. I think he's got grift sense."

"Grift sense?" Rondeau said.

"Don't get excited," Marla said. "It's not like a sixth sense or even spider-sense. It's old-time hustler lingo. Just means you have a knack for spotting gullible idiots who'll fall for a line of bullshit."

"I would've put it a little more elegantly than *that*, but basically. What do you think? I promise it won't interfere with your business."

"And your word is gold, right, brother? Rondeau, go downstairs for a bit while I talk to Jason alone."

Rondeau scurried away, and Jason looked after him with eyebrows raised, then turned to Marla. "You've got him well trained."

"He's been working for me for a long time." Marla

sat down, sighed, and picked up Jason's glass. She took a sip and grimaced. "Ah, should've known you'd have something other than tonic water." She put the glass of vodka down and gazed at her brother, drawing out the moment of silence to see if it would put Jason on edge, but he just looked patiently expectant. "You want to use Rondeau's connection to me to help you scam Cam-Cam. You already dragged my name into this to give it a whiff of legitimacy, and now you want to parade Rondeau past Cam-Cam so he thinks he's *really* on the inside track to magical mystery woo-woo stuff." She looked at him.

Jason looked back. After a moment he said, "I'm sorry, was that a question? Yes. You are correct. I didn't expect you to think otherwise. So what do you say?"

"I'd really rather not have Cam-Cam buzzing around and annoying me. *After* you rip him off and leave him penniless, he'll come sniffing around here after Rondeau, looking for restitution, and I don't want to deal with it. You can leave town and avoid the repercussions, but I've got a life here, and I don't want you fucking it up. Understand?"

"Ah, Marlita, but the blow-off I've got planned is perfect. Smoothest dismount you can imagine. This guy won't even know he's *been* scammed. He'll be flat broke, he'll give me his last dollar, and he'll thank me at the end of it. But in order for me to accomplish that perfect blow-off, I could really use Rondeau. I meant what I said. He handled himself well today."

"I'm sure he did. He's capable, in his way." Marla considered. If things went bad and Cam-Cam bothered

her afterward, she could always dose him with forget-
me-lots and send him back to his life as an irritatingly
clueless seeker after wonder. It wasn't likely to be a problem—Cam-Cam wasn't heavy, he wasn't connected, and
there were few downsides to messing with his memory.
She couldn't explain that to Jason, but she *could* pretend
she believed his line of patter about having the perfect
scam. Maybe it would help their relationship. She was a
bit surprised, after last night's dinner, to realize she
wasn't opposed to the idea of having a relationship with
him. Maybe she was going soft. And with B around to
take up the slack, she didn't need Rondeau quite so
much, not on a daily basis, and letting him do some
work with Jason would…well, not keep him out of
trouble, obviously, but keep him in trouble she *knew*
about. "Okay. But if I even *hear* about guns, knives,
hatchets, any kind of physical coercion at all, Rondeau
is out, understood? This has to be a clean and gentlemanly grift. Otherwise I'll go to Cam-Cam personally
and tell him you're a liar and a thief."

"Wow. You're protective of Ronnie, huh? Do I hear
wedding bells?"

Marla snorted. "Me and Rondeau? That would be
like—" *Like dating my brother.* Her standard answer
when people misunderstood her relationship with
Rondeau, but it would feel strange saying it to Jason.
"We're old friends, is all. He's saved my ass a few times,
I've saved his ass a *thousand* times, and that's the extent
of our interest in each other's asses."

"Understood." Jason reached over and clasped Marla's
hand. "I promise, no heavy stuff. Pure intellectual scam.

It'll be great, you'll see, and I'll cut you in for five percent, since you're kind enough to let the kid moonlight."

"Keep the money. Consider it eighteen years of over-due birthday presents."

"Wow, turning down cash. You *must* have a sweet operation in this city. Maybe I should become a legitimate businessman." He stood up. "Should I tell Rondeau the good news, or do you want to?"

"You can. Just do me a favor?"

"Name it."

"Make sure he has to wear a really bad fake mustache as a disguise at some point. Or, better—dress him in drag. Something slinky, red, and backless. Make him think it's absolutely essential to the scam."

Jason laughed, and it was so familiar it made something tear loose in her heart—it was the same laugh he'd had as a teenager, when something genuinely delighted him. "I'll do my best, Marlita. Can we get together again this week? I feel like we barely made it two blocks down memory lane last night."

"Sure, give me a call later, we'll work it out. Send Rondeau up for me, would you?"

After Jason left her, she sat quietly at the table for a while, then polished off the remains of his drink. Marla was never prone to introspection, but it was hard not to think about friendship, family, history, with Jason back in her life. Maybe that wasn't a bad thing. Time would tell.

Rondeau appeared. "Hey, thanks for letting me get into this. Sounds like it could lead to both fun *and* profit, which are each on my list of top-five favorite things."

"Mmm-hmm. Listen, I need you to spy on Jason for me."

Rondeau sat down and reached for his glass, swirling the pebbles of ice around. "Ah, right. Should've figured. You think he's got bad intentions?"

"Oh, he's definitely got bad intentions. I don't mind that—unless he's got bad intentions toward *me*. The guy shows up unannounced, with big plans I'm already a part of, like it or not? Damn right I'm suspicious."

"Gotcha. I'll keep my gimlet eye on him. Or is it my weather eye? Do you get one of each? Is it like 'port' and 'starboard'?"

"Just remember, like I said, no magic talk."

"I know, I know. So ... Jason's your brother, right? He loves you? I never had a brother, but it seems..." He trailed off.

"I'm just being cautious. Jason and I didn't part on such good terms. We're both smiling and pretending that stuff never happened, but it doesn't mean there's no old bad business underneath."

"Understood. I'll watch for signs of moral turpitude and spiritual decay, and report back. I've got my cell if you need me. Jason wants to introduce me to one of his buddies, and they're supposed to fill me in on the big con. I feel like I'm in *The Sting* or something."

"Movies aren't real life, Rondeau."

"Only because we don't try hard enough. What's wrong with being a little cinematic? Catch you later, boss."

*   *   *

Viscarro escorted B to a little waiting room near an access hatch leading to the surface, where Marla was lounging in a high-backed carved chair, reading a thick sheaf of paper. She folded it up and shoved it into the beat-up leather sack by her feet, then grinned. "So, B, is your head all full of esoteric knowledge?"

"Positively stuffed." He yawned hugely. "I think I've forgotten what the sun looks like."

"The sun went down half an hour ago, so you'll have to wait until morning to reacquaint yourself. Viscarro, was he a good student?"

Viscarro sniffed. "He was acceptable. He's learned some very basic pscyhometric techniques, so he should be able to help you should you encounter any more artifacts. Of course, some would say it's unfair you already have *two*."

"I thought you had, like, a hundred artifacts in the bank down here? All nicely sitting on shelves, not bothering anyone?"

"My inventory list is confidential." He waved his hand. "Begone. I assume I won't see you until next month's tribute is due?"

"Unless some metaphysical shit hits the fan before then." She stood up. "Come on, B, you've had a hard day. Want something to eat?"

This time they went up a dimly lit flight of stairs, emerging into some kind of power substation, all humming coils of metal, and then out into the night. They were in a fenced-off lot in who knows what part of Felport, but B didn't care where he was—the air was still pleasantly warm from the day's dissipating heat, and he'd never been so happy to have outside air in his lungs. "I think that place down there is where dust is *made*."

Marla led the way toward lights and bustle a couple of blocks away, where it looked like early nightlife of some description was gearing up. "Viscarro was okay? He didn't try to enthrall you and make you his Renfield or anything?" The question had an absent-minded tone—banter on autopilot.

"No, he was fine, boring and humorless, is all. I didn't get any... you know... twinges. Like we talked about. So what's on your mind?"

"Hmm? Just trying to decide where to eat. There's a good taqueria up past this movie theater, and a café with decent panini, and I think a pho place. What're you interested in?"

"Oh, anything. Seriously, I can tell something's bugging you, what is it?"

Marla started to walk faster, and B had to hustle to keep up. "I don't know. Maybe my brother. He's on my mind a bit. Family reunions aren't really my thing."

"Rondeau said you hadn't seen him in a long time?"

"Since we were kids. I left home when I was about fifteen. He was a couple of years older, already a high school dropout and small-time crook by then."

"Were you guys close?"

"Once upon a time, it was me and Jason against the world. Let's eat here." The taqueria was jammed into an alleyway between two closed shops, the counter manned by a surprisingly perky white teenager, who said, *"¡Hola!"* when they came in. They placed their orders—something heavy on the spice, called the scorcher special, for Marla, and a plain cheese quesadilla for B, who'd been forced to swear off hot sauce (along with caffeine and uppers) when his supernatural sensitivities developed some years earlier. They were the only ones in the place, and they took a table as far away from the counter as possible. Marla sipped her agua fresca and took a bite of her burrito, and B just waited, trying to be patient, knowing she would get to things in her own time.

"Okay. Jason did something really bad, right before I left town. I couldn't forgive him for it, and he was pretty upset about that—he thought I'd understand, maybe even that I'd applaud. After we had our big screaming fight over it, I told him I had a drunk for a mother and a psycho for a brother and I didn't see any reason to keep living in the cesspool with them. I packed my bags and started hitchhiking, and I eventually wound up here. I seriously never thought I'd see him again, especially not wearing a thousand-dollar suit and smile so sincere I can't help thinking it's phony."

"Sounds like an interesting guy. I hope I get to meet him." Insight into Marla's past—into anything about her personal life—was rare. "Is he in town for long?"

"Much to my dismay. He's running a scam on this rich magic-chaser named Campbell Campion. He's got Rondeau helping him out, and I know if I'm not careful, I'll wind up helping him, too. He can be very convincing."

"A real con artist, huh? I knew my share of hustlers back in Hollywood, but we're talking like a whole big con kind of thing, with accomplices and disguises and salting gold mines and stuff like that?"

"So it would seem."

"I thought all the con men were doing identity theft and Nigerian e-mail scams these days."

"Jason's old school. He says he doesn't even care about the money, that he's got plenty of money—he's just in it for the thrill. I can't say the idea of seeing Cam-Cam reduced to poverty upsets me. He's a pain in the ass with more money than sense who thinks he can buy the numinous with a checkbook. He's heard of me, though, and Jason parlayed our family ties into a meeting with Cam-Cam, and from there, some kind of con. But I can't help thinking, Jason being *here*, bringing Rondeau in on his grift...it can't be coincidence, can it? Did he just happen to find me and see an angle he could play, or did he come looking for me, and if so, why?"

"You can't just ask him?"

"I can ask, but how can I be sure he's telling the truth? I could cast a spell to reveal falsehoods, but I know for a fact Jason has faked out polygraph machines in the past, and I wouldn't necessarily trust the results—Jason's got the rare ability to make *himself* believe whatever lie he's telling, at least while he's telling it. That's why he's so damned convincing."

B chewed his quesadilla. Bland. He was so sick of bland things. "So why don't we go find an oracle and ask it if your brother has nefarious intentions toward you?"

Marla shifted uncomfortably in her chair. "Messing with that kind of magic just because I'm suspicious of my brother seems...trifling, somehow. Oracles can get pissed when you come to them with bullshit questions, you know?"

B shrugged. "Sure, but I'm an oracle generator, so it seems a waste not to use me—I can sniff out some supernatural node of influence and put the question to it. If whatever we summon gets pissed off, I'm good at soothing them."

"Maybe it's a good idea. This is kind of eating at me."

"I can't promise we'll get an answer that makes sense, but it's worth a shot."

Marla wiped her mouth with a wadded-up napkin. "Okay. Earn your supper, then, lowly apprentice. Find me an oracle."

They went back out into the night, and B opened himself up. Marla had explained to him that most of the supernatural beings he called into existence weren't actually hooked up into some cosmic information line— they were just telling him things he already knew, truths he'd discovered using his unique psychic senses but, for whatever reason, couldn't apprehend directly. Even if they were just a manifestation of his own powers, though, he needed them—without outside explanation, the secrets would stay locked up in his brain, coming out only in cryptic dreams that, more often than not, he required an oracle to interpret anyway.

So he tried to feel with senses for which he possessed no names, and sensed something down an alley filled with garbage cans and quiet skitterings. Marla followed him silently as he went a little way down the alley, stopping in front of a particular dented trash can, its round metal lid askew. "Hey." B prodded the trash can with his foot. "I've got some questions."

The lid stirred, then fell off, and a welter of brown rats came scurrying out. B didn't flinch—the rats were real, ordinary vermin, not what he was looking for. The trash in the can groaned and shifted, garbage welling up into first a vague heap and then a quasi-human shape, a head of melon rind and sodden coffee filters, the blossom end of tomatoes for eyes, mouth of shucked oyster shells, a beard of rotting banana peel.

"Crazy," Marla said. "Like Oscar the Grouch, if he was actually made of garbage."

"I am Shakpana, bringer of pox, healer of the sick, maker of madness." The voice was slithery and squishy and foul. The garbage thing shifted, raising arms of chicken bones with spaghetti-noodle tendons and gripping the edge of the trash can with fingers made from Popsicle sticks. "Who awakens me in this form?"

"My name is Bradley Bowman. I have a question."

"Ask, and hear an answer, if you can pay the cost."

"Does Jason Mason mean this woman harm?"

"Ah." The thing tapped its fingers against the side of the can, making a clattering noise. It looked toward Marla. "Ah. He is your brother. Brothers and sisters should not fight."

"I don't want to fight him," Marla said. "I want to know if he means to fight *me*."

"I can answer this. But the cost is disposition of these earthly remains. You must swear to make a compost of this body later, and return to the soil whatever the worms and beetles might wish to eat."

"Agreed."

"Then know this. Jason—" Shakpana stopped talking,

and gagged with the sound of bursting gases. The garbage shifted and sank and became ordinary refuse again, and then the metal can started to shudder on the pavement, vibrating and humming with noises that soon transformed into words, the same words—in the same voice—they'd heard on the car radio: "Darkness, oblivion, the emptiness beyond emptiness, the ceasing of being, the all-swallowing space beyond space—" B covered his ears and crouched, hunching in on himself, and then began keening. The thing speaking to him now filled up his whole head, he heard it in his ears and his mind all at once, and a pulsing welter of darkness pushed itself against his vision.

Marla shouted and kicked over the garbage can, which seemed to break the connection with whatever they'd encountered. B uncovered his ears and struggled to his feet, swaying a little.

"Was that about my brother?" Marla came to B and put her arm around his shoulder, propping him up. "Or something else?"

"I—Shakpana never had a chance to answer my question about Jason. That other voice just forced itself in, overrode everything. I don't know what it means." He was shaky, sick to his stomach, his thoughts sluggish and scattered. He felt on the verge of blacking out. Something horrible was trying to make itself known, pushing itself through him to get out. Marla came over and put an arm around him, helping hold him up.

"Mystical shit." Marla sighed. "Let's get you home. I'll explore some other avenues of inquiry. If that warning *isn't* about Jason, I'd like to find out what it *is* about."

B went with her, quiet and afraid. Not so much afraid of whatever danger the insistent voice warned about—with Marla at his side, he was fairly confident of their tactical superiority—but afraid of his own powers, and their failure. If he couldn't summon an oracle to answer his questions, and if his only dreams lately were dreams of sinking into pillowy darkness, what good was he to Marla? An oracle generator who produced faulty oracles? A prophetic dreamer who prophesied only the coming of night? What kind of successor could he be for her? He wanted to ask, but he didn't, afraid she would answer with her customary truthful bluntness. He didn't think he could bear that, not with his head pounding so hard.

"It'll be okay, B," Marla said. She paused. "For some given value of 'okay.'"

The messenger came down from his trip to find himself strung upside down in the high branches of a tree, with mushrooms growing on the back of his neck. "This is fucked up, right here." He swayed a little as he struggled against the ropes of moss holding him.

The thing—no, the *sorcerer*, Bulliard—chuckled in his ear, out of sight, but not out of smell. "The Mycelium says you can be useful to us. You feel the mushrooms there, at the base of your skull? Their roots are in your brain. You can be rewarded with euphoria.

You can be punished with terrible visions. You can be ridden like a horse. You understand?"

"I had a vision," the messenger said. "I flew up in the sky, and looked down, and the trees all melted away, and the dirt, and I saw this giant thing living under the ground, this . . . this . . . it had a *face*."

"The Mycelium chose to let you look upon it. You should be honored. You are being allowed to serve."

"That thing was *real*? It wasn't just a bad trip?"

A hard shove, and the messenger's face slammed into the tree trunk, banging his nose hard enough to make him see explosions of darkness.

"Do not blaspheme again, or I will hurt you. You can still serve without all your limbs. The Mycelium is real. It is the white rot, the father of foxfire, the mother of will-o'-the-wisps. It has destroyed this forest a dozen times over in the past, and it can destroy you. You will tell us where to find the spores."

Gasping through his pain, the messenger said, "Man, I don't *know*. I just get told to go places, and I go. The message I gave you was the whole thing."

Another shove, gentler this time, enough to send him swaying, which was terrifying enough, this high up. *Fuck*. Why'd he ever answered that ad in college? Becoming a "courier" for magicians had been a good way to get weed money, but eventually it had turned into a career, and now, apparently, it was rapidly mutating into a death sentence.

"Do not lie to us."

"Who the hell is 'us'?"

"The Mycelium," Bulliard said reasonably. "The Mycelium is listening."

The certainty in his voice chilled the messenger. The guy was clearly crazy, but was a sentient mushroom god that lived underground really that much weirder than the other shit he'd seen in his time? "I'm not lying."

"Then tell us who *gave* you the message, and I will go and ask *them*."

The messenger grunted. "I wish I could, but I can't."

Another shove, and a sickening pendulum swing that made the messenger's guts lurch. "This is not a negotiation." Bulliard reached out a hand and stopped the swinging. "You will tell."

"I didn't say I *wouldn't*, I said I *can't*. I'm a courier for sorcerers, dude, and that requires strict confidentiality. I'm under a geas, is what I'm telling you. I *can't* reveal my employer, not when they ask for secrecy, and this one did!"

"There are ways to read your mind. They are not pleasant."

"You're *one* of them, you know how sorcerers are—there are safeguards. My brain would just melt and run out my fucking ears if you tried to go rifling through it."

"Hmm." Bulliard didn't sound pissed, at least, just contemplative. "But the spores are in Felport?"

"That's what the message said, but it's not like I know shit about it. I don't even know what the spores *are*."

"They are many things. They are what you make them. They are a path to the total obedience of all mankind to the will of the Mycelium. We would like to have them."

"Great. Then I suggest you head to Felport and start knocking on doors."

"I will. I will do just that." Bulliard patted him on the back. "But I do not drive. You will drive me."

"That'll take *days*."

"Not at all. The Mycelium says perhaps two days. Less. You will not sleep, and you will drive very fast."

"And what do I get paid for this?"

"Serving the Mycelium is its own reward," Bulliard said, almost amiably.

5

"Pier 14," Marla said. "Smell that sea air!" She wore a black cloak with silver trim, and it flapped around her dramatically as she stood near the end of the concrete tongue protruding into the water. "Hardly even a whiff of sewage."

B had only his old camouflage army coat as a defense against the wind whipping in off the water, and probably didn't cut nearly as striking a figure as Marla did. *Maybe I should invest in a cape or something. Marla says style counts.* "So you're taking me fishing now? As part of our master-apprentice bonding?"

Marla snorted. "I wouldn't fish this close to the docks, any more than I'd go swimming in the Balsamo River. We've got the pollution pretty well under control, thanks to Ernesto's cleanup efforts, but you can't completely sanitize a port this heavily trafficked. Give these fish a tox screen and you'd never want to touch seafood again."

The sun was just rising in the bay, making the shapes of cranes on the other piers stand out starkly against in the sky. There was plenty of bustle up and down the docks, but Pier 14 was oddly deserted. "Why no ships here?"

"This pier is reserved for special business, B. What if *Naglfr* should come steaming into port? If a ship of dead men's nails rides into town, you'd better have a berth for it."

B couldn't tell if she was kidding or not. "Are we taking a boat trip, then?"

"Not exactly. We're meeting someone. And here she is now. Come take a look." B joined her at the end of the pier, and the water rippled and bubbled and rolled. A woman shot out of the water, rising into the air in a burst of spray like the birth of Venus on fast-forward, and landed nimbly on the pier beside them. She straightened and shook out her long blond hair, splattering B and Marla with droplets. The woman was gorgeous, in a surfer-girl way, dressed in a dark blue wetsuit. "Marla. New person. Hello."

"Bradley Bowman, allow me to introduce you to the Bay Witch, mistress of the watery realm and the islands therein and etc. Zufi, this is my new apprentice, B."

"Yes," the Bay Witch said. There was something profoundly weird about her, something that B couldn't pin down. She didn't quite look at either of them, and her vocal inflections were odd. "I will teach him a trick. A *good* trick. And then no pearls for you this month."

"That's the deal," Marla said.

"Okay." The Bay Witch stepped up to B, gripped both

his forearms, and kissed him. Startled, he tried to pull away, but she was incredibly strong, and her insistent tongue forced his mouth open. Her breath was salt, and storm, and perhaps a hint of fish, but more fresh salmon sashimi than stinking mackerel. After a moment, the Bay Witch stepped away. "There. Done."

"What's done?" Marla said, frowning. "Besides the molestation of my apprentice?"

"The gift of endless breath. He can swim underwater forever now, with no need to breathe." She paused. "Also: he cannot suffocate."

"Ah. *Forever*?" B said.

The Bay Witch nodded. "That's what makes it a *good* trick."

Marla laughed. "Well, hell, that is handy—even *I* can't do that—but I'd figured on leaving B with you all day to learn things. Guess I'll have to find something else for him to do."

The Bay Witch cocked her head and, for the first time, looked at B directly. "He is very attractive. Would he like to copulate for recreational purposes?" She unzipped the front of her wetsuit, revealing the side swells of her breasts, which B could appreciate only on a purely aesthetic level.

Marla seemed to be stifling a guffaw. "That's up to him, Zuf."

"Ah, thanks, but I'm gay," B said, a lot more apologetically than he usually did. "That was actually the first time since high school that I've had a girl's tongue in my mouth."

"Oh. Sad."

B was gay, but he was still a *guy,* so he put in a word for a friend: "I bet Rondeau would be happy to come down here for, um, recreation, though."

The Bay Witch shook her head. "He cannot breathe underwater. He would drown. Marla would be angry." With that, she dove cleanly back into the bay.

"Ha!" Marla said. "Even Zufi can't resist you, pretty boy."

"That woman is deeply strange."

"What do you expect? She spends all her time with fish. She forgets how to talk to people sometimes. We're lucky we got full sentences out of her today. Then again, on some days, if she's had human company recently, she could pass for an ordinary weirdo. She's got absolutely no guile at all, though, no matter what. It's a good thing her only political rivals are lobsters."

B nodded. "I definitely didn't get any sense of hostility or incipient betrayal off her." He pinched his nose closed with his thumb and forefinger and held his breath, but just for a few seconds. It was too bizarre. "So I'm amphibious now?"

"That's what the lady said, and she doesn't tend to lie. Why don't you jump in the bay and try it out?"

"Leap into the sea and try not to breathe? Hmm. I think I'll hold off and try it in Rondeau's bathtub tonight instead."

"Huh." Marla's face took on a speculative expression. "You know, I've only just now realized the sexual possibilities open to a guy who doesn't need to breathe—"

"Stop, please." B held up his hands. "Way ahead of you, don't need to go there."

"On the other hand, I hope you aren't into erotic asphyxiation, because I bet you can't do *that* anymore."

B covered his eyes. "Please, I beg you, stop."

"Heh. So modest. Okay, Captain Breathless, you'll have to come with me on my errands today."

"What's on the agenda? Any exposure to hard vacuum? Because I'm totally ready for that."

"Maybe if we have time in the afternoon we'll shoot you into space. I gotta visit the Chamberlain and talk about some hideous golf courses she wants to build. I want to put low-income housing there instead. We'll argue, and she'll insult my wardrobe. It should be a hoot. Then I was thinking I might pester my brother."

B thought of their failed attempts to consult an oracle the night before, and suppressed a shudder. Marla hadn't found any explanations for the oblivion voice in her studies the night before, but she said she had other possibilities to run down, and that he shouldn't worry yet—noise and random static and crossed connections were occupational hazards for psychics. "It'll be good to meet him."

"Maybe not good exactly. But it should at least be interesting."

Jason picked up Rondeau in a black Mercedes that was so comfortable and climate-controlled it was like a rolling living room. "Two stops today, Ronnie," Jason said. "Welcome to the crew."

Rondeau resisted his urge to fiddle with the radio, open the glove compartment, mess with the seat controls. He wanted to play the game, so he needed to play it cool. He couldn't quite manage silence, though, so he said, "What was it like, growing up with Marla?"

"She was a pistol. Too big for that little town. Just like me. Indiana, Ronnie, was not the right place for us. You know, in the old days, lots of the best grifters came from Indiana?"

"Oh? Why's that?"

"It was a crossroads for a lot of carnivals, and traveling carnivals, especially back in the day, were pretty much just roving grift machines with popcorn on the side. The carnival would come to town, hire some of the local mud-farmer kids to scoop shit and pitch tents, and along the way those kids would pick up a few little tricks. Some of them would decide they didn't want to stare at the ass end of a plow horse for the rest of their lives, and they'd go with the carnies when the troupe left town, and from there, on into a life on the grift."

"You've really made your living all these years by ripping people off?"

Jason spun the wheel smoothly, and the car zoomed around a curve and rolled with barely a bump over some old railroad tracks. "Never did an honest day of work in my life. Grifting is the most gentlemanly of the criminal trades. We don't hit people with iron pipes and steal their wallets. We get them to *give us* the cash, of their own free will. Hell, they beg to write us checks and wire us money, if we do our jobs right. I get the feeling

Marla's business is a bit more, ah, thuggish. She always did have a violent streak, even when she was young."

Rondeau squirmed a little. "I'm not privy to much of her business. I just run the nightclub where she keeps her office."

"Really? I heard you were her right-hand man."

Rondeau shrugged. "We're old friends. She takes care of me, and I'm there for her when she needs me. I, uh, do get the impression her business used to involve a fair amount of hitting people. She's at the top now, though, and she's not as hands-on anymore, I don't think."

"Just sits on top of the mountain, letting money roll uphill, huh? Sweet gig, though I imagine there's still a lot of pipe-swinging down in the trenches. It's not the life for me, but to be honest, I admire her willingness to do whatever's necessary to take care of herself. I always have. And I'm glad she got famous enough in certain circles for me to find her. I didn't realize how much I missed her until we had dinner the other night. We've got the kind of connection that a few years apart can't destroy. We've changed, sure, but she's still my little sister."

Except for the whole bit where she's been practicing magic for more than a decade, Rondeau thought, but the presence of the magical in Marla's life didn't necessarily change who she *was*—it just changed the way she did the things she was always going to do anyway.

"Here we go." Jason parked in front of a long low building with a rusting sign that declared it a metal shop, though judging by the boarded-up windows, it wasn't one of those anymore, and hadn't been anything at all for a long time. They got out and walked up the steps to the door, avoiding the rotted-through riser in the middle, and Jason knocked three times.

After a moment a bolt snicked loudly inside, and the door swung open, revealing a broad-shouldered, dark-haired man with sweat on his forehead and a grin on his face. "Jason, you bastard, it's about time somebody showed up to do the heavy lifting."

"Making good progress, then?" Jason stepped in past him. Rondeau followed suit, nodding at the other man, who regarded him without comment or greeting. The inside of the building was dark and dirty, an oil-stained concrete floor littered with bits of broken machinery, and a huge crate squatted in the middle of the space. The thing was easily three feet to a side, square, made of wood so old it looked petrified, and studded all over with rusty steel bolts. There were no hinges or other obvious means to open it, and the impression of permanent closure was enhanced by the black iron chains wrapped all around it, the links big enough to support an anchor for a medium-sized boat. Various mystical symbols were hacked into the wood beneath the chains, though they were oddly generic-looking, pentagrams and the sort of runes you could find etched on polished rocks at New Age bookstores.

"Good God!" Jason said. "We're gonna need a fork-lift to move that thing!"

"Eh, it's only about a hundred and fifty pounds. You said make it big and solid. And watch it with taking the Lord's name in vain, you asshole." The sweaty man scowled.

"Sorry, Danny." Jason walked around the crate, nodding appreciatively, prodding it with his toe. "This is good work. You came through again." He glanced over at Rondeau. "Ronnie, this is Danny Two Saints. Danny, this is Ronnie. He works for my sister."

"Oh, yeah? You a big spooky magician, too?"

"Just a humble tavern keeper." Rondeau cocked his head. "Danny Two Saints? Funny name."

"I never stop laughing," Danny said.

"Why do they call you that?"

"Because I'm so motherfucking pious."

Jason laughed. "Don't give him a hard time, Danny, he's good people. Danny got that name because when he was born, his head came out a few seconds before midnight, and the rest of him came out a few seconds after midnight, so his mom couldn't figure out which saint's day he'd actually been born on. Eventually she said he split the difference, and that means he's watched over by two saints. Given some of the shit he's gotten away with, she might've been right."

"Nothing compared to the shit Jason's pulled." Danny seemed to warm up a little—because Jason had vouched for Rondeau? "Having a couple of saints looking over your shoulder's nice, but Jason's got the devil's own luck."

"Which two saints?" Rondeau asked.

Danny laughed. "Most folks don't ask that. Peter Chrysologus and Ignatius of Loyola. Why, you Catholic?"

"Only in the sense of having broad tastes. I'm just nosy. Which is why I'm wondering—what's in the box?"

Jason crouched by the box and thumped it with his knuckles. "The Borrichius spores."

Rondeau waited, but nothing more was forthcoming. "What are those?"

"I thought you were into this whole fake mystical magical woo-woo shit," Danny said.

Rondeau shrugged. "I play along, but I've never heard of the.... whatever spores."

"That's okay," Jason said, "because Cam-Cam *will* have heard of them. I'll make sure of it. And once he does hear about them, he'll be desperate to get his filthy-rich hands on them. Not for the spores themselves, but for the corridors of power they'll open to him. They're a very sought-after commodity, you know, rare and expensive, and big-shot wizards will fall at his feet once they're in his possession."

"So where'd *you* get them?"

Danny laughed. "Get *what*? Imaginary magic shit? From the imaginary magic-shit store. And from the sweat of my brow. That box, which I built from scrap and scratch, has got a welded metal box inside it, and inside *that* there's nothing but a ton of padding and a sealed bucket full of sand and seawater, plus a lead pipe."

Jason stood up, grinning like a wolf in a Tex Avery cartoon. "The sand and pipe and water are an homage to a scam some guys pulled in France during the Cold War, the *bonbonne d'uranium*. They sold a box of rocks and sand and water to a baron who thought he was buying nuclear material to help fight the communists. It was kind of my inspiration for this." He kicked the box.

"Now we just have to make Cam-Cam want to buy them."

"So, what, we arrange a meeting, let him know we've got them for sale, and . . . ?"

Danny Two Saints clucked his tongue. "Jason, what'd you bring this amateur in here for? He's going to blow the whole thing."

Jason shook his head. "Nah, Ronnie's all right, he's got the grift sense, I can tell. He just needs a few pointers. See, Ronnie, you never try to sell a mark anything. You make the mark come *begging* to buy it. If somebody calls you up and says, 'Have I got a deal for you,' you hang up the phone. But if you hear about some amazing deal, and you try to chase it down, and they say, 'Oh, sorry, this is very exclusive, you don't qualify,' pretty soon you start shoving wads of cash at them, begging for the privilege to buy in. That's basic salesmanship. Like, at your nightclub, don't you keep a guy out front to let people in, and make sure he turns some people away?"

"Of course." Rondeau nodded, seeing the connection. "Nothing attracts a crowd like a crowd. A nightclub without a long line in front, a club anybody can get into, probably isn't worth getting into, right? Being all-inclusive is bad for business."

"See, Danny?" Jason beamed. "I told you he's got a natural sense for these things."

"How do you make Cam-Cam beg for it, then?"

Jason shrugged. "Word got around I was in town, and that I'm Marla Mason's brother. Maybe I hinted I'm doing a little work in the family business. Turns out Cam-Cam is a big fan of my sister, but she won't give him the time of day, won't acknowledge he exists—hell, he's never even *seen* her up close. He's been trying to arrange a meeting with me for days, and I keep ducking his calls. He's pretty eager at this point, so I dropped him a note telling him I'd come around his place this afternoon if I've got a minute. How'd you like to come with me?"

"Ah." Rondeau sighed. "Marla said it was going to be like that. That I'd pretty much be a prop to make your scam more convincing."

"I won't deny you'll be useful to me, Ronnie. But I wouldn't have brought you in on this if I didn't think highly of your potential. I've got other means of convincing Cam-Cam, believe me. After all, I just have to make him believe I'm Marla Mason's brother, and I *am*—I don't even have to make him believe a lie."

"Quit being offended and start getting rich," Danny Two Saints said, lighting a cigar with a welding torch. "We're gonna cut you in."

He'd get paid, just for being himself? Rondeau was *good* at being himself—better than anybody else in the world. "Sure. You really just want me to stand around looking like an associate of Marla's?"

"That's the *main* thing," Jason said. "But how about I give you a couple of lines to slip into the conversation, just to make sure you don't get bored?"

"Welcome to the Heights." Marla got out of the Bentley and gestured at the Chamberlain's mansion. Though the Chamberlain would insist it wasn't *her* mansion—she was merely a servant to the ghosts of the founding families of Felport who dwelled there.

B whistled. "I've spent a fair bit of time in mansions—for a while there, I even lived in one—but nothing like this."

"It was an English country house, brought over here and reassembled brick by brick." She paused. "I never understood that expression. How *else* are you going to reassemble a giant-ass house? Look at those gables. And the columns! I hate this place." She sighed. "Come on, we'd better go in." Marla led B up to the door and kicked it in lieu of knocking, as was her custom. She knew it was passive-aggressive, but didn't care. The Chamberlain and Marla had an uneasy relationship. They would have been enemies, maybe, if their goals weren't so complementary—of all the city's leading sorcerers, they were the two most concerned about preserving the prosperity and integrity of Felport itself. The city wasn't just a place they lived; it was a life's work. And, like two women in love with the same man, they inevitably clashed, despite—even because of—their shared passion.

The Chamberlain's butler opened the door and ushered Marla and B inside, leading them to the great house's library, a dark-paneled room crammed with orderly rows of volumes. Any existing windows had long since been sacrificed to make room for more shelving, which was for the best. Most of the books in the library were rare, and many were so old they shouldn't be exposed to sunlight anyway. The high ceiling kept the space from feeling claustrophobic, and there was more than adequate lighting in the form of tall antique lamps on the floor and short ones on the tables. The Chamberlain wore an elegant black-and-white dress, practically casual-wear by her usual standards. Though when the woman rose from a wooden chair to greet them, Marla noted she was wearing high heels, as always. That alone illustrated the yawning chasm that existed between them. A sorcerer in *heels*. How could she run, kick, fight? She didn't. She had people do those sorts of things for her.

The Chamberlain was beautiful, but she was so sophisticated it wouldn't have mattered much if she were homely. "Marla, how nice to see you." She glided in and air-kissed both Marla's cheeks. "Who's your friend?"

"My new apprentice, Bradley Bowman."

A tiny line appeared in the Chamberlain's smooth forehead. "Forgive me. I must have made a scheduling error. I understood you were bringing him for his magic lesson two days from now. Unless you've brought him today for a lesson in . . . sartorial matters? I'm sure one of the valets would be happy to counsel him."

She sounded so sweet, it was hard to take offense, but Marla always managed. "Okay, okay, we're filthy and disreputable. B doesn't get magic lessons today, you're right, he's just tagging along in an observational capacity, to learn how I handle the delicate act of negotiation." Marla thought of punctuating that with a nice hearty belch, but decided it would be too juvenile.

"He isn't a lovetalker like your *last* apprentice, is he,

brought to sway me into agreeing with your ridiculous plans?"

Crap. Marla hadn't realized the Chamberlain knew her last "apprentice" was one of the supernaturally charismatic types who could make people agree to anything. Joshua had been her secret weapon in delicate negotiations. Shame he'd turned out to be such an evil bastard. Marla tried for an airy tone. "Why, does B make your heart go pitter-pat and your panties melt? I practically had to pry the Bay Witch off him this morning, but no, he's not a lovetalker."

"I understand he is a psychic. Some such have powers of mental domination, a skill that's in short supply in Felport these days. I am . . . understandably suspicious." She turned to B, who'd been doing an admirable job of standing there quietly, a fine quality in an apprentice. "You used to be a film actor, isn't that right?"

B nodded affably. "A lifetime ago."

"Mmm. And you reached your modest level of fame through non-magical means? No . . . special charms?"

"No, ma'am. My charisma, such as it is, is strictly natural. Supernatural things kind of ruined my career— when I started seeing ghosts and monsters, it messed up my life. Hard to run your lines on set when you can see a parasitic demon sucking life energy from your director . . . and when you actually try to get rid of it and everybody thinks you were trying to choke your director to death, it suddenly becomes a lot harder to get more jobs. Even in commercials."

"I see. Very well, he can join us in the discussion. Come along to my office."

They followed the Chamberlain down a marble-floored hallway, her heels clicking as they went. B, bringing up the rear, tapped Marla on the shoulder. "Uh, Marla? There are some ghosts back here."

"I should think so." The Chamberlain didn't slow down or look back. "The ghosts of Felport's founding families all dwell here, and I am their servant. The fact that you sense their presence is some proof of your psychic abilities."

"No, ah... They're *here*. Lots of them. Behind us. And what they're doing... What I mean to say is..."

Marla turned around, surveyed the scene in the hallway, and blinked. "They're *fucking*, Chamberlain. I'm surprised at you. Don't you know throwing orgies in the morning is gauche?"

A crowd of ghosts—who didn't *look* like ghosts at all, but like living people—were tearing off one another's garments and setting hungrily upon one another, their pale bodies filling the corridor from wall to wall, their thrashings knocking over a couple of tables and shattering doubtless priceless vases.

The Chamberlain gasped. "Ghosts! What is the meaning of this?"

One muttonchopped old lech in an unbuttoned waistcoat looked up from the two women beneath him and said, "I don't know how you're doing this, Chamberlain, but keep it up. Care to join us? We've been wondering about you for *ages*."

Marla looked closely, but the Chamberlain's skin was too dark to show a blush. "How do they have enough substance for this?" Marla said. "I know they're more coherent than most ghosts, and they can even get a little corporeal on Founders' Day, but having enough substance to push a glass off a table once in a while is a far cry from being…ah…*solid* enough to manage penetration. They look a lot more like flesh than ectoplasm, too."

"I have no idea." The Chamberlain fluttered her hands, and Marla was amazed to see Miss Perfect Poise at a total loss. "The founding families have always expressed a longing to enjoy the gratification of certain appetites denied them by death, but this is the first time they've managed to *do* it."

The three of them regarded the grunting, heaving mass of ghostflesh for a moment. "It's a hell of a sight," Marla said at length.

"I, ah, think it might be my fault." B stared at his feet.

"Oh, right," Marla said. "B here is an oracle generator, you know, bringing the potential into actuality? His presence tends to, hmm, excite any nearby supernatural particles. He's a signal booster for magic. It's never been quite this *dramatic* before, but then, he's never been around this many really coherent ghosties at once. I don't think we could've predicted it." *Though if I could have, I would've brought him here even sooner.*

"In that case, I'm afraid I'll have to ask him to *leave*." The Chamberlain's glower encompassed B, and Marla, and the disporting horde of horny ghosts. "I'll give him his magic lesson at some neutral location, where he won't be so likely to disrupt my household."

Marla thought about digging her heels in, but in truth, a bunch of naked ghosts grunting and groping in the hallway *did* constitute a pretty serious distraction, and there was no telling what mischief the founding families would get into if they remained embodied— what long-suppressed appetites would they seek to satisfy *next*? "Be a little bitchier about it, why don't you," Marla said. "It's not B's fault that he's bubbling over with power. Look at him bubble!"

"You might consider teaching him how to *pop* those bubbles, or at least keep them under control. Until then, he should *go*." The Chamberlain stalked away toward her office.

"Sorry, you've gotta take a powder." Marla patted B's shoulder. "Don't worry about it. Hell, seeing the look on her face was priceless. You can find your own way out? Feel free to take the car and drive around awhile. I'll call when I need a pickup. I wanted you to get acquainted with the city anyway."

B nodded glumly. "I'm sorry. I keep fucking up. If I knew how to turn it off, I would, but this stuff just *happens*."

Marla glanced after the Chamberlain. If Marla kept her waiting much longer, the negotiations would be a real bitch. "Don't sweat it, we'll work on it later." She regretted giving B the quick brush-off—the guy was having a hard time, with his powers going haywire last night, and now this—but if he was going to be her apprentice, he'd have to get used to it. She wasn't the hand-holding type.

"You're the boss." He walked away, and the ghosts cried out complaints as their temporary fleshiness subsided, leaving them with nothing but their old forms of airy nothing.

"Quit your bitching," Marla said, and the founding fathers scowled at her while the founding mothers rearranged their spectral skirts. "If you guys behave yourselves, maybe I'll bring him back next Founders' Day, okay?" The ghosts cheered her in their thin voices, and Marla went toward the Chamberlain's office.

B started the Bentley and began the long trek down the Chamberlain's winding driveway. "Well, you suck," he told the reflection of his eyes in the rearview mirror. Being able to call up ghosts and monsters was undeniably useful under certain circumstances, but the Chamberlain was right—why didn't he have more control? Control had always been his problem. His lover had died overdosing on drugs B gave him, and if his psychic awakening hadn't ended his acting career, his self-destructive partying would have done the job eventually. Since he'd become aware of the twilight world, he'd exerted a lot more willpower, eschewing even such mild stimulants as coffee in order to spare his oversensitive nerves, but sometimes he felt he was barely holding it together. That was why he'd wanted to be Marla's apprentice—she was made of control, and he wanted to learn how she'd gained such mastery of herself. But what if such mastery was inborn? What if B just didn't *have* it, and would never be more than an apprentice? He'd spent months under the tutelage of the legendary sorcerer Sanford Cole, but he still couldn't bring on his prophetic dreams at will, or make himself less attractive to ghosts, or read minds with any reliability. He couldn't even summon oracles effectively anymore, it seemed, not since coming to Felport. His magic still controlled *him*.

B knew from his time as an actor that talent alone could only take you so far. Eventually, you had to back the talent up with more practical capabilities. But he'd only been Marla's student for a few days. If anyone could whip him into shape, it was her. He just hoped she wouldn't resort to actual whips.

B turned the car down the first major street he reached, thinking he might check out the outdoor Market Street Market Marla had told him about, when the landscape abruptly shifted around him. Buildings and traffic lights and other cars were replaced by a dense forest of sick-looking trees, dark and parasite-ridden. Every trunk was riddled with mushrooms in white, green, and yellow, clinging to the bark like a thousand leeches on a hundred bodies. B braked the Bentley hard, slamming to a stop, and heard blaring and horns and the crunch of metal around him, though he saw nothing but trees leaning under their fungal burdens. *A vision.* Somewhere around him there were other cars, shouting drivers, but this vivid hallucination hid them from view. Worst of all, it showed no signs of subsiding, and second-worst, he had no idea what the vision *meant*—he'd always needed an oracle to interpret *those* dreams, and now his oracles were malfunctioning.

B caught sight of himself in the mirror. His nose was bleeding, which was not unprecedented—he sometimes woke from particularly strong prophetic dreams with a

bloody nose. But there was blood welling from the corners of his eyes, too, and as B wiped the bloody tears
with the back of his hand, he felt horribly mortal. Was
his death coming *now*? Did he have some kind of supernatural Ebola?

Something moved in the forest. Trees shivered and
deliquesced into pillars of rapidly collapsing slime as it
approached. B couldn't make out details—there might
have been a human shape beneath it, but all he could see
were fans of fungus, gilled mushroom caps, strands of
mossy lichen hanging like misplaced beards. The thing
extended an arm, pointed at him, and said—

Nothing. Before it could speak, the vision vanished—
overwritten, pushed out, replaced by blotted clouds of
darkness. He couldn't see anything at all, and that
cursed voice thundered in his head about oblivion and
darkness and the end of everything. B gasped and
flailed, sounding the car's horn accidentally and grabbing on to the wheel in the desperate need to hold something solid. *I'm blind. Fuck me, I'm blind, I'm—*

A man's voice cut into B's consciousness: "Dude, did
you have a *stroke* or something?"

B blinked. He could see again. He turned his head,
and the man who'd spoken was knocking on the
Bentley's driver-side window, looking in with concern. B
took in the scene outside his windshield. Two cars had
collided around B, one swerving to avoid B's sudden
stop, probably, and slamming into a car in the next lane.
Judging by the people standing around talking, nobody
had been seriously hurt—B was the only one with blood
on his face and hands.

"I'm sorry," B said, rolling down the window. "I'm really sorry. Is everybody okay?"

"You're the one with blood coming out of your eyes." The guy backed away once B opened the window. "What the hell's wrong with you?"

B shook his head. "I don't know, man. I really don't." He thought about calling Marla, but did he really want to interrupt her meeting? He flipped open his cell and dialed another number instead. "Hey, Hamil? This is B. I could really use that other kind of sympathy, if you've got a moment to spare."

6

Y ou never heard of a hit-and-run?" Marla said as she entered Hamil's apartment.

B grunted from the couch. "I thought you were a law-and-order chief sorcerer. I really should have hauled ass out of there?"

"No, but police records regarding my Bentley aren't welcome, B. I'll have to make a whole phone call to get that shit expunged, and I hate talking to bureaucrats."

"It's taken care of." Hamil brought her a drink. "I paid off those involved generously, in cash, in exchange for their discretion."

She sniffed the glass. "What's this?"

"Scotch, neat. I thought you might need to relax."

"True enough." She flopped onto the other end of the couch and took a drink, grimacing. "Even the good shit tastes bad to me. Why didn't you call *me*, B?"

"You were in a meeting, and I'd *already* pissed off the Chamberlain, so I didn't want to make it worse."

Marla sighed. "You can always call. I would've probably just told you to call Hamil, but still, I don't like it when shit happens I don't know about. What *did* happen? Hamil said you managed to wreck two cars."

"The Bentley didn't even get scratched, at least," B said.

"Of course not, it's magically protected. You think I'd ever let Rondeau drive it if it was possible for the thing to get wrecked? Stop avoiding the question. *Why* did you make cars go boom boom against each other?"

"I had a vision. Like a dream, but I was awake, and it kind of...overwrote reality. I could still hear the cars and stuff around me, I just couldn't *see* anything except trees, and this thing made of mushrooms and moss and fungus coming toward me."

Marla grunted. "Was this an ominous vision, or a happy, tasty-delicious-truffles-in-our-future vision?"

"Definitely ominous. I'd try to interpret it, but every time I call up an oracle, I just get that 'darkness and oblivion' stuff."

She leaned back in the couch, considering. "Think it's a safe bet the two are connected? Fungal apocalypse equals darkness and oblivion?"

"It's a working theory, at any rate," Hamil said from his giant armchair. "Since Bradley's powers are...behaving erratically, perhaps we could consult some other seer?"

"Sure, but who? Since Gregor died, we've been strictly small-time when it comes to future-seeing around here. Hell, that's part of why I was so happy to get B on our team. Langford is good at divination when he knows what he's looking for, but if I brought this to him, he'd just say 'insufficient information to proceed.' We need somebody with a deep connection to the mystic. Whatever happened to Sauvage's crazy seer, the one who giggled all the time?"

Hamil shook his head. "He vanished after Sauvage died."

"Would you sniff around for him a little? He's not as cute as B, but he's got a line on starry wisdom. It's not a major priority, but..."

"I'll see what I can do," Hamil said. "I did hear a rumor, years ago, that he was in Gregor's service, but Gregor denied it."

"Gregor was a big fat liar."

"Indeed," Hamil said. "But in the meantime..."

"We're flying blind," Marla said.

"Oh, yeah," B said. "And my eyes bled."

Marla whistled. "Fuck, B. Okay, we're taking you to Langford. He's the closest thing to a doctor for magical malfunctions we've got. If you picked up some kind of mystical parasite, he'll be able to figure it out."

"I'm so sorry, Marla. I'm supposed to be saving you work, making your life *easier*, and instead I'm dragging you down."

"Eh, I'll just work you twice as hard once we get your wires uncrossed. Don't worry." But she was worried. A seer with bleeding eyes? That *couldn't* be good symbolically, and in magic, symbolism mattered.

* * *

Campbell Campion, last scion of one of Felport's oldest families (though not, to his dismay, one of the *founding* families), paced up and down his cavernous but sparsely furnished living room. This was the moment. If he did this right, if he made the proper impression, he might finally—

The doorbell rang. He'd sent the maid home, of course—this wasn't a meeting he wanted overheard by a domestic—so he hurried to answer it himself.

Jason Mason was tall and handsome, if a little tired around the eyes, and wore a suit of immaculate cut. He radiated confidence and power, and Cameron had no doubt he was a powerful sorcerer in his own right, in addition to his close familial connection to the elusive Marla Mason. The Hispanic man standing behind him, sniffing the summer damask roses in their oversized planters, was far less impressive—he wore a hideous brown suit with wide lapels that might have been fashionable for fifteen minutes in the '70s.

"Mr. Campion?" Jason looked at his watch. "I can only spare you a few minutes, so . . ."

"Of course, please, come in, Mr. Mason, and your . . . associate?"

Jason glanced behind him. "Oh, this is Rondeau."

Cam-Cam—as his mother had always called him and, to his eternal shame, how he automatically thought of himself—stood, stunned. Jason and Rondeau— Rondeau!—went past him into the foyer. Rondeau was said to be Marla Mason's right hand, though Cam-Cam didn't know much else about him. *He must be a person of tremendous power, too.* Cam-Cam ushered them into the living room and offered them seats, though only Jason sat. "Thank you, both of you, for agreeing to meet with me."

Rondeau laughed. "I'm not meeting you. Pretend I'm not here. I'm just along for the ride." He wandered over to a tall bookshelf that contained first editions of H. Rider Haggard novels—one of Cam-Cam's reliable pleasures—and began thumbing through the volumes. Cam-Cam bit back the urge to tell him not to manhandle the books, that they were valuable, but snapping at the man would hardly serve his purpose. His assertiveness had ruined his other attempts at finding entry into the society of sorcerers, and he wasn't about to make the same mistake again.

"Rondeau and I have a meeting after this." Jason looked at his watch again. "There wasn't time to go back and get him after, so I had to bring him along. Now, what did you want to meet with me about? I have to say, I've never been pursued quite so aggressively."

"Yes, well, I ... I'm not quite sure how to say this. ... I am a man of some means, Mr. Mason."

Jason raised an eyebrow and took an ostentatious look around the huge living room with its expensive works of art and antique furniture. "Yes, so it seems. Good for you."

"My family's money comes from mining, mostly, but I've never had a great interest in precious metals, so I leave things in the hands of my employees, many of whom have been with the business since before I was alive. My interests ... lie elsewhere."

Rondeau wandered over to stand behind Jason's shoulder, yawning. "That's a great story."

Flustered, Cam-Cam said, "The occult. I'm interested in the occult. I always have been."

"The occult," Jason said blankly.

"Yes. Magic."

"And this involves me how?"

"You're Marla Mason's brother," Cam-Cam said. "I *know* about her. I paid a lot of people very good money to find out about her. I've never been able to arrange a meeting with her, which is why I was so happy to hear you were in town, and amenable to a talk."

"You know *what* about my sister?" Jason was frowning, and Cam-Cam felt it slipping away. He was going to be stonewalled again.

"That she's an important person. A powerful person. That she's...a *sorceress*."

Rondeau snorted. "Call her a 'sorceress' and she'll kick your ass. She's a *sorcerer,* just like a woman who acts is still an actor, not an 'actress.' I'm guessing you're not much of a feminist?"

"What Rondeau *means* to say is, what are you talking about, there's no such thing as sorcery, don't be ridiculous." Jason's voice was perfectly level.

"Mr. Mason, I *know* about...people like you. I don't know why you all persist in pretending I'm crazy."

"Crazy people never think they're crazy," Rondeau offered. "Listen, Jason, we should go, that guy's not going to hand over sacks of gold if we disrespect him by showing up late. He's *serious* people." Rondeau looked scornfully at Cam-Cam, who shriveled a little inside.

"Okay." Jason rose. "Mr. Campion, I'm sorry we wasted each other's time, I think you've got the wrong idea—"

"You need money?" Cam-Cam said desperately, falling back, as always, on the one thing he could offer most freely. "You're going to meet, what, an investor? *I* have sacks of gold. Literally, even—my family has gold mines."

Rondeau made a *thpppt* noise. "You think you can buy us?"

"Rondeau." Jason looked at the ceiling as if doing math in his head. "You know, that other guy's only good for half, and if we can't afford to buy this thing soon—"

"*No,*" Rondeau said. "You know what Marla would say if we brought in an outsider? What she'd *do*? Nuh-uh. This isn't some ordinary business deal."

Jason nodded, but regretfully, Cam-Cam thought. "You're right. I'm sorry, Mr. Campion, we should really be—"

"I can help you. Let me help you. Gold. Currency. Anything you need."

Jason looked thoughtful again. "You know, Rondeau, I really don't know who else we're going to tap—Marla doesn't want word about this to spread too far."

"Sure, but if we take his money, he's an *investor,* he'll think he's got the right to tell us what to do and how to do it." Rondeau shook his head.

"I swear, I won't make any demands, I just want to be involved. I'll swear a sacred oath, with blood, anything you want. I *know* real magic exists. I just want to be part of it."

"The man says he knows," Jason said. "If he knows, he knows."

Rondeau scowled. "I don't think it's a good idea."

"I'll give you *everything*," Cam-Cam said. "Cancel your other meeting, I'll supply all you need, just tell me how much, and what it's for."

"A single investor would be a lot simpler," Jason said. "And we can make excuses to the other guy, he won't mind as long as we're polite about it."

Rondeau sighed. "We should call Marla."

"Nah, nah," Jason said. "Leave her to me, she's my sister, I can make her see how this is a good thing."

"It's your funeral." Rondeau shoved his hands in his pockets. "I guess if he gets out of hand we can always erase his memory."

"That won't be necessary!" Cam-Cam cried. The thought of learning about magic, finding real proof, only to have it *unlearned*, was horrifying. "I am utterly discreet and trustworthy."

"What, you won't tell your girlfriend, your wife, your mommy and daddy?"

"I have no family left. No close connections. I've dedicated my life to the study of magic, as the two of you have also, I'm sure."

Rondeau chewed his lower lip. "Okay," he said finally. "You're in, chump."

Cam-Cam blinked. "Did you call me a chump?"

"He said 'champ,'" Jason said. "He calls people champ. That's his thing."

"Yeah," Rondeau said. "It's my thing."

"Ah. Well. Gentlemen. What will I be helping you buy?"

"A big fucking box, and that's all you need to know right now," Rondeau said. "I don't care what you say, Jason, I'm calling Marla." He stalked off.

Jason stepped close to Cam-Cam. "Don't mind him. He gets a little touchy. And don't worry. I'll tell you about the details later. Wait for our call." He patted Cam-Cam on the shoulder and departed.

That's it, Cam-Cam thought. *I'm in*.

"You know, I bet we could've gotten him to write a check for pretty much any number we cared to name right then and there." Rondeau fiddled with the passenger-side window in the Mercedes, powering it up and down, up and down.

"No doubt, but I don't want to take him for a hundred grand, or even a million. I want it *all*, and that takes a deeper game and more finesse and a perfect blow-off. If we'd done a take-the-money-and-run tonight, he'd just hire some hard guys to chase us down."

Not if we erased his memory, Rondeau thought, but didn't say it, because Jason didn't know magic was real, and anyway, Marla would kick his ass if he tried something like that. Apparently scamming people was more acceptable than straight theft, in her eyes—it gave the victims a sporting chance.

"This magic shit's great, though," Jason said. "Normally you have to predicate a scam on something illegal—you know, fake stock tips the mark thinks you got from insider trading, like that, so they can't run to the cops and tell on you without implicating themselves in a crime. But this magic thing is cop-proof. Even if Cam-Cam twigs to the fact that we're ripping him off—which he *won't*— what's he going to do? Call up the attorney general and tell him the money he gave to a couple of *wizards* was obtained under false pretenses? I guess he could try to get us with fraud, but that would require admitting he was dumb enough to believe we actually had magical powers, and nobody that rich and well established likes to look like an idiot in public."

"Pretty good. So what happens next?"

"We let Cam-Cam stew for a day, then give him our regrets. Tell him Marla vetoed our idea, and we can't take his money, after all."

"But why pull back? He's so gung-ho now!"

"Buyer's remorse, Ronnie. I guarantee, next time we see Cam-Cam, he'll be all narrow-eyed and suspicious. People are easily dazzled in the short term, but give them a night to sleep on it, and they worry. Cam-Cam will start mulling it over and thinking about how he *likes* his money, and how all his past attempts to cozy up to sorcerers have failed. He'll ask us difficult questions, and he'll be on high alert for fishy answers. But if we short-circuit all the moaning and wailing by telling him he's out, it'll take the wind out of his sails, and reinforce the impression that we're on the level. Pretty soon he'll beg us to let him back in."

"This is more complicated than I'd expected," Rondeau said. "When do we agree to accept his money again?"

"Alas, that decision is out of our hands, as we are

mere underlings. It's Marla's call, so the best we can do is set up a meeting with my little sister, so he can try to convince her personally."

"Um, Jason, I don't think Marla's going to go along with that."

"Ah, but Cam-Cam has never even *seen* Marla."

Yes he has, Rondeau thought, *but his memory of the meeting was erased, so I guess . . .* "Ah."

"If he meets some woman wearing a cloak in a dark and suitably occultish location, her face shrouded in shadow and so forth, why wouldn't he think it was Marla?"

"Heh. Who do you have in mind to play the part?"

"Nobody. I figured, you're local, you know people, I can tell you probably have a lot of ladies on speed-dial. Bring me a prospect—somebody who can keep her mouth shut."

"That I can do. But I have to say, it strikes me as kind of elaborate."

"Remember that old con I mentioned, about the Frenchman who thought he was buying a crate of uranium? The guys who scammed him milked him for about two *years*. All the while they were taking his money, they made the guy feel like he was in the middle of a spy novel, fighting off the commies. They strung him along, and yeah, a scam like that, it's elaborate. That's the kind of thing I'm working on here, Ronnie. I want to squeeze Cam-Cam long-term. I'm not looking to burn the lot."

"Burn the lot?"

Jason chuckled. "Old carnie term. If a carnival was

hard up for money, they'd sometimes pull out all the stops—cheat more than usual, use every dirty trick they knew to part rubes from their bankrolls, even outright theft with pickpockets circulating in the crowd. *That's* what they call burning the lot. Of course, the downside to pulling shit like that is the townspeople get pissed, and they won't be real happy to see your carnival, or *any* carnival, roll into town anytime in the next few years. If you do return, you're apt to get your head busted by the locals, including the cops. So the town is burned, metaphorically. Get it?"

"Got it."

"Good. We're not going to burn Cam-Cam. We're going to string him along, give him a lot of thrills and chills, make him think he's in some kind of supernatural action thriller, and then blow him off." Jason puffed up his cheeks and exhaled a loud spurt of air. "And him, poor sap, he'll just float away when we're finished, like so much dandelion fluff."

"You sound confident." Rondeau was both doubtful and admiring.

"I've always been a confident man, Ronnie."

"So what the hell's wrong with him?" Marla said.

"Hmm." Langford stared into a wide-screen computer monitor that appeared to display a bubbling green fluid. "We'll see."

"What are you staring at?"

"My cauldron," Langford said absently. As usual, he wore a white lab coat stained with suspicious splotches, steel-rimmed round glasses, and a distant expression. "It's a quantum cauldron. Less messy than the conventional sort."

He tapped at the keys, and B shouted, "Holy fuck!" and jolted in the chair, jostling the odd helmet he wore— like a metal colander with bare-wire leads running out to one of Langford's computers.

"Sorry." Langford didn't even look at B. Marla knew that when he got into the zone, into the flow, he was barely aware of his surroundings. B was, just at the moment, not a person to Langford, but a collection of interesting data.

Marla peered over Langford's shoulder at the screen, which had developed some black bubbles now. "Does this even do anything, or are you fucking with me for a generous hourly rate?"

Langford turned toward her, blinked a couple of times, and frowned. "Would you like to engage in repartee, or would you like me to finish my diagnostic series? I'm fine either way. My consulting fee doesn't vary based on the nature of your demands."

"Do your work, then." Marla hooked a stool with her ankle and pulled it away from a nearby lab table, sitting down beside B, who was understandably looking a little freaked-out. Langford's lab didn't inspire comfort in a patient—it was all bubbling beakers and tubes, shelves full of pickled things that used to be alive, and cages of varying sizes that were mostly, blessedly, empty at the moment. "You all right?" Marla asked her apprentice. "Being hooked up to one of Langford's contraptions can be stressful. I always get the sense he could switch my brain with a chicken's if he wanted."

"That's reassuring." B peered out dismally from beneath the helmet. "Is that a Tesla coil over there?"

Marla looked at the spark-spitting machine and nodded. "When I bought this new lab space for Langford—which was not cheap, but he earned it—I threw that in as a joke."

"Marla considers me a mad scientist." Langford kept tapping keys in a rapid-fire rhythm that Marla found oddly comforting. "Though I am not mad, and am only intermittently a scientist." He leaned so close to the monitor that his nose almost touched the screen, said "Aha" in a satisfied voice, then leaned back. "I see."

"See what?" Marla hopped off her stool. The screen didn't look much different to her.

Langford drummed his fingers on the table for a moment. "Imagine that Bradley's brain is a program for reading e-mail."

"I don't use e-mail." Marla crossed her arms. You couldn't effectively threaten someone over e-mail, was her feeling.

"Then you'll have to work very hard to imagine it," Langford said equably. "So: incoming messages are stored on a server—that's a big computer, off-site somewhere, Marla. The e-mail program fetches those messages, pulling them down over phone lines or cable or a wireless network, to your local machine."

"You download the messages, right," B said. Marla glared at him. "What? You're the only Luddite in the room, boss."

"Occasionally," Langford went on, "there's a message on the server that's too large to download, and the e-mail program times out—essentially, it gives up on trying to pull down the message. Meanwhile, new messages arrive, but they can't be downloaded, either, because that enormous message is sitting in the way."

"Clogging up the tubes," Marla said.

Langford winced. "Yes. In a manner of speaking. The program keeps trying to download the message, and it keeps failing, though it may manage to download a truncated version of the message, producing a lot of gibberish that can't be read."

"So I've got some huge vision my brain can't handle?" B said. "And it's keeping all my other normal-sized visions from coming through?"

"That's my working theory. The big vision is arriving in garbled form, at best—that's the persistent voice of doom. Meanwhile, the program—which, I'm afraid, is your brain—keeps crashing. Hence the bleeding eyes. You can't cope with...whatever's trying to drop itself into your brain."

"Huh," Marla said. "Ain't science grand. What do we do about it?"

"This is where the analogy breaks down a bit." Langford swiveled back and forth on his stool. "With e-mail, you can often access the server directly and delete the offending message. But in this case, the 'server' is wherever Bradley's mystical dreams come from, and that is a place beyond my understanding."

"So if you can't get to the server?"

"You can tell the program to simply ignore messages

over a certain size. The program will then stop trying to download that message, leave it on the server, and just move on to the next message. No more crashing. No more bleeding eyes."

"You can make B's brain do that?"

"Of course." Langford said.

"Without giving him a stroke or lesions? Or the brain of a chicken?"

"Your faith is all that sustains me. There should be no permanent damage." Langford spoke in that bland way that managed to sound completely confident yet totally nonreassuring. "The alternative will almost certainly cause Bradley great harm as more visions pile up, increasing the psychic pressure on his mind until . . . something breaks."

"What do you think, B? It's your brain, so I won't decide for you."

"I was crying blood earlier. I'm willing to try alternatives. But, and maybe this is an obvious question . . . even if this works, doesn't that mean we're ignoring the giant-sized monster vision pressing down on my head?"

"Yep."

"Isn't it likely to be kind of *important*?"

"Probably," Langford said. "Psychics are . . . resistant to analysis . . . but broadly speaking, in my experience, such powerful visions tend to be either items of vast universal importance—apocalypse or the like—or else something profoundly life-altering for the psychic personally."

"Great. So whatever it is, we'll be flying blind?"

"Don't sweat it, B." Marla patted him on the shoulder. "There are billions of people who go through their lives and never have a single dream that comes true, and who even manage to decide what brand of toilet tissue to buy without consulting the oracle of the paper products aisle first. We've got other options to figure out the nature of this oblivion-threatening danger we might have to face. At least we know there's *something*, right? Forewarned is forearmed, even if we're not quite as well armed as we'd like to be."

"All right," B said. "It's not like I'm faced with a lot of choices here. Work your magic."

"You heard him, Langford. Let's flush out those tubes."

"All right. Be aware, once I remove the blockage, you may be flooded with all your backed-up visions. And Bradley, in case you should die, I'd like to say I'm a great admirer of your films." Langford tapped a few keys. The bubbling mass on the computer screen roiled furiously.

Judging by the way B's eyes rolled back in his head, and with him falling out of the chair while shouting in a strange tongue and all, Marla figured Langford was right about the whole vision-flood thing.

Langford checked B's vitals and arranged him a bit more comfortably on the floor. "He's likely to be out for a while. Would you like to see a little something I made with you in mind?"

"You want to show me gadgets while my apprentice is twitching in a vision-coma?"

"You'd rather sit over him and make small talk?"

"Good point. Let's see what you've got."

Langford led her to one of his lab tables, reached

underneath, and came back with a pair of steel-toed boots, not unlike Marla's current pair in shape, though these were made of dark green leather.

"You're a cobbler now?"

"Only incidentally. The U.S. military has been trying to develop footwear and gloves that can enable wearers to cling to virtually any surface. In theory, soldiers so equipped could scale sheer walls as easily as they'd climb a ladder. The technology is based on the microfibers that geckos have on their feet, called setae, which enable them to stick to practically anything, even vertical sheets of glass. Most sticky creatures are literally sticky, with secretions that help them cling, but with geckos, it's all in the structure of the skin, tiny hairs that interact with surfaces. It's fascinating, really, the van der Waals forces—"

"You're going to lose me talking like that," Marla interrupted. "Synthetic gecko feet is all I need to know. So you've done what the military couldn't? Made sticky boots?"

"Well, yes, though I cheated—I used real gecko skin and sympathetic magic." He stroked the boots. "I've got a pair of gloves you could wear, too."

"What do I want to climb walls for?"

Langford shrugged. "I can't imagine. I just thought it was an interesting challenge, and now that I've exceeded my own expectations, I'm bored and looking to sell the results. I'm sure you'd find a good excuse to go walking on a ceiling."

"Fair enough." Marla stroked the boots. "Can you put a nasty inertial charm on these, too? The boots I've got on now can kick through a concrete wall without even stubbing my toe."

"The magics shouldn't interact badly, so I don't see why not."

Marla sighed. "They had to be green lizardskin, didn't they? Rondeau's going to give me shit about my fashion sense. Ah, well. I'll just jump on him from the ceiling for revenge."

B woke up in a puddle of his own drool, which he decided was marginally better than awakening in his own vomit, if no less sticky. He sat up, groaning, and took stock. He was on a hard little cot in a corner of Langford's lab, squeezed between a black taxidermy goat and a crude clay jar sealed shut with wax. Marla approached and handed him a bottle of water, which he greedily gulped. "Thanks, boss." He did a quick interior survey. "I feel . . . better."

"Good." She dropped down to squat on her heels so their faces were on the same level. "So what's the news from dreamland?"

"Mushrooms," B said. "Beyond that, I'll have to consult an oracle. I saw lots of things, but I'm not sure what most of it means."

"Langford says you oughta be able to talk to oracles and get straight answers again. As straight as you ever did anyway."

"They tend to be crooked as Lombard Street, but as long as I'm not blind or bleeding, I can cope. Can we find an oracle now? It's the only way to get this taste out of my brain."

"You sure you feel up to that, iron man?"

"No, but some knowledge is better out than in."

"Langford, give Hamil a call and tell him I said he should send you a big sack of money. We've got to hit the streets—"

"No." B started at the clay pot beside him. It was old, and from far away, he could tell. He could *feel* it. "No, I think I can call up an oracle right here."

Marla backed away. "Langford, is that jar a container for some malevolent desert spirit? Some dark genie from the center of the Earth? Some kind of…" She paused. "I'm trying to come up with a joke using the phrase 'djinn and chthonic,' I've been waiting *years* to use that, but I got nothing."

"Alcoholic jokes are apropos," Langford said, "though it's not gin in that pot, but exceedingly elderly wine. You sense a spirit in the clay, Bradley?"

B didn't answer—*couldn't* answer, because he was thinking too hard, his brain straining to produce an oracle.

The pot shivered and rattled and hissed, though the wax seal remained unbroken. An oily smoke began to coalesce in the air above the jar, with a smell like a dusty tomb's inner chamber. Two sparks that might have been embers and that could pass for eyes winked into existence in the cloud's depths. "I am Il-a-mo-ta-qu'in," the cloud said in a raspy sandstorm of a voice. "Master of traps and deceptions, killer with a poison kiss. What would you ask of me?"

"I had a dream," B said. "One of *those* dreams. About mushrooms, and a man with the snout of a pig, and a mad slave, and a rotting forest, and an empty box, and—"

"I know of this dream," Il-a-mo-ta-qu'in said. "It heralds the coming of a servant of the Mycelium. He will arrive soon, seeking powerful magic, and willing to strike down any who oppose him. His madness has a terrible clarity that I admire, even as I despise him for being so . . . moist. He would not survive an hour in the burning sands of the empty quarter, where even lichen on rocks have been known to die of thirst."

"Thank you, Il-a-mo-ta-qu'in," B said formally. "How may I repay you?"

"A kiss. I developed a taste for kisses when I killed a prince with one."

Marla said, "How are you supposed to kiss a cloud of dirty smoke?" But B didn't hesitate, just leaned in and shut his eyes, and the smoke closed over his face for a moment, then began to dissipate.

B coughed hard a few times, throat burning, and picked up the water bottle, finishing it off. The water eased the pain in his throat, but some of the oracle's substance remained in his lungs, probably shortening his life. Maybe Marla knew a way to make him live longer, to help balance things out. That was worth looking into.

Marla was already on a cell phone borrowed from Langford. "Hamil? B had a vision. There's some out-of-towner coming to make trouble, looking for some big magic. No, I don't know what. No, we don't have a name, either, all I know is he's a servant of something or someone called the Mycelium, and he's got something to do with mushrooms—"

"A mycelium is part of a mushroom," Langford said. He knelt by the clay pot, prodding it with a wooden tongue depressor. "The underground, vegetative part—mushrooms are merely the fruit of the mycelium."

"Langford says a mycelium is like the roots of a mushroom," Marla went on. "Run this guy down for me, would you? Fungal magic. Icky. Can't be too many big scary practitioners of *that*. Let me know if we need to lay in a supply of athlete's foot cream or something." She snapped the phone shut. "Oh, goody. It's been like a *week* since I've had to beat the crap out of some invader muscling into my city. Way to be an early warning system, B."

"Happy to be of service."

"So . . . nothing about my brother in all those visions you had? Just the Fungus Channel?"

"No, nothing about Jason. But my visions tend to center on mystical stuff, trains to Hell and dead gods and scary magic, so family matters might be a little outside my area of expertise. I got mugged last year, and I never had a dream about *that*, though I could have used the warning . . . I think it was just too mundane to trigger my gift, such as it is."

"You have a *brother*?" Langford said.

"I do," Marla said. "Don't get any ideas. You aren't allowed to dissect him."

"When the subject is still alive, it's called vivisection."

Marla rolled her eyes. "To be safe, B, could you call

up ol' long-ass-name there again and put a few questions to him about my brother? Ease my mind?"

B shook his head. "It wouldn't work." He wasn't sure how to explain. "This is the wrong oracle for that question. It would be like asking a bricklayer for medical advice, or a piano tuner to fix your car's engine. He's the wrong guy for the job."

"But a desert spirit was the *right* guy to ask about mushrooms, which are pretty distinctly nondesert?"

"I don't claim it makes sense, though I think Il-a-mo-ta-qu'in hates squishy wet things, and hate is a sort of affinity. I can try to find another oracle to tell me about your brother if you like, later."

"What, another little garbage god? Maybe we should. I wonder if it's symbolically relevant that the oracles who know about my brother are made of trash?"

"We can ask the oracle about that, too. It'll be totally recursive. But could we get something to eat first? I'm *ravenous.*"

"Sure," Marla said. "You still interested in meeting Jason? Maybe we can all grab a bite together. Who knows, seeing him could spark one of those visions of yours. It'll do you good to quit talking shop for a couple of hours anyway."

The messenger shut the rear doors of his van, closing Bulliard in. He considered running for it while the doors were locked—but the tickle at the back of his neck changed his mind. He reached back and gently patted at the nape of his neck, and his fingers encountered the rubbery sponginess of mushroom caps. He shuddered and wiped his hand on the front of his rather filthy black T-shirt. The messenger had done courier runs to rain forests and river basins, and had picked up his share of disturbing parasites and infections in the course of business, but this was the first time he'd ever been *deliberately* infected with such a thing by another human being—assuming Bulliard was human, something it was tempting to doubt.

He went around the van and climbed into the driver's seat. The back of the van was just open space, the rear seats long ago ripped out, various hooks and D-rings welded to the walls to help fasten down whatever strange cargoes he might have to transport. *Never anything stranger than this.* He looked in the rearview mirror, but Bulliard was still playing coy. "Why don't you want to let me know what you look like?"

The shapeless darkness in the mirror swelled and loomed closer. "I do not care if you know what I look like. But the Mycelium wishes you always to remember that your mind is under its control. That your perceptions are nothing but a courtesy extended to you in exchange for your continuing good service. Whenever you look upon me and see only darkness, you will know your eyes are not your own, that your senses and body belong to the Mycelium alone."

"So I'm still basically hallucinating, is what you're saying, and the reason I'm hallucinating is, the Mycelium is on a power-trip."

"I am saying you should drive. I am saying we have some distance to go."

"Across the freaking country. With you as a traveling companion. This is going to be worse than the vacations I took in the family station wagon when I was a kid."

"You are very insolent, for a slave."

"The worst thing you can do is kill me, Bulliard, and I'm starting to think that wouldn't be so bad."

Bulliard chuckled. It was a wet laugh, like fruiting bodies were bursting apart with every sound. "Silly messenger. I can do so many things that are worse than death."

"And on that note," the messenger said, and shifted the van into drive.

7

"You sure you're okay with driving?" Marla asked, hesitating by the passenger door. Just because she almost never drove didn't mean she'd forgotten *how*.

"No, I'm all right, it's not the Bentley's fault I caused a five-car pileup." They got in the car and pulled away from the run-down residential neighborhood where Langford's lab was hidden, behind the façade of a ranch house with flaking paint.

"Hand me your cell, would you?" she said.

B dug it out of his pocket and passed it over, keeping his eyes carefully fixed on the road the whole time. "No offense, just curious, but why don't you carry your own?"

"Don't you watch TV? Criminal kingpins don't carry their own phones. Helps avoid wiretaps and cell cloning and all that stuff." She flipped his open and began stabbing at buttons. She wasn't entirely sincere—she had a cell of her own, one magically rigged to get reception just about anywhere, but she seldom remembered to keep it charged, and it was currently a worthless paperweight in the bottom of her bag. Langford said he could make it so the phone never had to be recharged again, but apparently that would involve ovary-melting levels of radiation, which Marla reckoned was too high a price to pay for convenience. "I can't get over how weird it is knowing my brother's phone number again." She finished dialing, hit the little green phone icon, and listened to the ring.

"Marlita! I was just about to call you."

"Great minds think alike. You up for an early dinner? I want you to meet my, ah, business associate, Bradley Bowman."

"Didn't there used to be an actor with that name?"

"Same guy. He's in a different business now."

"You never cease to surprise me, sis. Sure, let's eat, I've still got Rondeau with me, and I get the idea he's always hungry."

They made arrangements, and Marla flipped the phone shut. "Better double back and go over the west bridge. Jason wants us to meet at some pub near the college, he says the food is really good."

"You never did tell me what caused your falling out with him." B spoke in a careful tone Marla recognized: he didn't want to sound like he was prying, but yeah, he was prying. She considered. B was one of the handful of people she trusted with her secrets, and wouldn't it be better for somebody to know about Jason, about what he'd done? Her brother could be charming, and if she was the only one on the lookout for shady behavior, she might miss something.

"When I was a teenager, there was this kid at my school with what you'd call a history of violence. He hurt a couple of my friends pretty badly and made it clear he was going to come for me next. So I...made sure that wouldn't happen. I got *him* before he could get me, and things went too far, and he wound up dead."

B whistled. "Marla, I'm sorry. How old were you?"

"Fourteen. Pretty much the end of my innocence, not that I ever suffered much from that. Jason was there for me, though. He helped me get rid of the evidence. He protected me. Pretty good brother, huh? I think he was even proud. Everything I ever learned about bushwhacking and ambush, I learned from him. At that time he was fleecing people pretty regularly—nobody expects to get conned by a fresh-faced seventeen-year-old, and he didn't have those tired eyes then. He was no stranger to the wrong side of the law. But helping cover up a *murder*? That wasn't something he'd do for just anybody."

"Family."

"Right. So a few months later, Jason calls me up, kind of panicked, and asks for my help. All I had was a learner's permit, and it was after midnight, but I took Mom's car and drove across town to the address he gave me, in a swanky subdivision, and parked a few blocks away like he said I should. It was a big house, turned out it belonged to a deacon at the church, a widower who lived alone, kids all grown up and moved away. Jason was there...along with the deacon. His body anyway. Jason had killed him with a kitchen knife. The guy was in his underwear and a wife-beater T-shirt, bled out on the linoleum by the sink.

"Jason was trying to act all in control, but his eyes had this crazy gleam I'd never seen before, like a trapped animal. He told me he'd been working on a blackmail angle for a while—the deacon was queer, and Jason got wind of that somehow and started to put himself forward as a willing plaything. He got the deacon on tape talking about what he wanted to do to him, you know? Jason came over that night to let the deacon know about the tape and start squeezing him for cash, or whatever."

"Damn. That's cold."

"Jason was never overly encumbered with a conscience. Deacons who preach damnation for gays on Sunday while cruising teenage boys on Saturday nights don't get a ton of sympathy from me, but they don't deserve to get murdered. Jason said it was self-defense, or an accident, or both. Said he came over, played the tape, and things... got out of hand. 'Things got heavy' is how Jason put it. I'm not sure of the precise chain of events, but the end result was Jason stabbing the guy."

"You don't think it was self-defense?"

"How do I know? I didn't see any other weapons, and how big a threat is an out-of-shape guy in his fifties against a tough seventeen-year-old? But to Jason, it was all very simple. When I had a dead body on my hands, he'd helped me. Now that he was the one with a corpse to get rid of, he expected me to return the favor."

"I'm guessing you didn't grab a shovel and ask where to dig."

"I flipped my shit, B. I was still messed up about the

guy I'd killed, full of guilt and remorse and emotions I couldn't even name, and now my brother had killed a guy? I couldn't deal with it. Plus—and I told Jason this—my murder had been a matter of life or death, me or him. Jason's had been a matter of profit. That was different, couldn't he see that? I'd done murder to keep myself alive. Jason had done it to save himself from his own stupid decisions, to keep a mark from beefing to the cops, whatever. But Jason didn't get the distinction. He said we were family, we were in it together, and I had to help him. But I didn't. I packed my shit and left town. Jason's little killing spree wasn't the only reason—my mom's latest boyfriend was getting a little grabby, and I was afraid I might lose my shit and do something violent to him if I didn't leave soon—but Jason's little problem was what pushed me over the edge. I left that night, and my last interaction with my family was a very low-pitched screaming match with my brother in a dead guy's kitchen."

"Ah. So he didn't take it well."

"Called me an ingrate, and a hypocrite, and worse. Said I was betraying my family by refusing to help him. Said as far as he was concerned, I wasn't his sister any-more. Said I better hope I never got myself into shit again, because he wasn't going to help me climb out next time. I never thought my brother was a good guy, exactly, but up until then, he'd always been a bad guy who was on *my side*."

"Wow." B shook his head. "And now he's back. No wonder you're suspicious."

"Sure, but—it's been eighteen years. He says he's out

of that heavy stuff, that it was a youthful indiscretion, a one-time thing. Honestly, B, I'm sure I've got more blood on my hands than Jason does. I like to think my violence is in the service of a greater good, and usually it is, but there are some definite borderline edge cases in my past where I didn't have motives all that much purer than Jason's were. He seems willing to forgive and forget, and I'm trying to show willing, too—letting him pull Rondeau into helping him out with his latest scam, like that. He's my *brother*. He's a big part of the reason I am the way I am. I don't know if I would have survived as a teenage runaway on the streets of Felport without the things he'd taught me. At the very least, he deserves a chance to be part of my family again. Maybe I deserve a chance to be part of his, too."

She went silent, and B let the silence hang there—he was good like that. Marla directed B to take the next left and pull into the lot next to the Foxfire Tavern, where Jason's Mercedes was already parked. After they got out of the car, Marla turned to B. "All right. Time to meet my brother. Don't mention anything about magic, and, ah, don't let on that you know...that stuff I just told you."

"Discretion is the soul of me." B patted her on the shoulder.

He's a good apprentice, she thought. *And a better friend.*

The Foxfire Tavern was a typical pub—dark wood, brass accents, vintage beer signs on the walls—and Rondeau and Jason were lounging in a booth big enough to sit six comfortably, beers already before them. Marla slid in next to Rondeau and B sat beside Jason. They made a strange foursome—B in his camouflage coat, Jason in his immaculate suit, Rondeau in a hideous brown outfit, and Marla in loose unbleached cotton pants and shirt. To an outside observer they would have looked like one of those wildly mismatched merry bands on a fantasy quest.

"You kids have a good day ripping off morons?" Marla flipped open a menu.

"I think it was a good learning experience for Rondeau," Jason said. He turned to B and stuck out his hand. "I think my sister forgot to introduce us. I'm Jason."

"Bradley. My friends call me B."

"I hope I qualify for that honor soon," Jason said. "I've seen your movies. You left Hollywood behind for a life of crime, huh?"

"More like Hollywood left me behind, and I had to take what I could get."

"Let's hear it for upward mobility," Jason said.

After that they all sat, no one sure what to say, fiddling with their beer mats and looking at their menus a little too intently. Marla had no problem with uncomfortable silences as long as *she* was the one causing the discomfort, but being uncomfortable herself was no fun.

Rondeau rescued them. "Hey, B, the table service in this place is glacial, and Marla said you were starving. Let's go to the bar and get drinks and make pointed remarks about how hungry you are, whaddya say?"

"Good boys," Marla said. "Bring me a lemonade."

Left alone with Jason, it would have been weird to

keep sitting quietly, so Marla decided to broach one of the many subjects she'd been wondering about. "So, uh, how's the rest of the family? You in touch with anybody?"

Jason shook his head. "Haven't seen or heard from any of the cousins in years. We were never all that close-knit anyway, I'm sure you remember."

"I do. Uh, how's Mom?"

Jason rolled his beer glass back and forth between his palms, a nervous habit Marla recognized. "I've been meaning to tell you. I wasn't sure how to bring it up.... Mom's gone. Five years ago. Her funeral's the last time I saw any of the rest of the family."

Marla winced. "Shit. Shit. I'm sorry, Jason. You shouldn't have had to deal with that on your own."

"It was okay. I mean, not okay, but I had money for the funeral and everything, it wasn't a problem. I would have told you when it happened, but I wasn't sure how to get in touch."

"That was one of my unreachable years." Five years ago she'd been a ragged up-and-comer in Felport's magical underworld, not the kind of person who had a fixed address. "Still, it was a shitty thing, you having to face that alone, and I'm truly sorry." She paused. "For everything. For leaving...the way I did."

"I never blamed you for taking off. Too many of Mom's boyfriends thought you and her were some kind of package deal—I'd catch them looking at you, and I know you saw it, too. I sure got tired of secretly beating their asses. It made sense you would leave."

Marla laughed. "You beat up Mom's boyfriends?"

"Sure, the ones who needed beatings. Of course, Mom's own fine interpersonal skills ran off more of them than I did."

B and Rondeau returned bearing drinks.

"Jason just broke the news that my mom passed away five years back," Marla said. B and Rondeau murmured condolences, which Marla waved away. "It's okay, I feel bad I didn't go to the funeral, but it's all right." She'd never had a particularly good relationship with her mother—to be honest, her mother had basically been walking poison—and it was hard to grieve for her now. "She was young, though," Marla said. "What did she die of? Was it . . . ?" Marla mimed tipping back a bottle.

"Cirrhosis of the liver." Jason raised his beer glass ironically. "Guess we're lucky neither one of us inherited the alcoholic gene, huh?"

"Well, it's not like we don't have other . . . compulsive issues. We didn't exactly choose safe lines of work, either of us, so there's got to be some kind of danger-seeking thing going on. Not to get all psychoanalytical."

"You've got a point. But better chills and thrills than booze and pills. You know the most messed-up thing about Mom dying?"

"What?"

"She wrote us out of the will. Assuming we were ever *in* it. Left everything she had to one of her scumbag ex-boyfriends—I guess the guy she was seeing when she thought to make a will." He shook his head. "She didn't have much anyway, but it's the principle of the thing, you know? Some random asshole she met in a bar has Grandma's antique silverware. It's fucked up. Family, huh? Ah, but I shouldn't bitch. I doubt we have a monopoly on screwed-up familial stuff."

"Hell, Jason," Marla said, "you've been in my will all along, even when I didn't own anything but the shoes on my feet and the bruises on my knuckles."

Jason blinked at her, and Marla was pleased to see genuine surprise on his face. "Really?"

She shrugged. "I wasn't going to give anything to Mom, and you're the only living relative I ever gave a damn about. I figured if I died, and they had to get word to somebody, I'd just as soon it was you and not one of the cousins. The least I could do for making you deal with that crap was leave you my dirty laundry and the leftovers in my fridge, right?"

"Marlita, you've just restored my faith in family." Jason raised his glass to her.

"My parents kicked me out of the house when they found out I was gay," B said, stirring the straw in his glass of iced tea. "Then, when I started making money in Hollywood? They appeared on my doorstep one day and said all was forgiven. I believed them for about ten seconds, but my dad wouldn't hug me, and Mom wouldn't look at me, and pretty soon they were asking if I could help them out with a loan. So yeah . . . family."

"Fuck all y'all," Rondeau said. "Parents? I grew up in an alley eating out of trash cans."

"All right, Rondeau wins," Marla said. "That's why I never play fucked-up family with him. He's always got some story about how his only friend was a dead cat, and it tops everybody."

"I *wish* I'd had a dead cat for a friend," Rondeau said.

"I had to make do with a dead *rat*. But I grew up and made a new family. Marla. Bradley. A few other people. My brothers and sisters in arms. Here's to the family you *choose*."

"I'll drink to that," Jason said, and they all clinked glasses. "I know you got stuck with me by birth, Marla, but I'm hoping we might get to the point where we'd choose each other for family anyway."

"It could happen, big brother."

After another couple of hours of chitchat and assorted deep-fried finger foods, B started yawning conspicuously. Marla poked him. "Lightweight. Why don't you go home and get some sleep?"

"Bless you." B pushed his half-full water glass away. "I know you're going to have me up at some unhallowed hour tomorrow."

"I just want you to be healthy, wealthy, and wise, B."

Rondeau checked his watch. "I should bail, too, see how things are going at the club. Can we take the car, or...."

"I'll give Marlita a ride home," Jason said. "If that's all right with you, sis?"

"You haven't had enough family bonding, huh?" She munched a cold mozzarella stick, then nodded. "All right, sure. See you two in the morning."

B and Rondeau said their farewells, leaving Marla and Jason facing each other across the booth.

"The food here isn't bad," Jason said, "but what do you say we hit some places that are a little more *fun*?"

"I'm not sure I can handle your idea of fun."

"Have a little faith. Remember those little tricks I used to show you in the kitchen, or the yard? Didn't you ever want to try them out in real life?"

"I'm not a big fan of recreational stealing, Jason."

He rolled his eyes. "Who's talking about stealing? Stealing is boring. I'm just talking about, you know, magic tricks. Bets. Not even halfway serious money. If you insist, we can play for funsies—"

Marla laughed. Funsies. As opposed to playing for keepsies. She'd forgotten that phrase. When they were kids and Jason offered to make a bet with her or show her a card or a dice trick or even something fancy with glasses or matchboxes or peas or walnut shells, she'd always insisted they play for funsies—at least, after the first time, when she'd lost her milk money betting him that bats were blind. She'd been about seven years old at the time. She hadn't believed him until he'd shown her the encyclopedia article about it—not that faking such a thing would have been beyond his abilities, even then. "That's nice of you to offer, bro. But I guess if we're talking about five or ten bucks a pop from the kind of people who are dumb enough to make bets with guys they meet in bars, you can play for keepsies."

"Oh, good. It's just so much more *fun* when there's money on the line."

The first bar they went to was a trendy crowded joint with blues on the jukebox and abstract neon artwork on the walls. Jason bellied right up to the bar, next to a yuppie in steel-rimmed glasses who'd just ordered a nice glass of scotch. Marla lingered near the end of the bar, watching.

Jason was suddenly *drunk*. He didn't look like a guy pretending to be drunk, hamming it up—he looked like a guy who'd started out the night having a good time and had proceeded to have a *blitzed* time. Everything about him, from posture to body language to voice to facial expressions, radiated good-natured inebriation. "Hey, buddy," he said. "I'll bet you, I'll *bet* you, I can drink that glass of scotch without touching the glass." He held up his fingers and waggled them. "No hands! No elbows! Nothin'!"

The guy raised one eyebrow and shook his head. "No way. Seen that one before. You pick up the glass with a napkin, or your sleeve, or something, forget it."

"Nope." Jason spoke with the exaggerated seriousness that only a total lush could muster. "No hands, no nothing, if I touch the glass at all, with anything, you get, uh…" He groped in his jacket. "Five bucks. Yeah? Look, look, we'll get a partial, no, whatsit, *impartial* judge." Marla thought he was going to beckon her, that she was going to be his shill, but instead he plucked the sleeve of a cute young woman passing by. Jason beamed at her—even in drunk mode he could charm birds down from trees and panties down around knees. "Hello, there, hoping you can settle something for us." He explained the bet—having neatly skipped over the part where the mark actually *agreed* to the bet, Marla noticed, but the yuppie was going along with it—and said,

"If you think I'm violating the, whatchamacallit, spirit of the thing, you just give the money to *him*."

She agreed, and the yuppie put a fiver on the bar next to Jason's bill. Jason made a great show of shooting his cuffs, waggling his fingers, leaning close to peer into the glass, extending his tongue until it almost touched the liquid inside, then rearing back. "Here goes." He plucked a straw from inside his jacket pocket, put one end in his lips and the other in the scotch, and in a couple of seconds had slurped up the entirety of the drink. He winced. "Not the best way to sip good whiskey," he said, "but better than going dry."

The judge awarded the point to Jason, and the yuppie laughed. "I'm going to try that at my next party."

Jason sketched a little bow. "Tell you what. Order another, and I'll drink that without touching it *and without using a straw*. Same stakes? You still willing to judge?"

"This I gotta see," she said, and the yuppie bemusedly agreed, glancing at the girl. Maybe he was hoping that when the drunk fell over, he could start charming her. Jason had certainly provided him with a conversation-starter. The yuppie called for another glass, and Jason went through his whole rigamarole again, peering into the glass, waggling his fingers—and then frowning. "I saw this earlier tonight," he muttered. "Guy showed me this trick, I swear, he . . . He . . . Ah, fuck it." Jason picked up the glass and downed it one gulp, over the protests of the judge and the yuppie.

"You lose," she said, laughing.

"Next time." Jason swayed a little. "I'll get you next

time." He pushed a five over to the yuppie and made his way down the bar toward Marla.

When he'd settled in beside her, Marla said, "Well, you broke even, I guess, but what happened with that second bet?"

He grinned. "What happened is, I just paid five bucks for a couple of twenty-dollar glasses of whiskey. That was eighteen-year Macallan he was drinking. Or, rather, *I* was drinking." Jason sighed. "Of course, now he's chatting up the Honorable Judge Hotness there, so maybe he's getting the better end of this deal, after all."

"You got a lady in your life, Jason?"

"Just lady luck, and I cheat on her all the time. You got a fella?"

"I don't have time for one. I was seeing a guy earlier this year, but it didn't work out. He tried to screw me—and not in a good way."

"Men are pigs," Jason said. "This place is too hoity-toity for my tastes. Want to find something a little more down-and-dirty?"

"I thought you'd never ask."

The next bar was a dive apparently much beloved by students—one of those townie bars that gets colonized by self-consciously slumming college kids during the academic year—and Jason did a trick where he put a coaster on top of a beer glass, then balanced a cigarette on its end on the coaster, then put a quarter on top of the cigarette. "Bet I can get the quarter in the glass without touching the glass, the cigarette, the coaster, *or* the coin," he said, and he had a couple of takers. Marla even scared up a couple of side bets, as Jason had suggested. Jason bent over the bar, turned his head, and blew a puff of air *up* at the underside of the coaster, sending the coaster and the cigarette flying—while the coin's greater weight sent it plunging straight down, to land in the bottom of the glass.

"Anybody want to see another trick? I've got a great one, if the bartender will be so kind as to lend me an empty pint glass." Burned by their losses, the clustered college kids hesitated, so Marla stepped forward. "What's the trick?"

Jason took the glass and said, "If we measure with a piece of string, which do you think is greater, the circumference of the glass, or the height of the glass?"

One of the kids stepped forward. "The circumference. Duh."

"Spoken like a true math major," one of the others said, and everyone laughed.

"How about now?" Jason took a pile of coasters about an inch thick and put the glass on top of that. "From the top of the glass to the bar, is it still less than the circumference?"

"Maybe about the same," the math major said, squinting.

Jason added another inch of coasters. "Now?"

"That's definitely taller," he said firmly.

"Care to place a wager?"

"You're not allowed to measure with, like, a rubber band or something," Marla said. "And you can't move the glass down *off* the pile of coasters, either."

Jason glared at her for just an instant—long enough for the kids to notice—then was all smiles again. "Come on, we're all friends here—"

"Nope, I'll bet, but under her terms." Math Major plopped a bill on the bar.

"Okay, kid. Lend me one of your shoelaces? So you don't think I'm cheating?"

After unthreading the lace and trying to hand it over, Jason said, "No, you're the expert, you do the measuring."

Math Major carefully wrapped the lace around the mouth of the glass, measured off the circumference, then let the string dangle down the side of the glass . . . where a significant amount of its length rested curled against the bar. He gaped. "Shit, shit, *shit*."

"Don't blame me," Jason said. "I never got past basic algebra in high school." He picked up the money and breezed out of the bar.

Marla commiserated with the kids for a few minutes, then left herself. Jason was around the corner, smoking a cigarette. "See, not even a con. Just a little optical illusion. Best part of that bet is, if the guy gets pissed, he can't even chase you, because he's got one shoe off, with the lace pulled out."

"Heh. You do figure all the angles, don't you?"

"I love this shit. The old-school stuff, you know? The *classics*. You can learn this stuff out of books now, off the Internet. It's not like it used to be, but you can still find takers for just about any bet you care to name."

"In bars full of drunks, sure. Talk about choosing your audience."

"God must love fools, because he sure made a lot of them. In bars and out of them. Want a smoke?"

Marla hadn't had a cigarette since she was a kid, when she'd smoked them in secret with her friends behind a barn, but she and Jason were *bonding* now. "Sure." They puffed in companionable silence for a while, though Marla didn't inhale as deeply as he did.

"I liked that," Jason said after a moment. "You know. Teaching you tricks."

Marla thought of Bradley's magic lessons, and was amused at the idea of herself as a student—everybody had something to teach somebody, she supposed. "Big brother being a big bad influence, huh?"

"This from the crime queen of Felport?"

"It's a dirty job, but someone's gotta do it."

"I'm proud of you, sis. You really made something of yourself."

"Doesn't look like you turned out so bad yourself, bro."

"Maybe we didn't become doctors and lawyers, but we're not selling shoes in a strip mall in Nowheresville, either. We're living life on our own terms."

"I'll drink to that."

"Then we'd better find a place that's got drinks. And maybe a game. Have you ever played liar's dice?"

"I've heard of it. Bluffing game, right?"

"Yep. I love games where lying is part of the *rules*."

"Didn't, like, pirates used to play that game?"

He presented her with his most charming, cockeyed grin yet. "We still do."

8

The next morning B opened one eye and saw Marla sitting at the tiny desk in the corner, an open manila folder before her.

"Sweet dreams, sleepyhead?" She didn't look up.

B groaned. "More mushrooms. Not sweet. Earthy. Would somebody tell the vision dispenser in the sky that I *get* it? Beware the fungus among us."

"Mushrooms are interesting," Marla said. "Just about anything is, if you look at it hard enough, but mushrooms . . . very interesting."

B picked up an alarm clock from the floor and squinted. "It's, what, 5 A.M.? Don't you ever *sleep*?"

"Sure. Four hours a night, usually, though Jason and I rambled around too much for that last night. I'm good, though."

"You and Jason are getting along?"

"Better than I expected we would. Given my position, it's hard for me to find someone to just hang out and

raise hell with—not that I usually have time for shenanigans. Last night was kind of like the old days, when we
were kids, only with more booze and profanity." She
paused. "Well, maybe about the same level of profanity."

"I'm glad. You could use more people you can trust."

Marla made a pfft noise. "Just because I enjoyed his
company doesn't mean I *trust* him."

"But maybe it's a start." B got up and rummaged in
his duffel for some fresh clothes. Eventually he'd get un-
packed and get settled, and that would be nice, but in a
fundamental way he already felt he was home. Working
for Marla was frustrating, dirty, and very likely dangerous, but it was right. They were protecting the city, and
even if the city wasn't in his blood and bones the way it
was in hers, that connection would come, in time. The
bad parts of Felport weren't so different from the bad
parts of Oakland anyway—just as dirty and junky and
dangerous, albeit with fewer stucco houses and a total
lack of palm trees. He yawned. "Maybe we can sleep in
tomorrow? Lack of sufficient sleep can lead to psychotic
breaks."

"Psychotic breaks can be useful if the timing's right."
She tossed the folder and its contents onto the mussed
covers. "Give that a look."

There wasn't much there, a computer printout with a
thumbnail bio of a sorcerer named Bulliard, resident of
some forest in Oregon, with a special affinity for—

"This is our mushroom man?"

"The world's leading mycomancer, apparently. Not
that there's a lot of competition, though I gather it
can be pretty potent magic—poison, rot, hallucination.

Hamil says Bulliard is probably our impending visitor. If it's not him, it's somebody we've never heard of, and that's too depressing to contemplate, so let's go with this theory. We don't have a photo, and no real history, not even a first name. Bulliard could even be an alias. The guy's a hermit, eats roots and bugs, talks to himself, shit like that."

"Then how do we have any information on him?"

Marla shrugged. "Got it from *Dee's Peerage*. Used to be a book, now it's on disc, sort of a *Who's Who* of sorcerers. Hell, you'll probably be in there next year. Nobody knows who compiles it—presumably some fucker named Dee—or where they get their info. It's just basic biographical shit, but it's helpful if you're going out of town and want some idea who you're likely to encounter. Which is how we know Bulliard worships a giant honey mushroom colony. Now, I ask you—do you think a giant mushroom colony is likely to be sentient, let alone possessed of godlike attributes? I'm thinking no. I'm thinking you might as well worship a coral reef or a pile of rocks, and I'm sure there are wackos out there who worship both. I don't know what it is with sorcerers pledging allegiance to weird gods. It happens a lot. Even when the gods are real, the relationship seldom ends well."

"So we know who we're looking for. What's the plan of action?"

Marla shrugged. "Hamil's calling people, alerting them to be on the lookout. When and if Bulliard shows up, I'll have a little talk with him, and if he's not the talking kind, well...maybe his name won't be in *Dee's Peerage* next year. Dead sorcerers don't get included."

B frowned. "If we're just hanging tough, then why did you wake me at 5 A.M.?"

"Magic lessons. You thought your little supernatural head cold would get you out of your chores? Get dressed. We're going to the biggest junkyard in the universe."

"Think fast!" Ernesto hurled most of a carburetor at B's head.

B swore, lurched left, slipped on oily gravel, and landed on his ass in the shadow of a pile of wrecked cars.

"At least the carburetor missed him." Marla sat in a sagging lawn chair drinking from a bottle of Mexican Coke—"the good kind, with *sugar*, none of that high-fructose shit," she'd said.

"I guess falling to the ground qualifies as thinking fast," Ernesto said. "But I don't think it counts as thinking *well*."

"I'm getting flashbacks to dodgeball in junior high." B got to his feet, not even bothering to brush the dirt off his jeans—after all, the lesson wasn't over, and he would only get dirty again. "Is this really—"

"Again!" This time Ernesto threw a hubcap, spinning it through the air like a discus, right at B's face.

This time B resisted the urge to dive and instead drew on the techniques Ernesto had spent all morning drilling into him. Space was a flexible thing, B knew, and could be distorted by forces as everyday and ubiquitous as gravity. With the right training, a sorcerer could twist space, too—exerting a sort of gravity of *will*. B stared at the oncoming hubcap, watching the light glint from the shiny scratches on its edge, and time slowed down. Since space and time were inextricably linked, the ability to alter one incorporated the ability to alter the other...if you could keep the balance right. He could feel sweat beading on his forehead—forget walking while chewing gum, this was closer to conducting neurosurgery while juggling pineapples.

Only B's subjective sense of time had changed, so his body couldn't move any faster than usual, but his mind could, and the feat Ernesto and Marla expected from him was a feat of the mind.

B *flexed,* the space around him curved slightly, and the slowly spinning hubcap lazily shifted in its course, describing a parabola around his body, avoiding contact with him entirely. Normal time slammed back onto him, and B stumbled, gravity yanking on him harder than usual for a moment and blurring his vision, but fuck, he'd *done* it, by the gods, that was *sorcery*—

An empty Mr. Pibb can bounced off the side of B's head. "Aw, fuck you, Ernesto, no fair."

The salvage sorcerer laughed. "When the bad guys start chucking grenades at you, and you need to make space-time twist like a pretzel to send the bombs back at them, is that gonna be fair? Still, pretty good, kid, for your first time. That's how we dodge bullets, you get it? Don't move yourself, and don't move the bullet, just move the space the bullet *travels through*. Keep it up and you'll be able to do all kinds of neat tricks with geometry."

"Give my apprentice a soda, Ernesto." Marla rose from her chair. "Fucking with reality is thirsty work." She sauntered over to B, grinning, while Ernesto went into his trailer to get a drink. The trailer was a tiny silver tin can of a thing from the outside, but B had gotten a glimpse through the open door, and the place was the size of a palace on the inside.

"How big is this junkyard?" B said. They'd walked a long time after passing through the wire-and-sheet-metal gates, and B had the feeling if he climbed to the top of one of these scrap-metal mountains, there'd be nothing but junk as far as he could see.

"Hard to say." Marla passed him a handerchief, and B blotted at his sweaty face. He was *beat,* and his head thudded like someone was pounding a drum inside it. This made doing sympathetic magic seem about as strenuous as taking a nap. He was going to sleep hard to-night, and he already dreaded the certainty that Marla would have him up again tomorrow at the crack of dawn.

"Ernesto's our resident spatial specialist, and he's carved all sorts of folds and scallops into the geometry here. If the whole junkyard took up the surface area it actually contains, it'd be—"

"Bigger than Felport itself. Which makes me a more important civic leader than Marla here, right?" Ernesto said, emerging from the trailer and handing B an open bottle, which B quickly tipped back. It *was* better than the usual stuff.

Marla snorted. "Right. Except Ernesto's only constituents are rats and oil-stained apprentices."

"Wow." B looked around, a little unnerved at the yard's weird immensity.

"Anybody ever get lost?"

Ernesto shrugged. "Not *forever*, though I've had a couple of apprentices come stumbling out after two or three days of drinking puddle water. Some of them come out raving about finding other people in there, and things that aren't exactly people, but I don't know how seriously to take all that. One apprentice went hiking in with a pack and enough food and water to last a few days, and came back telling stories about some kind of dragon sleeping on a pile of wrecked ocean liners, but come on. Dragons? Thpt."

"I heard about him," Marla said. "Markov, right? Didn't he go back in, and never come out again?"

"Yep." Ernesto shook his head. "But I don't count him as lost. He went in with no intention of ever returning."

"So you've never seen anything weird in there?" B said.

"I didn't say *that*. There may have been a short-term interdimensional breach or two, I won't pretend otherwise, though I've got all kinds of safeguards to keep anything that comes in from getting out of the yard. If I didn't, Marla would have my head on a stick."

"That's just good city management," Marla agreed.

"Last week I found this big old landshark of a car, looked like it was in decent condition, and on the trunk it said it was a Chrysler Wendigo. That's no model of Chrysler *I've* ever heard of, and I know 'em all, even the concept cars." Ernesto shook his head. "I went looking for it a couple of days later and it was gone. So, sure, weird stuff. But think of the money I save on property taxes! Whenever I need to expand my operation—which is really lucrative these days, the way the Chinese are buying up scrap metal—I just *think* really hard."

"So, ah, your will holds all this together?" B said. "What if something happens to you?"

"Oh, we got binding spells. Don't worry."

"If he *didn't* have binding spells," Marla said, "all this stretched-out space, and everything occupying that space, would collapse into the *real* space here, and that would get ugly. Hell, theoretically, it could even squash down tight enough to make a black hole."

"I call bullshit," Ernesto said. "Maybe if I tossed a few hundred *planets* in here, or a *star*, but otherwise, we're a long damn way from the Schwarzschild radius for my yard. Marla just likes contemplating end-of-the-world scenarios."

"What can I say? I get hung up on contingencies."

"You've got a contingency for a black hole coming to Felport?" B found the idea amusing, scary, and comforting all at once.

Marla tapped her temple with her forefinger. "You wouldn't believe what I've got up here."

"Better let the kid get back to practicing," Ernesto said. "He doesn't seem half bad. I've got ten apprentices now, and most of 'em can't even rebuild an engine without fucking up."

"Well, they don't have *me* for a teacher," Marla said.

"I see you doing a lot of teaching out here today, drinking all my Cokes and talking shit."

"I'm teaching B how to *delegate,* Ernesto."

"All right, all right. Remember, B, rearranging space is good for more than playing dodgeball, so we're gonna work on a couple of other things. Reality here is nice and prestretched, so you'll be able to do some cool shit that might not work so well outside my yard, get it?" He paused. "You going to hang around getting in the way, Marla?"

"Nah." She held up B's phone, which she'd pretty much commandeered. "Rondeau sent an ambiguous text, said he has something to tell me about Jason, but 'not to worry,' which makes me worry more, naturally. Anyway, I'm supposed to meet him in an hour or so. I hope it's not black treachery. I was starting to like having my brother around."

"A brother, huh?" Ernesto said. "There's *more* of you!"

"Not all Masons are made alike, Ernesto."

"Let me know if you need me," B said.

"Sure thing." She tossed him his phone. "But I wouldn't sweat it. I've handled worse things than Jason will ever be."

Rondeau followed Jason into the living room and sat down in the nice armchair Cam-Cam had used in their last meeting. Jason had instructed Rondeau to act arrogant and entitled, and Rondeau was willing to give it a shot. Jason took the far end of the couch, leaving Cam-

Cam with no choice but to sit between them, glancing nervously from one to the other. Cam-Cam looked older than Rondeau had first supposed—in the window-light his crow's-feet were visible, as were the frown lines around his mouth.

There were several chains around his neck—silver, gold, and baser metals, all disappearing into the collar of his tailored shirt. Rondeau suspected the poor bastard was wearing a bunch of amulets, always a favorite fake artifact for charlatans to sell to the credulous.

"Gentlemen," Cam-Cam began, "I have some concerns—"

"I'm afraid I have some bad news, Mr. Campion." Jason played disappointment tinged with embarrassment perfectly. "My sister says we can't involve you in this."

Cam-Cam blinked, straightened, and said, "The money's not a problem. I can—"

"It's not the money, it's *you*," Rondeau said. "You're an outsider. Them's the breaks. I'm annoyed, too. Now we have to shake some other trees and hope money falls from the branches."

"This is ridiculous! I assure you, I'm perfectly trustworthy."

"It's not even that," Jason said. "It's just . . . this is dangerous and delicate business, confidentially trafficking a highly sought-after commodity, and some people—"

"And things that *aren't* people," Rondeau chimed in.

"—are going to be interested in stealing it," Jason went on. "Marla doesn't want your demise on her conscience."

"Sorcerers worry about karma," Rondeau said. "Because karma pays extra-close attention to them."

"Marla says sorcerers know what they're getting into, and they're prepared to deal with stuff that would drive most people insane. I'm sorry, Mr. Campion. You're just, well, a mundane. A muggle."

"An ordinary," Rondeau said.

Cam-Cam clenched his fists. "I may not be an initiate, but I've studied magic, from Paracelsus to Grant Morrison, sacred rites to profane rituals and points in between. I'm *ready* for this."

"A theoretical grounding isn't much comfort when things from behind the stars try to suck your mind out through your face." Rondeau tried on a look of contempt. "Shit, you've got *no idea*."

"But I want an idea. I want to know. I've been trying my whole life to pierce the veil, to see the true reality beyond the illusions of the known world. Can't *anything* be done?"

"Like I said, it's out of our hands," Jason said. "It's Marla's call."

"Can I—can I *talk* to her?" Cam-Cam asked. "Plead my case?"

"Oh, I don't know." Jason held up his hands.

Cam-Cam narrowed his eyes. "Would a cash donation help grease the wheels?"

"Oh, this guy," Rondeau said. "You think we're fishing for a bribe? We're *sorcerers*. Money is not, generally speaking, a problem. I can walk up to an ATM and whisper sweet nothings in its card slot and have it spitting bills at me until I can't close my wallet." Rondeau enjoyed the speech, even more because it was mostly true. That was the reason Cam-Cam had never found much traction in his quest to become intimate with the workings of truly powerful sorcerers—all he had to offer was cash, and real sorcerers seldom hurt for money, unless they were choosing to be impoverished for ritual reasons.

Cam-Cam didn't deflate. He laughed, though it sounded more like a cough. "Then why did you come here *asking* me for money?"

Jason sighed. "Rondeau's right about charming an ATM, but we're talking about *big* money for this deal. The kind of money you can't just filch without people noticing."

"You can rob some random guy of the cash in his wallet and then erase his memory with magic," Rondeau added, "but you can't erase the memory of the entire Internal Revenue Service. Even sorcerers don't fuck with the IRS." In truth, sorcerers mostly just *avoided* the IRS, but even Marla had extensive money-laundering operations to make her cash flow look legit.

Jason went on. "Without getting too heavily into specifics, we're gathering funds to purchase a ... certain item ... that Marla would rather not have traced back to her. We're then going to sell that item to a third party, and Marla doesn't want to be connected to him at *all*. Basically, Mr. Campion, there's a war going on between a couple of magical factions, and Marla wants to help one of them out. But for political and personal and otherwise complicated reasons, she can't be seen taking sides. This quantity of money doesn't get moved around without attracting notice, so she'd rather not risk dipping into her personal accounts." He glanced at Rondeau, who took up his end of the spiel.

"We're collecting some money here, and some money there, and approaching people like it's an investment—which it is, should be a hell of a return, too—so it's not obviously connected to Marla. But there could be blowback, still, and she doesn't want you to get splashed with acidic monstrous death."

"I tell you, I don't care about the dangers, and I'll pay *all* of it!"

Jason looked at Rondeau. Rondeau shrugged, almost imperceptibly. Jason said, "We can ask. Tell her we explained the dangers, see if she's willing to talk to him."

"*You* ask," Rondeau said. "You're her brother. She won't kill *you*."

"All right." Jason stood up abruptly. "Mr. Campion, we'll be in touch."

Rondeau went to Cam-Cam and shook his hand "I gotta hand it to you, champ, you're braver than I expected. You've got that real seeker's fire in your heart, I can sense it. Maybe Marla will sense it, too. Take care of yourself." He went toward the front door after Jason, and they let themselves out.

Back in the car, Jason grinned. "That was good, Ronnie. That was really, really good. Now we just need to find somebody to pretend to be Marla."

"Piece of cake," Rondeau said. He already had a very intriguing idea for who should play that role. At first he'd thought of asking Lorelei, using the fun of the game as a way of getting back into her good graces and her panties both, but then he'd had a better idea.

"Rest stop." The messenger parked the van and rubbed his eyes. Even with the mushrooms on the back of his neck pumping stimulants into his blood, he was exhausted from driving so far for so long, stopping only for gas every several hours. Bulliard was not the most pleasant traveling companion. He stank of rot and body odor, and though he didn't talk much, he was always back there, *rustling*.

"No rest. Back on the road."

"I need to piss, and I need *food*. Maybe you're happy back there eating the morels that grow out of your armpits or whatever, but I need a godsdamn cheeseburger."

An ominous silence. Then: "You are an impertinent slave."

"You're right. You'd better kill me, then." He turned around and confronted the eye-twisting blot of darkness that was his master and passenger. "Motherfucker, I've got mushrooms growing into my *brain stem*. I'm enslaved to, forgive me, the smelliest, craziest, scariest freak I've ever met. I know my glimpse of the Mycelium was supposed to convert me to your way of thinking, make me into a zealot in your cause or whatever, but here's the thing: seeing the face of a giant mushroom god just convinced me that some things in this world are way too fucked-up to even bear thinking about. I had every expectation of dying back there in the woods, and

I don't hold out a lot of hope of getting out of this alive. So either let me piss and get some food, or kill me and drive yourself to Felport, if you can figure out which pedal is 'go' and which one is 'stop.'"

"I could just...hijack you, you know. The mushrooms in your brain. They allow me that power, to use you, like a puppet."

"Would your puppet know how to drive a stick shift, stinky?"

"Go, then. But make haste."

The messenger pushed down the handle on the van door.

"While you're in there, bring me some food," Bulliard said.

"Sure thing, boss."

The messenger washed as well as he could in the bathroom, trying and failing to get a glimpse of the mushrooms at his neck. He tugged on one, gently, and the pain that erupted in his head was blinding. Once he recovered from the agony, he turned up his collar to hide the mushrooms from sight before exiting to place his order. Returning to the van, he tossed a wrapped sandwich back to Bulliard. "There you go."

The sound of paper rustling. "This," said Bulliard, "is a mushroom swiss cheeseburger."

"That's right." The messenger started the van. "I'm a funny motherfucker."

9

Marla slid into the red vinyl booth at Smitty's Diner, where Rondeau was playing drums with a pie-stained fork and knife. "This better be important. I had to drive myself over here, and you know I hate that. I think I broke the horn from honking it too much."

"Nice boots." Rondeau leaned way over to look under the table at her feet. "What did you do, lose a bet? Those look like—"

"Like what? Like something *you'd* wear? Shut it. I like them. So what's the bad word?"

Rondeau shook his head. "If Jason has nasty nefarious stuff in mind, he's keeping it to himself." Rondeau ran his thumb over his plate and then sucked off a gob of smeared pie filling. "I really like the guy, boss."

Marla grunted. "He's likable. Professionally."

He sighed. "Maybe this was a bad idea. Never mind. Forget it."

Marla rolled her eyes. " 'Never mind, forget it'? And now the mark, that's me, is supposed to be consumed by curiosity and say, 'Oh, no, please, tell me,' right?"

"I'm not as cynical as you are, Marla. I'm kind of jealous you've got a brother, honestly, and I wouldn't mind seeing you two get close again. I think it'd be good for you. Lord knows Jason can actually keep up with you, and he's not afraid to give you a little crap, and he can probably absorb all the crap even an accomplished crap-flinger like *you* can fling. Crap style."

"He's certainly had practice. So, Mr. Reconciliation, what do you want from me?"

"In the spirit of family, how'd you like to help us out with the scam?"

"Oh, it's 'us' now, is it? You and Jason, hustlers for hire?"

"What can I say? The guy has drawn me to his very bosom. I'm supposed to find somebody to pretend to be you, so Cam-Cam can have a meeting. It's part of the convincer—give him an impressive meeting with the head of Felport's magical underworld, so hc knows he's involved with serious people. How funny would it be if the actress was *you*? Jason would shit."

"The only reason I'm okay with you guys ripping off Cam-Cam is because he's annoyed the ever-loving shit out of me every time I've met him. Why would I want to meet him *again*?"

"Ah, but it's so much more fun when you're running a game on the guy, Marla. I'm having the time of my life here. Remember when Cam-Cam showed up in your office and offered to buy you your own private island if you'd take him on as your apprentice?"

Marla laughed. "I said I'd show him a good trick, and blasted him in the face with a dose of forget-me-lots potion. Then we dumped bourbon all over his head and took him to Mary Madeline Monroe's brothel, left him snoozing in the lobby. I wonder what he thought when he woke up with no memory of the previous two days?" She shook her head. "He's got all that private-jet privilege shit going on, for sure. Too much money and not enough sense, thinks he can buy anybody."

"And you hate people like that."

"Truth."

"So why not give us a hand taking his money *away*, so he can never bribe another alley witch into telling him your whereabouts? I know he's pestered Hamil and Ernesto in the past, too. They'd thank you."

"His memory's been erased so many times I wonder if we've done permanent brain damage," Marla mused. "There's never been a test on the long-term effects of forget-me-lots, though there's some evidence that it works less effectively the more often it's administered. We did have to give him a pretty big dose the last time."

"See? By taking away his money, you're saving him from future brain damage! It's win-win. I still say you should've let him buy you an island and *then* erased his memory, by the way."

"If I wanted an island, I'd get an island. Hell, there's Shrove Island out in the bay. It's technically under the Bay Witch's protection, but she wouldn't care if I used it.

She's only interested in the bits that are below the water-line anyway, the caves and shit under there." Shrove Island, a couple of miles offshore, had once been chosen as the site for a federal prison in the bay, a sort of East Coast analog to San Francisco's Alcatraz. Partway through construction one of the caves under the surface had collapsed, killing a dozen construction workers, and the project had been abandoned for safety reasons. The remains of the prison complex were still out there, con-crete and rebar ruins overgrown with scrub pines and full of treacherous sinkholes. Marla'd been out there once or twice to investigate reports of things living in the caves, though neither she nor the Bay Witch had been able to confirm or disprove the rumors. "You know," Marla said, "if you're going to dazzle Cam-Cam, you need a suitably impressive setting. Just sitting him down with somebody in a bar won't do the job. And even if it would, it lacks style."

"You have any ideas?"

Rondeau had a self-satisfied smile on his face, and that was *almost* enough to make Marla change her mind. But, hell, Jason was back in her life, and she had to admit, it would be fun. She'd never had the chance to play even a bit part in his scams when she was a kid—he'd kept her out of that stuff, because she was too young, and he didn't want her to get in trouble, though there were times she'd begged for the chance to be a shill or an extra. They'd certainly had a blast carousing and making bar bets and playing games the other night—he could do things with dice she would have almost sworn were literally magical. "I might have one or two thoughts."

"You're willing to play the part of Marla Mason, witch queen of Felport?"

"Fuck it. Okay. You going to tell Jason?"

"Only if you make me. Otherwise, I think it'd be a nice surprise."

"Let's do it that way. It'll do Jason good to *not* be five steps ahead for once. Set it up for tonight. Midnight, dark of the moon, like that."

"Okay, but where are we going?"

"For a boat ride."

B was sweaty, disheveled, and covered in oily slime when Marla came back for him. "How you doing, kid?" She lounged against the side of the Bentley.

B limped through Ernesto's gates, which were festooned with bits of scrap metal and decorated with old hubcaps. "The guy collapsed a tower of cars on top of me."

Marla whistled. "I'm guessing you passed that test, seeing as you aren't squashed like a bug."

"I made the whole cascade of cars roll around me, walked out without a scratch. Would he have let me die?"

"I can't say for sure. He knows your death would've led to his own, and it's possible he has a death wish. But I doubt it. There were probably safeguards in place. I asked him to teach you, not test you to destruction. That's *my* prerogative."

"That's reassuring." He groaned. "This was a lot more physical than I'm used to. With Sanford Cole, we mostly sat around talking, reading, *thinking*."

"Playing canasta, talking about the good old days when men were men and fire hadn't been invented yet? There's a different vibe out here. You bothered by that?"

"No, ma'am. I always wanted to be an action hero. I'm just achy."

"I've got some stuff at home that makes tiger balm look like applesauce. Langford whipped it up for me, so I wouldn't ask too many questions about what it's made of, but it does wonders for muscle soreness."

"I won't say no to medical intervention." He went around to the driver's side and opened the door. "Where to?"

Marla squinted at the twilight sky. "I guess I'll feed you. Then I'm going to make you work some more. Then, around midnight, we're going to have some fun."

B groaned. "Sleeping is fun. How about sleeping?"

"No, we're going to help my brother run his con. It'll be a blast."

B climbed into the car, and Marla followed. "So you're helping your brother?"

"Well, why not? Maybe I've been unnecessarily paranoid. Not that 'unnecessary' and 'paranoid' are two words I ever expected to put together. I figure I'll extend the hand of sisterly love by giving him some help with his latest gig. We'll see what develops."

B grunted and pulled the car from the lot. "And you don't have any . . . moral qualms about ripping off this guy?"

"Cam-Cam? You ever heard of blood diamonds?"

"Sure, the mines in Africa that fund warlords."

"That's his family business. One of 'em anyway. The Campions have been into the Earth-pillaging business for a long time, from back in the silver and gold rush days out west, and their interests range a lot further than that now. Cam-Cam never met a wildlife refuge he didn't want to drill." She paused. "Well, okay, maybe not Cam-Cam *personally*. His family's company is a machine that runs without him paying much attention, I suspect, which is damning in its own way, mind you. Cam-Cam's only interest is his obsession with magic, and he's made a nuisance of himself in the city for years. Take away enough of his money, and he'll stop being a nuisance anymore, right? Maybe we can even scare him away from the supernatural entirely."

"Okay," B said. "I didn't realize we were grifters, but okay."

Marla sighed. "You don't have to help. You want to take a moral stand, I'm totally okay with that. But believe me, if you met this guy, you'd know he's a fool who needs to be parted from his money, posthaste. And be aware, this isn't the only shady business I've got a hand in. Mostly those businesses are based on giving people things they want that society deems illegal or inappropriate, and not so much on outright stealing, but down at the lower levels things go on that I don't question too carefully. If you're not comfortable with that..."

B shook his head. "No, no, it's okay. I know all that. I've always had too much empathy, I guess."

"Part of what makes you a good seer, B. Me, I'm an

ass-kicker, and if you have too much empathy when it comes to kicking ass, you wind up with a sore ass of your own. I'm sure me and you will figure out how to strike the right balance. You're an actor—think of tonight as a chance to do a little acting, you know?"

"Well, when you put it *that* way . . ."

After they finished eating dinner, B said, "Did you still want me to find an oracle and ask about Jason?"

Marla stirred her postmeal coffee and looked thoughtful. They were in a little café where the only notable décor was a vast quantity of towering ferns in giant pots, so it was a bit like eating steak and fries in the late Cretaceous. "I know I did earlier, but now it feels . . . unkind, I guess, to supernaturally spy on him. Like a family should have trust, you know?"

"Sure."

"Ah, screw it, let's find an oracle."

B grinned. He felt a lot better having replenished some calories, and now the muscle ache felt almost pleasant, proof he'd done an honest day's work. He was looking forward to the chance to use his magic to call up another oracle. He *liked* doing that stuff, now that it worked again. It was awesome.

They went out the front of the restaurant, and then Marla immediately led him to an alley around the back, where the Dumpsters were overflowing. "Garbage again, I'm guessing? Will this do?"

"I'm not sure, let me think—ah. Right there." He could feel the presence of an oracle, a tug like he was iron and the oracle was magnetic. B flung open the plastic lid of a trash bin and stood on tiptoe to look inside. "Hello in there?"

"THIEF!" the garbage can screamed, and a towering figure of reeking refuse loomed out of the bin. B caught a glimpse of a mouth lined with teeth of broken glass and eyes made of cantaloupe halves, and then the garbage thing snatched him up in rotten-meat arms. He opened his mouth to shout, and the stinking thing from the can jammed a wad of moldy bread between his jaws. It was still screaming, calling him a thief, an oath-breaker, a liar, and B thought clearly, *This is how I die, eaten by leftovers.*

Naturally, Marla saved him. He wasn't sure what she did, but the thing in the garbage screamed in pain and Marla dragged B back, well away from the Dumpster, and propped him against the brick wall across the alley. B spat moldy bread out of his mouth. Marla stood, legs wide, a dagger in each hand, a pile of garbage—maybe they'd once been the thing's arms?—scattered before her. "Bring it, little god. I've cut up bigger deities than *you.*"

"I am Shakpana. I will make your flesh eat itself."

"Now that the mutual threats are out of the way, what's your grievance? We can work this out."

"He did not *pay,*" Shakpana hissed, swaying like some improbable serpent. "He asked a question, terms were set, an answer given, and he *did not pay.* There is no balance. Thief! THIEF!"

"Enough already!" Marla shouted. Without looking

back, she said, "B, help me out here. I'm a little hazy on the care and feeding of psychotic oracles."

B rose shakily to his feet. Shakpana rippled and seethed and hissed. "Crap. It's the oracle I asked about Jason, when that voice started up and drowned it out. I was so shaky then, so out of it, I never *paid*."

"Looks like this is your past-due notice."

B cleared his throat. "Oh, oracle, please accept my apologies for my failure to follow the forms. When I summoned you before, we were interrupted, and—"

"You *asked,* I *answered,* it is of no consequence to me if you did not *hear* the answer."

"What was the answer again?" Marla said.

Shakpana ignored her. "You promised to dispose of my temporary body, to make sure it was returned to the earth, and you *lied*."

"I accept full responsibility for my error. It was unforgivable." And it was. B knew the rules. You had to balance the books. He'd just been too freaked out by the voice of doom. "I present myself now to make amends. Only tell me what I should do."

Shakpana swayed. "You are truly contrite?"

"I am."

"Then . . . this garbage. All this garbage in the alley. It is wasted. It should be returned to the cycle, to make plants grow, to nourish beasts."

"You want me to compost . . . all this?" B looked up and down the length of the alley. They were on a restaurant row, and there were a lot of Dumpsters there.

"Yes."

"It will be done," B said.

"Then our business is finished."

"Damn it, what's the answer?" Marla said. "We never *heard* you, do I need to worry about my brother?"

Shakpana began sinking down into the Dumpster. "Jason Mason," it wheezed.

"Yes?"

"He is..."

"*Yeah?*"

"He is a liar." And with that, Shakpana was nothing but a bin full of garbage again.

"No shit!" Marla yelled. No response. "That was informative."

"Sorry," B said. "If it had gone right before, we could have asked follow-up questions, maybe, but the oracle isn't willing to cut me a lot of slack. I can't believe I didn't do what I promised before. That was so careless."

"Eh, I figured the connection was broken, too. I didn't realize the oracle went on talking when its voice was drowned out by that other mystery vision. Shit. So Jason's still an unknown quantity. Knowing he's a liar doesn't help much. Tonight I'm going to *help* him lie."

"Maybe that's all the oracle means, that he lies for a living. Jason's a liar, you're tactless, and I'm beautiful but unlucky."

"You really have to sort all this crap and compost it? Want me to scare up some apprentices to give you a hand? I can tell Viscarro I heard there was an artifact in one of these bins; he'd have all his people down here in a snap."

B shook his head. "I should do it on my own. That's the way it works. I don't want to risk pissing off the oracle further. But . . . where the fuck can I compost all this stuff?"

"Let me call Granger." She borrowed his phone again. "You haven't met him yet, though you will soon, for a magic lesson. He's the sorcerer who runs Fludd Park, nature magic, shit like that. He's got a giant compost heap there for the gardens, I'm sure you can contribute to it. I'll get him to send a guy with a wheelbarrow." She looked up and down the alley. "Actually, make that a *truck*. There's a lot of organic nastiness back here, B."

"The life of a sorcerer is a glamorous one. At least if I'm going to be neck-deep in garbage all night, I can hold my breath indefinitely. What time was that thing with your brother?"

"Midnight, but I have to get out to the island before that. I'm thinking you won't be done by then."

"I'm sorry, Marla, I wish I could help—"

"Forget about it. It's extra-curricular. Besides, I'm the one who asked you to call up the garbage oracle again; I'm not going to bust your chops for dealing with the consequences. I'll see you in the morning, all right?"

"Bright and early, I'm sure. Give me a hand climbing into this Dumpster?"

Cam-Cam opened the door in his pajamas, and found Jason and Rondeau on his doorstep, each dressed all in black. "Come with us, Mr. Campion," Jason said. "Marla will see you now."

"Now? But it's after eleven." His mouth was running

on autopilot. He knew sorcerers didn't keep banker's hours, but he hadn't expected them to come here now.

"And if we aren't on the island by midnight, she won't wait a minute longer," Rondeau said. "Grab a coat. Even in summertime, it's cold out on the bay."

"I—what island?"

"Shrove Island. She doesn't want to have this meeting in the city proper." Jason looked around warily. "Too many potential spies."

"I understand. Let me get dressed."

"*Quickly,*" Rondeau said, and so Cam-Cam hurried. When he came back downstairs—dressed in black himself, because it seemed best to fit in, adorned only with a few of his more potent protective amulets—they were standing by the French doors that led to his terraced backyard, with its bay view. "This way," Rondeau said. "She sent a boatman." Cam-Cam thought he saw him shudder, and felt a cold knot grow in his belly. Was this a trap? Were they going to send him to a watery grave? But—*why?* He was just being paranoid.

They led him down through the back gardens, past the swimming pool, to the little dock where he kept his smallest boat—the big yacht was berthed at the marina.

But they didn't go to his boat. There was a little boat tied up on the other side of the dock, with a figure in a voluminous hooded robe sitting by the tiller. As Cam-Cam drew closer, the figure in the boat looked up. A pair of huge glowing green eyes, set inhumanly far apart, regarded him balefully from the black depths of the hood, then vanished when the figure turned his head away.

Cam-Cam balked. "What—what is this? Who is that?"

"One of my sister's creatures." Jason put a hand on Cam-Cam's arm. "Nothing to worry about. He's ... under her control." Jason stepped into the boat, followed by Rondeau, but Cam-Cam noticed they sat as far away from the boatman as they could. Cam-Cam followed, legs shaky, and sat down upon the hard wooden bench.

Rondeau untied the boat from the dock. The tillerman—if he was a man at all—started the boat's engine, and they puttered off into the darkness. The bay had never seemed so vast and dark and empty before. The sky was clear, the stars hard and bright, the moon nowhere visible—was it new, or under the horizon? Shouldn't he know that? Shouldn't anyone who wished to know the ways of sorcery also know the current disposition of the moon?

Nervous with the silence and the buzz of the engine, Cam-Cam said, "I went to Shrove Island once, when I was a child, before they started building the prison—"

"Be *quiet*," Rondeau whispered. "Don't you know how voices carry on the water? You have no idea what *things* live out here. Bad enough we're running the engine."

Jason nodded solemnly, and Cam-Cam hunched down, silent. No, he didn't have any idea. He wanted to, though, and this was his chance, if he didn't screw it up.

After about twenty minutes Shrove Island loomed into view, a dark shape over the water, blotting out stars behind. The island was an unlovely lump of rock covered in straggly trees. The boat pulled up to the sagging remnants of the old dock, which decades ago had welcomed construction crews and equipment. The federal government still owned the island, technically, though they didn't show any interest in doing anything with it, and neither did anyone else.

Rondeau climbed out of the boat and tied the rope. "Walk carefully," he whispered as Jason and Cam-Cam disembarked. The boatman didn't move. "There are things living in the caves under the island that don't like visitors, and while they're afraid of Marla, I doubt they're afraid of *you,* champ. Stay close." Rondeau switched on a flashlight and led the way along a barely visible path, toward the ruins of what would have been the prison's administrative building. The structure was roofless and exposed to the elements, but there were still tall unadorned walls, covered in climbing vines. "Watch your step." Rondeau pointed out a set of concrete steps leading up to a walled space about the size of Cam-Cam's living room. "Here we are." He switched off his flashlight.

"Now what?" Cam-Cam whispered.

"We wait for midnight, and for Marla," Jason said.

Suddenly a dozen torches jammed into crevices and cracks around the room burst into flaming life, illuminating the space with flickering light. Cam-Cam jumped and instinctively huddled toward his new associates. He looked around frightfully. "Where's Marla?"

"Up here, Cam-Cam," a voice said.

Cam-Cam looked up.

Marla Mason, the greatest sorcerer in Felport, reputedly one of the greatest in the world, stood before him, arms crossed, wearing a flowing black cloak trimmed in a glistening silver. Which would have been impressive enough.

Even more impressive was the fact that she was standing sideways ten feet up a stone wall, with no visible means of support, utterly indifferent to gravity, staring down at him.

And she was grinning.

"We're here." The messenger stepped on the brakes and eased the van to a stop on the side of the road.

Bulliard stirred behind him. "This is Felport?"

"That's what it says on the sign we just passed." The van was parked in a grim district, nothing but dark warehouses and empty lots, though the lights of tall buildings twinkled off in the distance.

Bulliard grunted. "I am unaccustomed to cities." He climbed into the passenger seat...and the cloud of darkness that had shrouded him for the entire journey dissolved like black fog blowing away. Bulliard was revealed to the messenger as a giant of a man, dressed in what seemed to be nothing but mosses and lichen, hair a forest of matted dirt, beard vast and unkempt. He turned to look at the messenger directly. Bulliard had a plastic pig snout attached to his face with a dirty rubber band, covering his nose. It was so ridiculous the messenger wanted to burst out laughing, but he stifled the impulse as best he could—he'd pushed his luck already with the mockery, and this seemed like a bad time to get snarky.

The mushroom sorcerer tapped the side of his snout. "I cannot smell the spores. I can find *anything*...but I suppose something as powerful as the spores would be disguised."

"Drat the luck. Guess we should call it a lost cause then, huh? You can catch a Greyhound back to the forest tomorrow morning."

"If I cannot find the spores, I will need to search. But I do not know the city well. Which means I will need allies, willing or otherwise."

The messenger yawned. "That's great. Good luck with that."

Bulliard sniffed, a deep snuffling inhalation. "Drive. Drive straight. I have found someone who can help us."

The messenger sighed and put the van in gear. "Would this someone be a replacement for me?"

"The Mycelium has let you look upon me directly." Bulliard sounded almost aggrieved. "In recognition for your swift travel and steadfast service. Do you not feel honored?"

"Honored? Is that what this feeling is? And here all these years I've been calling it revulsion."

"Drive," Bulliard growled, so the messenger drove.

10

Marla stood on the wall gazing down at Cam-Cam's upturned, distinctly sheeplike face, confident that gravity and the bay breeze were doing impressively flappy things to her cloak. She'd emptied her pockets before activating the gecko boots and walking up the wall—having her spare change and keys fall out and land on Cam-Cam's nose would rather have spoiled the effect.

She almost never got to show off. This was fun. "So you want to work for me, Cam-Cam?"

"Ah, that is, I'm at your service, Ms. Mason."

Marla decided to take pity on their bent necks, and her own screaming abdominal muscles. She walked down the wall, then stepped onto the ground, relaxing at last—locking her knees and holding her body out perpendicular to the wall had been a greater strain on her core strength than she'd expected, despite all the crunches she did every week. It was worth it for the dazzled expression on Cam-Cam's face, though.

Jason, on the other hand, hadn't betrayed a flicker of surprise, either at finding Marla here in person, or at her gravity-defying feat. She strolled over beside him, and Rondeau moved over to join them, so the three formed a semicircle with Marla at the center, all facing Cam-Cam. "Let me ask you something," Marla said. "Are you afraid of vampires?"

"I'm not sure I've ever considered it. Are vampires real, then?"

"All kinds of things are real, Mr. Campion. You really have no clue. Fucking undead. I hate them all, but vampires are the worst. They're so goddamn *smug*. I want to wipe them out like the vermin they are."

"That seems reasonable." Cam-Cam was trying hard to maintain eye contact, keep his spine straight, all those tricks his daddy had probably taught him about looking strong and cool in business negotiations, but Marla could see the sweat on his forehead despite the cool air, the little tremor in his hands, the slight widening of his eyes. He was tense, anxious, afraid...and he was also excited.

"I wish everyone was as right-minded as you are, Cam-Cam. There's a whole nasty colony down in Virginia, the biggest in America, living underground, an actual organization with leaders and rules and laws. Like they're something more civilized than mosquitoes in opera cloaks. A long time ago one of Felport's chief sorcerers signed a nonaggression pact with that colony. Sure, we get the occasional rogue vamp, and I've beheaded and barbecued a couple of those myself, but I can't move against the main body directly, for political reasons. The bloodsuckers are old, smart, powerful, and connected, which some people think is reason to let them go on living. Or unliving. You know what I mean. If I declared war on them, that would be the end of me—the other sorcerers would turn on me in a heartbeat as an oathbreaker and a betrayer. So, since direct action is off the table, I've been exploring, what do you call it . . ."

"Covert ops," Jason said.

"That's it. Funny, huh? Sorcerers are already a secret society, and I want to keep secrets from *them*. It's that kind of business. Anyway, there's this guy I know—or, rather, I know *about*—who also hates vampires. He calls himself the Aeromancer. We've been in back-channel communications through blind intermediaries—literally and figuratively blind, people who are trustworthy because they'd die if they weren't, get me? The Aeromancer leads a band of vampire killers, sniping at the edges of the Virginia vamp settlement—the leaders of which, incidentally, claim they ate the *Roanoke* colony, the *lost* colony, if you can believe that. But the Aeromancer isn't even making a dent in their numbers. Vamps don't have to brainwash new recruits. They can just take anybody they want and turn them into one of their own. So the Aeromancer is looking for more efficient means of attack than wooden stakes and flamethrowers. I've been thinking about how to help him, but my options are limited. I can't risk anyone discovering my involvement."

"Of course." There was a shine in Cam-Cam's eyes that might have been reflected torchlight, but Marla thought it was the look of a man seeing his lifelong dream come true. It was almost enough to make her feel bad for what they were doing to him.

"I've found out about an opportunity," Marla said. "There's a weapon—well, it can be used as a weapon—that, in the Aeromancer's hands, would mean vampire genocide in this country, maybe in the world. But it's expensive, and the guy selling the stuff isn't swayed by moral arguments. He's not willing to donate it free to a good cause. I could afford his asking price, barely, but it would require a lot of liquidating of assets and shifting of funds, and if I did that, it would get noticed by the other sorcerers in the city. Questions would be asked. It wouldn't end well. So we've been looking for outside investors, people who won't be linked to me. Frankly, that's the only reason I've agreed to talk to an ordinary like you—you're so far outside sorcerous circles that *nobody* would connect me with you."

"How much does this weapon cost?"

Marla marveled. It was just like Jason said. The chumps begged you to take their money.

On cue, Rondeau said, "Before we get into that, Mr. Campion, you need to know what we're talking about here. Vampires have gotten a serious makeover in books and movies in the past century or two. We're not talking about suave guys wearing silly medallions, or hot chicks in velvet who just happen to like a little blood-play. These are flesh-devouring immortal monsters, and they're about as sexy as a shark attack. You have to understand, if you get mixed up in this, they might *come* for you. Hear what I'm saying? Your role would be to pay for the weapon in question, keep it safe while we make arrangements to meet the Aeromancer, and then help us transport it to him. Marla's name would never come into it, but the vamps might get wind of this, so your name *might*. Jason and I would do our best to protect you, but we can't make promises. And with vampires, you're lucky if they kill you. They can do worse."

"I understand," Cam-Cam said. "The dangers are acceptable. How much will it cost?"

"Ten million dollars," Jason said.

Marla was gratified to see Cam-Cam's furious spate of blinking.

"That's ... a lot of money. I'm not sure I can ... Huh."

Marla turned away, flipping her cloak. "Told you his financials were overestimated." She put as much disgust into her voice as possible. "He doesn't have that kind of liquidity, his money's all tied up in holes in the ground and bulldozers and shit."

"I *could* get the money, I just couldn't afford to lose it, not all at once—"

Marla whirled, frowning at her brother. "Jason, what is he talking about?"

"We didn't get into details." Jason held up his hands. "We wanted you to talk to him first."

Marla sighed. "We're not asking for your charity, Cam-Cam. I hate vamps, sure, but I'm a businesswoman, too. We buy the spores from my weapons guy at ten million, but we sell it to the Aeromancer for fifteen million. My organization takes two million for our trouble, you pocket your original investment plus another three. That's what we're talking about."

"That's a thirty percent return," Cam-Cam said thoughtfully. "That's quite good."

"Eh, the weapons dealer owes me a favor, so he's cutting me a she-once-saved-my-life-and-she-can-take-it-away-again discount. The price we'll offer the Aeromancer is still a bargain. If the spores went on the open—well, not 'open,' more like secret sorcerous—market, they'd fetch a lot more, probably. But my guy's got a conscience, at least by arms dealer standards, and he knows I won't use the spores for anything too nefarious. In the wrong hands . . ." She shuddered.

"The weapon is . . . spores?" Cam-Cam said.

"Wow, Jason and Rondeau really didn't let anything slip. I'm impressed by their discretion. The way they've been trying to sell me on working with you, I was afraid they'd already spilled some secrets into your lap and were trying to cover their asses. Yeah. Spores."

"They're called the Borrichius spores," Jason said. "Like any kind of spore, they're tiny and easily inhaled. There are some famously nasty spores in the world—anthrax. Stachybotrys. Ugly stuff. Tear you up inside, kill your lungs."

"These Borrichius spores are a biological weapon?"

"Only if you want them to be," Marla said. "They were designed by an herbomancer who'd pretty much gone around the bend, a guy unsurprisingly named Borrichius, and he made his spores self-replicating. Once one person inhales them, the spores start reproducing, and with every cough, the infected spews out more spores, which float in the air looking for new hosts.

But the spores don't just copy themselves—they're programmable. A sorcerer with the right skills can tell the spores to affect only very specific types of people. Want to kill everyone on Earth with green eyes, or red hair, or both? The spores can do that. Don't want to kill people? Just want to paralyze them, or give them hallucinations, or make them go blind, or make them your mindless slaves? The spores can do that instead. Anyone who inhales the spores who doesn't fit the template is just a passive carrier, spreading the contagion, but once the spores find their appointed target...they work fast. Or slow. Whatever the engineer wants."

"That's extraordinary," Cam-Cam said. "A weapon like that..."

"It's a war crime in a bottle," Marla said. "Fortunately, the spores can be configured to destroy nothing but vampires, and mass-murdering the undead is more like burning out an infection than killing people."

"Once you buy the spores, why can't you just program them yourselves?" Cam-Cam said. "Spare all the cloak-and-dagger stuff?"

Because the cloak-and-dagger stuff is helpful for scamming you, Marla thought, but Jason had worked out an answer for that, too. "Truth be told, we don't know how to program the spores. It's not exactly common knowledge. The Aeromancer *does,* though—he was once Borrichius's apprentice, before the old gardener went nutso—and once we get the crate to him, the Aeromancer can make them work. In the meantime, though, we have to be *really* careful with the stuff after we buy it. We don't know what the spores are *currently* programmed to do. Erase our brains? Make us into ravening zombies? Kill women, or white people, or guys over forty, or trust-fund babies? No telling. This shit is more dangerous than plutonium, but it's wrapped up nice and tight in a magically shielded box, where it can't hurt us as long as we don't break the seals."

"How do you know the weapons dealer isn't scamming you?" Cam-Cam asked. "That it's not just an empty box?"

Marla smiled her least-nice smile. Cam-Cam paled. "Because," she said, "very bad things happen to people who try to cheat me, and the seller knows that. Now, what do you say? Are you up for it?"

"I'll put up the money," Cam-Cam said. "But I have one additional condition."

Here it comes. So far Jason had predicted Cam-Cam's responses so perfectly that the guy might have been reading from a script, and she supposed he'd turn out to be right about this part, too.

"I want you to teach me magic," Cam-Cam said.

"I'll tell you what," Marla said. "Help us pull this off, and kill the vamps, and I'll make you my motherfucking *apprentice*."

Cam-Cam shook his head. "That's not good enough. I want—"

"Fuck that. I don't care what you want. Your money isn't the only money in the world, Cam-Cam. Yes or no."

He set his lips grimly, and for a minute, Marla thought he might say no. That would be interesting. She wondered how Jason would make that work, though she had little doubt he would, somehow.

"All right," Cam-Cam said. "I suppose your word can be trusted."

"My word is my bond." True enough. "Help us eradicate the vampires, and I will make you my apprentice."

"Agreed." He stuck out his hand, and Marla shook it.

"Rondeau and the boatman will take you back home. Jason and Rondeau will be in touch to work out the details. For safety's sake, you and I won't talk again until the last bloodsucker runs dry. Good luck. Try not to get eaten." She turned, doused the torches with a gesture, and vanished into the night.

But not very far into the night. She hung out in the shadows of the trees while Rondeau got Cam-Cam moving. After she heard the boat engine start up and buzz away into the distance, Marla sauntered back, relit one of the torches with a snap of her fingers, and clapped Jason on the shoulder. "Surprised to see me, bro?"

"You, my dear, are the greatest little sister that ever has been or ever will be. That was a command performance. Christ, I almost believed you were a witch *myself.* How in the hell did you manage that standing-sideways-on-the-wall thing? That was fucking uncanny. It was like watching one of those remakes of a weird Japanese horror movie. And those torches lighting themselves! Great stuff!"

"All done with wires and pyrotechnics, Jason. This is a spooky island. I use it sometimes when I need to scare somebody, so I've got it rigged up nice. Who's the guy driving the boat?"

"Old friend of mine named Danny Two Saints. Jack of all trades, absolute workhorse of a grifter, plays all parts, can get his hands on anything you need, you know the type."

"Nice touch with the glow-in-the-dark paint on his cheeks. Otherworldly demon eyes. Good stuff."

"Oh, I thought Cam-Cam was going to shit himself when Danny let him get a glimpse of the spooky eyes. No doubt you're the master of the hoodoo grift, but admit it, I'm coming along okay, too."

"You were always a quick study. I wish I could've worked out some more of the details of this scam with you beforehand, though. A huge colony of vampires living in Virginia?"

"The Old Dominion," Jason said. "What, too much?"

"Eh, big groups of vampires living in harmony don't make much sense ecologically. That many apex predators, eating humans? It's silly. You don't find dozens of tigers hunting in the same small area—it takes a ton of prey to support even one predator."

"I can see you've given this a lot of thought."

"It's my business, Jason. But it doesn't much matter. There's no such thing as vampires anyway. So technically, I didn't lie when I made my promise to Cam-Cam. If he manages to eradicate a race of supernatural monsters that doesn't even exist, he deserves to become my apprentice."

"You know," Jason mused, "the apprentice thing could be a good scam, too. Find some rube who believes in magic and charge him money for 'lessons.' Grifters do that kind of thing sometimes, find a mark who wants to become a con artist because they've seen one too many

episodes of *Hustle,* and then scam *them.* Somehow they
never see it coming."

"There's a lot of stupidity in the world."

"From your lips to God's ears."

"Want to ride on my boat back to the city?" Marla
said.

"What, you didn't fly here on a magic broom? I'm disappointed."

"Brooms are for amateurs. Give me a twenty-two-
foot Spencer Runabout with a three-eighty horsepower
motor anytime."

"Thank you for helping arrange that introduction."
Cam-Cam no longer seemed discomforted by the dark
figure at the tiller—maybe he believed himself under
Marla's protection now.

"No worries." Rondeau was attempting to segue into
the buddy-buddy relationship that Jason had suggested
for the next phase of the con. "Marla's blustery, but the
truth is, you're really helping us out. Controlling information flow—not to mention providing protection—is a
lot more difficult when you've got a bunch of people putting up money. A single investor makes things simpler.
And, hey, not a bad deal for you, either."

"Hmm? Oh. You mean the money. I suppose. I don't
really care about that part. It's the chance to work with
her, to learn her secrets." Cam-Cam smiled—the first
smile Rondeau had ever seen from him, maybe the first
to grace his face in a long while. "I'm very excited about
this."

Rondeau tried not to shift or show his discomfort. Personally, he'd take a few million bucks over learning cantrips, but wasn't that always the way? You want what you don't have. Cam-Cam didn't think money was important, because he had all the money in the world. Once that money was taken away from him—and the ten million up-front investment was just the start of the cash Jason expected to extract from Cam-Cam—he might feel differently. "Not to pry," Rondeau pried, "but why the, ah, abiding interest in magic?"

Cam-Cam stared out at the dark water for a moment, then said, "My father tried to teach me the fundamentals of the family business. Mining. It's an unforgiving business, dirty, messy, practical, hardheaded. Dependent on engineering. I remember my first tour of the smelting factory, the noise, the heat, the obvious misery or vacancy of the workers, and I thought, 'Is this all there is?' I knew there had to be more to life than tearing wealth out of the earth. Mining is . . . this sounds silly, but . . . it's not spiritual."

Rondeau pondered that. He suspected laboring in a dark crevasse miles below the surface of the Earth was actually very conducive to mystical experiences, if not necessarily pleasant ones. Though he was willing to accept that hanging out in the business office at a smelting plant probably didn't attune one to the numinous.

"That was the start. I read fairy tales and novels about magic, but my real interest was always in nonfiction—stories about cryptozoology, UFO abductions, psychic phenomena. I was foolish and credulous, of course, I believed almost anything, but even once I became more jaded and skeptical there was still a part of me that was desperate to believe. And then, one day when I was about fifteen, my mother called me into her bedroom and calmly told me she had recently begun conversing with angels."

Rondeau whistled. There were certainly beings that claimed to be angels, but Marla said they were almost certainly anything but. "You believed her?"

"She...knew things about me, secret things...I don't think she could have found out on her own, that no one should have known. I thought she would be angry, but she was forgiving, and loving. She told me she was dying. The doctors diagnosed her with a brain tumor, which caused temporal lobe epilepsy, and they said that was the cause of her angelic visions." Cam-Cam smiled faintly. "Of course, then she told the oncologist the angels had told her about the affair he was having with a radiologist half his age, and I could *see* the doubt flicker across his face. From that point on, I was convinced there were forces beyond physics and chemistry and finance, and I devoted my life and my fortune to studying them. My father was...disappointed by my interest. But I was his only son, and he let me inherit the business when he passed away, though he begged me not to run the operation personally. He was afraid I'd turn all his drills to the purpose of finding a passage to the hollow Earth, or start digging for the underworld."

"You can't get to the underworld by digging," Rondeau said. "I don't know about angels, but sometimes people with psychic powers get their visions in a weird kind of external way—a radiant being whispering secrets in your ear doesn't seem that far-fetched. And the tumor could have activated some latent telepathic power your mother had."

Cam-Cam nodded. "That's interesting. I can't decide if it's more or less interesting than the possibility of literal angels."

Rondeau shrugged. "I don't know about glowing flying hall monitors, you know? The universe, in my experience, has no underlying morality. Though there do seem to be consequences. If you do a lot of damage, damage will be done to you, in the long run. I'm not sure it has anything to do with God, though. Marla says karma is just a law of the universe, no more conscious than the laws of thermodynamics, and just as inescapable."

The boat bumped up against Cam-Cam's dock, and Danny Two Saints, in the guise of the terrifying boatman, extended his arm and pointed: *Get Off.* Before disembarking, Cam-Cam solemnly shook hands with Rondeau, who promised to get in touch soon.

Danny piloted the boat away, back out onto the water, and once they were a good distance from the land, he threw his hood back and lit a cigarette. The glow-in-the-dark paint on his cheeks made him look like an extraterrestrial clown. After a long silence, he growled, "Don't get soft."

"What?" Rondeau looked up from his study of his hands.

"I see you getting all pensive and shit. 'Oh, no, the mark is a human with hopes and dreams and a dead mom, I feel so bad for fleecing him.' Forget it. Cam-Cam's rich, self-obsessed, and fuckin' delusional, just like his mom was. You hear me?"

"I do, I just... he's an ass, but he doesn't seem like a bad guy."

Danny grunted. "My grandpa was a coal miner. The guys who own mines aren't good guys. Period. You want a tale of woe? How about your granddad coming down with black lung, and he dies still *owing* money to the company that employed him and killed him?"

"Is that why you're ripping off Cam-Cam? Because he owns mines, and you want revenge?"

"Nah, fuck that." Danny flicked the butt of his cigarette into the water. "I just want his money."

Bulliard sniffed and snuffled along the street like a bloodhound, down on all fours, pressing his nose against the cold metal discs of manhole covers and pausing at storm drains. While his tormentor was engaged, the messenger considered reaching for a nice chunky loose half-brick crumbled off one of the shithole buildings on this street and using it to cave in the mycomancer's head. That seemed like a good idea. Practical. But his body wouldn't oblige, the mushrooms growing into his brain regulating his actions too closely for that, and the messenger couldn't even work up much rage in the face of the coercion. Part of that was probably simple exhaustion, but he feared his brain chemistry was being tweaked, too, and wondered, in the way one occasionally worries about cancer after encountering a suspicious mole during a shower, what exactly the Mycelium had planned for him. He reflected, not for the first time, that meeting Nicolette was the worst thing that had ever happened to him. He wished he *could* tell Bulliard she was the one who'd sent the message about the spores, but the geas on him was too strong for that. Too bad. Seeing Nicolette tussle with old mossface here would be a treat.

"What are we looking for?" he asked, as Bulliard pressed his nose against the thousandth manhole of the night.

The sorcerer swung his head around and peered up at the messenger without rising from the ground. "A point of entry. And I think this is it." He hooked his grubby fingers into the holes on the manhole cover and lifted the weight as if it were only an imitation of metal, carved in balsa wood or Styrofoam, then descended the ladder, going down headfirst like some kind of lizard. The messenger followed more conventionally. Bulliard apparently had no trouble with the dark, scurrying along the low nasty tunnel at a rapid clip, while the messenger groped and stumbled along after him.

After many twistings and turnings, the messenger glimpsed a light, and Bulliard made a strange snuffling noise of glee. The light turned out to be a dusty bulb set in a rusty cage over a door of dull gray metal. At least, the messenger assumed it was a door—it had no handle, and there was no pushbell or intercom in sight.

"Dead end," the messenger said. "How about we go back up top and find a hotel? Someplace with room

service? I could eat a horse. A caribou. Just about anything—except mushrooms."

Bulliard ignored him and placed the palm of his hand
against the seam where the door met the brick around it,
a crack so narrow a credit card could not have been inserted. After a moment, bright orange mushrooms began to sprout up in the cracks in the brick, showering
down fragments of displaced stone and mortar as they
grew. Bulliard stepped back as the mushrooms sprang up
all around the door, their progression swift as flame
along a line of gasoline, and the metal door made a low
strange groan.

Bulliard suddenly surged forward, planting both
hands on the door and *shoving*. The door popped loose
from the wall and fell inward. A thin man in a button-
down shirt, a tie, and a leather helmet like an old-time
football player's stood gaping at them beyond the door-
hole, then lifted a double-barreled shotgun to firing position.

The messenger dropped to his belly. Good to know his
motor functions weren't compromised when it came to
basic ass-saving measures. The gun didn't go off, though,
and when the messenger looked up, he saw Bulliard take
the gun from the man's hands. Brown mushroom caps
sprouted from both the weapon's barrels.

"Take me," Bulliard said, "to the master of this
place." The man tried to run, and Bulliard reached out
and grabbed the back of his neck. "Don't run, or I will
kill you. The Mycelium won't mind."

Lucky bastard, the messenger thought. *Why's the
Mycelium have to be so fond of me?*

The disarmed man—a servant, an apprentice?—led them through narrow corridors, and after a few moments they entered a large space crammed with shelves and lined with vault doors. The room appeared to be deserted, and the messenger pointed to a low rounded concrete structure tucked between two support pillars. It looked like a World War Two bunker with a profusion of cameras and microphones bristling above the concrete door, on which the word "Management" was neatly lettered. "Viscarro is in there."

Viscarro, the messenger thought. *Hell, I've done work for him. Lousy tipper.*

Bulliard rapped on the concrete with his filthy knuckles. "Hmm. Are you there, sorcerer?"

"I am," crackled a voice from a speaker near the door. "I don't appreciate being roused from my studies. This bunker is rather cramped, but it has the advantage of being impregnable. Do please leave, or I'll have to deploy the poison gas, and I'm sure to lose an apprentice or two in the process. There are always a couple of them lurking about in the night."

The apprentice who'd led them in bolted away, though Bulliard took no notice. The messenger rather wished he could skedaddle himself.

"Hmm." Bulliard sniffed at the door. He placed his hand against it, but no mushrooms sprang up—the bunker was probably wrapped in fifty layers of magical protections. "My nose thinks you can help me. The Mycelium thinks you can help me. Perhaps...we can help each other."

"I rather doubt that. Perhaps I'll use mustard gas. The canisters are old, but of a good vintage."

"I am the deadly dapperling," Bulliard said. "Poison does not frighten me."

"For what it's worth, it frightens me!" the messenger said.

"Then convince your associate to leave," the speaker crackled.

"Sorry, it's more of a master-slave relationship, and not in a good kinky way."

"Tell me," Bulliard said. "In these vaults. You have... many wonderful things?"

"Wouldn't *you* like to know."

"I think I shall." Bulliard went to one of the great gleaming round doors. He pressed his hands against the door... and the vaults apparently didn't have quite the level of magical protection the bunker did, because mushrooms began to burst from the edges of the door, making the metal squeal and producing a loud pop when the seal broke.

"Stop!" Viscarro shouted.

"I will not even steal them," Bulliard said. "Your treasures. I will rot those that rot. I will break those that break. I will defile those that are pure, and purify those that are cursed. The others, I will shit on. Some of them I will *eat*." Bulliard grabbed the handle on the vault—round like a ship's door—and began hauling on it, grunting. The metal shifted, just a bit, but noticeably.

A hiss of dead air on the speaker, then, "What do you want?"

"The Borrichius spores."

"They are imaginary."

"Perhaps not. I have reason to believe they are in Felport."

"That is ... interesting. But they're not *here*, so why are you?"

"This is not my city. I am unsure where to search for the spores. Help me find them, and I will share them with you."

The messenger wanted to say, "Oh, *please*, if you believe that I've got some beachfront property in Idaho to sell you," but his tongue and lips and breath betrayed him, and he stood silent. Apparently Bulliard—or the Mycelium—was only willing to tolerate so much sass out of him, and not during delicate moments.

"Perhaps we can reach an accommodation," Viscarro said.

"We are reasonable men," Bulliard said. The messenger tried to laugh, but couldn't.

The bunker door hissed and unsealed, and a bald, pointy-eared man in a stained brown bathrobe shuffled out, carrying a pistol that looked comically oversized in his small hand. "Whom do I have the pleasure of addressing?"

"I am Bulliard, a servant of the Mycelium."

"That thing on your *nose*." Viscarro's gun hand sagged, and he hurried forward. "It's magical, isn't it?"

Bulliard tapped his pig snout. "It helps me find what I need. What the Mycelium needs. And it believes I need *you*."

"I could use something like that," Viscarro said. "I

need many things. The spores are imaginary, but that thing on your nose *isn't*." He lifted the gun again.

Bulliard held out his hand, palm up, and blew. A puff of dust flew from his hand into Viscarro's face, and the sorcerer dropped to the ground, writhing and screaming, pistol dropped and forgotten. "Rise for me," Bulliard said, and Viscarro stood jerkily, mushrooms doubtless sprouting from the back of his neck.

The messenger, able to move again, sighed and gave Viscarro a wave. "Welcome to the Mushroom Monster Slave Corps. I won't lie to you. It fucking sucks. But tall, dark, and mossy here just wants to know where to find the bullshit spores."

"As I said, the spores are *fictional*." Viscarro's voice grated as if scoured by a sandstorm. "Borrichius was a boastful liar prone to self-aggrandizement. Since his spores don't exist, may I have control of my body back? You *could* have set up an appointment for a consultation with me. Your *slave* has a prior business relationship with me, so that level of etiquette should have been possible even for someone facing your obvious challenges to hygiene and socialization."

"You know this creature?" Bulliard turned on the messenger.

"We've done business. Couldn't mention it before. You know. Geas."

"Your limitations begin to outweigh your usefulness."

"Better euthanize me, then."

Bulliard turned back to Viscarro. "The spores do exist. I have received a message, telling me they are here, in this city."

"A message from—oh. An *anonymous* message, sent by special courier. I see. I'm not certain that enslaving the messenger is any more reasonable than killing the messenger, by the way. You believe this message is genuine?"

"Why would anyone lie to me? The Mycelium does not like having its time wasted."

"You've been living alone in the woods too long." Viscarro shook his head. "Sorcerers have many reasons for lying. Some lie just because they *like* it. But I suppose it's possible the spores are here. I've seen unlikelier things come to pass. I'm not sure what I can do to help you, though."

"You know the city's sorcerers. You can make inquiries without arousing suspicion. You will find the spores. You will tell me their location. I will take them to the Mycelium."

"After dividing them with me, of course." Viscarro's eyes were beady, but sharp.

Bulliard snorted. "I think we are beyond such pretense. My mushrooms are in your brain, and your body is mine."

"Well. Much good the spores will do you. Once I'm loosed from your thrall, I'll kill you. Then I'll add your pretty pig nose to the vault I keep for souvenirs taken from vanquished foes. It's a very large vault, and quite full already, but I'll make room."

Bulliard shrugged. "Once the Mycelium has no further use for you, I will use your corpse as feed for fungus."

"Oh, you'll find me harder to kill than *that*." Viscarro

smiled a rather horrible smile, full of oddly pointed, yellowed teeth. The messenger had to admire his chutzpah, and Bulliard actually looked uncomfortable for a moment. The messenger was almost cheered, seeing that . . . but then Bulliard's usual blank, focused affect returned. "I am only a servant of the Mycelium, as you are—but I am a willing servant, and am thus exalted, while you are lowly and base. Your threats mean less to me than the chewing of earthworms in the dirt. Now, slave: where will you begin your inquiries regarding the spores?"

"It's a fool's errand, but as in all such situations, I may as well start at the top. I'll set up a meeting with Marla Mason."

"You will do this now."

"I will do this in the *morning*. Asking Marla for a meeting at this time of night would definitely arouse suspicion."

Bulliard appeared to ponder. "Very well. But *early*."

The messenger yawned. "So where do you keep the guest rooms around here? I haven't slept in days."

11

Rise and sparkle, movie star." Marla prodded B with her boot.

He groaned and rolled over in bed. He was fully clothed, and still smeared with garbage. Marla wrinkled her nose. "You might want to change your sheets. I think you got some alley slime on them."

"So...much...disgusting." B sat up and rubbed his face. "I feel like I just went to bed an hour ago."

Marla picked up the clock beside his bed. "Oh, maybe two hours, assuming Rondeau can be trusted about what time he heard you stumbling in."

"Day off?" B said hopefully.

"Nope. No rest for the weary, or the wicked, or you. You're going to the *park*." She said "park" the way another person might say "garbage dump" or, possibly, "gulag."

"Shower? Coffee?" The hope in his voice was pitiful and endearing.

"Sure, I'm not a monster. You can have ten whole minutes to clean and change, and get coffee on the way out."

B crawled out of bed and stumbled down the hall, toward the bathroom. Marla followed and leaned against the doorjamb outside while he undressed and got into the shower. The spectacle of unselfconscious, naked Bradley would normally have been satisfying, but he was covered in Dumpster-juice, and she had other stuff on her mind.

"How was the thing last night?" he called from the shower. "The big scam?"

Marla watched steam billow and begin to fog the mirror. "Scamtastic. My brother's chosen line of work might be low-down and reprehensible, but he's got a gift for it. And Cam-Cam was pretty much as annoying as I remembered, so my conscience isn't twinging a bit, thanks. Anyway, the scam rolls on without me now. I was just the convincer, really."

"I still don't approve, but it's nice you're spending time with Jason."

"Some siblings play in bands together or join a softball league or something. We, apparently, rip off chumps. It's the new family bonding."

"Whatever works. What's on the agenda today?"

"You're going to see Granger, the idiot."

"He's an idiot?"

"He oughta be. His parents were siblings. So were their parents. He's the only hereditary sorcerer in Felport. His great-great-something-great grandfather was one of the first sorcerers here, the nature magician who put the beast of Felport into hibernation for a couple of centuries and made the place safe for colonists.

He was also in charge of the village commons, which, eventually, became Fludd Park, that ugly green blight in the middle of my nice concrete-and-asphalt city. The original Granger was…kind of fanatic about family. Married one of his cousins, or something. Believed magic ability was linked to bloodline, and cast a spell to ensure his descendants would inherit his powers and re-sponsibilities. At this point, those responsibilities mostly entail making sure the duck pond doesn't overflow and the trees don't fall down or whatever. Which is good, since I don't think the original Granger counted on all the inbreeding his kids would do. The current Granger has a seat in our high councils, but he doesn't exactly bring a lot to the table, except for the boogers he wipes underneath. He mostly just hangs out in the park."

"So you're sending me to *learn* something from this guy?"

"He's not totally useless. He's a potent nature magi-cian, actually. And a hell of a gardener. Just not much of a conversationalist, unless you find compost really inter-esting. After last night, I'm guessing you *don't*. He can teach you how to, I dunno, whistle in the language of songbirds or harvest magical herbs or some crap. Who knows. Not really my area." Marla had grown up sur-rounded by cornfields, and had spent most of the past two decades trying to get as far from flora as she could.

B turned off the shower. "So while I'm learning at the feet of the master, what will you be doing?"

"It's the damnedest thing, but *Viscarro* asked me for a meeting this morning. He's actually coming *here*."

"Our friend the Nosferatu? I got the feeling he'd been

T. A. Pratt

in that spider hole of his for years." B climbed out of the shower and started toweling off.

"He came out into the sunlight earlier this summer, actually, but only against his will. I think that was the first time he'd seen daylight in decades, if not longer. He comes to council meetings, but they're usually after dark. He wouldn't tell me what it was about, just that it was important, and he needed to discuss it with me in person. He knows I hate his dried-up undead guts, so it's not a social call." She looked at B's face reflected in the mirror as he brushed his teeth, and was pleased to see the concern there. He was worried about her, which was sweet, if unnecessary.

"Let me know if it's anything I can help with."

"Oh, I will. You can take the Bentley over to the park, if you promise not to cause another multicar pileup."

B tapped his temple. "All the bats are cleaned out of my belfry. No worries there."

"Good. There's a map in the glove compartment. Park near the east entrance, by the statue of the family of bears. Granger will meet you there. You'll be able to recognize him—he'll be the fat slovenly dude grinning like a moron."

"Will do, boss. Good luck with the walking corpse."

Bradley walked into the park, and instantly felt soothed. Fludd Park was a little oasis from the honking horns and crowded sidewalks of nearby downtown Felport, a place of trees, paths, statues, and neatly tended flower beds. A wide-shouldered man crouched near a plot of bright yellow-and-white flowers, his fingers plunged in the dirt, his waistband sagging to reveal far too much butt-crack. "Mr. Granger?" B said.

The man rose, turned, and smiled. He was ugly as a jack-o'-lantern and just as merry, extending one dirt-smeared hand in greeting. B shook it, deciding not to be annoyed at the damp earth soiling his hand. The wizard of the park said, "Just call me Granger. Mr. Granger was my father, and my grandfather, and on and on. I'm the last and there's no little ones, so no mister needed for me."

"I'm Bradley. My friends call me B."

Granger got a sad and faraway look in his eyes. "B, bee, buzz buzz. Some bad wizard is stealing the bees away, you know, all over. Wild honeybee workers just disappear, colonies die, and then plants die. A bad wizard. At least, I hope it's a wizard. Somebody can fight a bad wizard, beat him, make him stop, bring back the bees. But if it's just the world, just the working of the world that's stealing the bees away, then I don't know. I just don't know. The poor flowers. The poor trees. The poor everything." Then he grinned again. "But the bees here are good, plenty good, I tend them, I do, I keep my little patch of the forest healthy." He slapped B on the back with a hand that seemed as broad as a tennis racket, but it wasn't a painfully hard slap—Granger seemed like a man who knew his own strength.

B decided he disagreed with Marla. He liked Granger. Maybe the guy wasn't all there mentally, but it seemed more likely his thoughts just ran in directions that were incomprehensible to Marla. She didn't have a lot of patience for the natural world, but B had always liked green spaces. B suspected Granger didn't have a particle of malice in his whole being...which was also probably part of why Marla didn't like him. She distrusted the gentle and the kind. "It looks beautiful here," B said. "I can't wait to see what you have to teach me."

Granger made a puffing noise that, perhaps, indicated uncertainty. He tucked his thumbs in his waistband and whistled low. "Well, now, well. Well well well. Marla said I had to teach you a trick. Something good. I said I'd teach you how to make beautiful things grow, and she said, 'No no, Granger, no no, that won't do, teach him *magic*.' I said I'm not so good at seeing where tending the land and doing magic come unmixed, and she said do my best, do what other gardeners can't do, no matter how green their thumbs are. So I thought. I thought and thought and *thought*." He stood for a moment, gazing down at the flower bed.

B gazed down with him. After a couple of minutes, he said, "So what did you decide?"

Granger looked up at him, expression strangely searching, as if wondering who B was, and what he wanted. Then he grinned that face-crossing grin again and said, "I'm going to teach you how to be a *bird*." Granger snapped his fingers, and the trees and Granger himself and the whole world rushed away fast and got very big and tall, and when B tried to shout, he produced only a startled sort of coo, and when he flapped his wings—

Oh, shit. B hopped in frantic little circles on the ground. *I'm a fucking pigeon.*

"Pretty bird," Granger said, and B flew away in a flurry of terrified fluttering, his bird-body reacting with panic before his human brain could intervene.

"I *have* to take a gift." Viscarro slammed his palms down on the long library table. "You idiot, I'm going to see the *chief sorcerer of Felport,* and I *must* come bearing a gift! You wish me to offend the woman I'm supposed to be gently interrogating?"

"I do not trust you." Bulliard crossed his arms.

"What, do you think I'll try to smuggle her a special mushroom magician–destroying *sword*? If you want her to be angry and suspicious, then, by all means, send me empty-handed. I can't be responsible."

"You know, mossface," the messenger said, "it's not exactly unheard of in social protocols for somebody lower in a hierarchy to bring a gift for someone higher in the hierarchy. I know your social sphere is limited to you, the bugs you eat, and the Mycelium, but—"

"I sometimes bring the Mycelium gifts," Bulliard said slowly. "Hikers. Campers. Careless park rangers."

"This is just like that," the messenger said. "Only instead of, you know, dead bodies, Viscarro wants to take Marla Mason a scented candle or something."

"She's more partial to jewelry," Viscarro said. "That vault there is full of pretty things. There's a particular necklace—"

"No," Bulliard said. "I will allow a gift, but I will not let *you* choose it. Messenger. Go to the vault. Bring back something appropriate."

The messenger went to the vault, used the combination Viscarro provided to open it, and stepped inside as the lights automatically came in.

The vault was a treasure cave, walls lined with hooks, shelves lined with stands, all holding necklaces, bracelets, rings, brooches, circlets, and tiaras, all the colors of the Earth, silver and gold and platinum, adorned with diamonds, rubies, sapphires, black pearls, and more and more and more. He cast around, overwhelmed by the splendor, knowing that if he filled his pockets here he'd never have to work as a courier again, he'd be able to pay off *all* his debts (except the karmic ones), and live in a mansion eating foie gras topped with caviar washed down with champagne *forever.*

"Quickly!" Bulliard shouted, and, as quickly, the messenger's fantasies shimmered and dissolved. He chose a necklace at random—a simple silver choker with a large and somehow luminous black stone in the center—and carried it out.

"Here," he said, and tossed it to Viscarro, who caught it, looked at it, grunted, and nodded.

"Fine," Viscarro said. "It will do. Perhaps Marla will like it enough that she will refrain from *beating* me for wasting her time with inquiries about imaginary spores."

"I don't mind if you're beaten," Bulliard said.

"He really doesn't," the messenger agreed.

B landed in a tree . . . and Granger was already there, improbably perched on a branch as wide as a park bench. He was chewing on an apple, and looked like he'd been waiting there patiently for hours, though B had only flown away from him seconds ago.

Granger wiped juice from his mouth with his sleeve, and said, "Sorry. Too quick? Should have been slower. Explained more. But, see, you're a *bird*. The hard part of being a bird is being a bird the *first* time. After the first time, your body remembers, your mind remembers, you know how to do it, if you aren't careful, you can go birdie in your sleep just from dreaming it. But, oh, to fly . . ."

B squawked impatiently.

"Oh, yes." Granger snapped his fingers again, and suddenly B was all big again, and falling out of the tree—but Granger caught him, almost offhandedly, grabbing him under the armpits and hauling him up to sit on the branch beside him. B was closer to the trunk, and he grabbed on as tight as he could, hugging the bole. "Did I do bad?" Granger said, sounding miserable.

B glanced down. He couldn't even see the ground, which seemed impossible—hadn't he flown to just an ordinary little tree with a few sparse branches? This tree seemed huge—shouldn't it have seemed smaller, now that B himself was bigger?

"I—no, you didn't do bad. I was just . . . startled. I've never been a bird before."

"Being a bird is great. Flying, when you're a person, is hard." He shook his head. "Lot of sorcerers can fly that way, but you have to make gravity angry, hurt gravity's feelings, and even then it's not so much flying as falling away from the center of the Earth. Like skydiving, only *backwards*. But when you're a bird . . ." He flapped his arms, apparently unconcerned about the vertiginous drop below them. "It's nice to fly when you're a bird."

"It ... was nice. I think. Once you take away the terrified. But why a pigeon?"

"Could've made you a hawk. A bald eagle. Those get noticed, though. Marla said teach you something *good,* something *useful.* Owls are okay but bad in the daytime. Gulls are okay but only by the water or the garbage dump. Pigeons? Pigeons are okay fast, okay good fliers, best of all nobody notices a pigeon, day or night, anytime, pigeons are just pigeons. You can be a pigeon in this city and nobody will think anything about it."

"That makes sense. Keep a low profile. I get it. So, ah, now that I've been a bird once, I can—"

"Yes." Granger reached over, grabbed B by the arm, broke his grip on the trunk, and tossed him out of the tree.

"Fuuuuuuck!" B shouted, but by the time he got to the end of the word, it wasn't so much a shout as a caw, and he was a bird again. Granger was perched on a limb below him, holding out his hand, palm up, and B landed on it. Without intending to, he pooped in Granger's hand.

Granger laughed and laughed and laughed. He set B down on the branch, wiped his shat-upon hand on the branch, and said, "Okay, change back."

"How am I supposed to—Oh." B looked around. He was himself again. "That was ... surprisingly easy."

Granger shrugged. "Like I said. First time's hard. Almost impossible, to do by yourself. So I did it for you. Not the, ah, responsible way? My daddy made me learn to do it by myself. I had to watch birds. Talk to birds. Live with birds in the trees. Eventually, I understood. Daddy would say this is a shortcut, a bad shortcut, teaching bad habits, but it's okay for you, you aren't a Granger, you don't have to watch out for the park." He sighed. "Nobody but me to watch out for the park."

"Are we . . . even in the park anymore?"

"Sort of. *Sort of* the park. You know. Daddy called them fishbowl worlds. . . ."

"Pocket universes?" B was thinking of Ernesto's lessons with twisted space.

"Yes. This is . . . next to the park. Above the park. This is where the trees go as big as they want, as big as they can, without worrying about water, sun, food, gravity, weight, parasites. Trees tall as mountains here. Up higher, there are branches so wide that other trees grow on them. There are branches as wide as streets. And the sun up there . . . it's the best sun ever. It nourishes all. Being connected to this place, it helps the park."

"This is a beautiful world, Granger." B wondered if Marla had any idea how amazing this place was, the power Granger truly had. Probably not. It wasn't the sort of thing she was likely to investigate.

"You come here when you want. When you're a bird—only when you're a bird. You can't climb high enough when you're you. I like you. You're nice, B."

"I like you, too, Granger. Thanks for teaching me to be a bird."

"Practice. Be a bird for a little while every day, until it's as easy as blinking, as easy as stand-up-sit-down. But don't be a bird too long, or you'll be more interested in eating bread crumbs than going to work and brushing your teeth. Not too long, or when you're a person again, you might forget the rules and just poop wherever you are as soon as you feel like it instead of going to the bathroom." Granger looked at his hand and giggled, a very childlike giggle. "You pooped on my *hand*. You showed *me*."

"And you showed me," B said. "So...should we get down now?"

"You can fly down. Just fly down. I want to stay here for a while. The air smells better up here."

B took a deep breath. Granger was right.

"If I can ever do anything for you..."

Granger looked hopeful, almost embarrassed. "Would you...could you...ask Marla something? I don't like to talk to her. She gets mad. She gets impatient. Worse than Daddy."

"Sure, Granger, anything."

"Ask her if the new nature magician is here to be my apprentice? I'm the last Granger. No sisters, no cousins, no babies. The ducks have babies, the bees have babies, the trees have babies, but no babies for me. But Daddy said, 'If no babies, an apprentice is okay, somebody to take care of the park.' I will live a long time yet, but there's a lot to learn, and this new one should start studying—"

"New one? I'm sorry, Granger, I don't understand."

"The sorcerer," Granger said patiently. "He came last night. I felt him come into the city, a big force of green, as powerful as me, nearly, maybe more stronger, even, except for I have the park. Not the same as me—I am trees and leaves and things that fly, mostly, and he is things that crawl and squelch, I am canopy and he is undergrowth, not what I would choose, but he's *nature*, he knows *nature*, he will do."

B blinked. "Is he . . . this sorcerer you felt . . . he's connected to fungus? To mushrooms?"

"Oh, yes," Granger said. "Fungus among us. Fungi. Fun guy!" He frowned. "Maybe not a fun guy."

"He's . . . I don't think he's here to learn from you, Granger. I'm sorry. But I'll talk to Marla about helping you find an apprentice, okay?"

"That's good." He nodded. "Good good good. You go, be a bird. Don't eat too much birdseed! Don't poop on anybody who doesn't deserve it!" And he laughed and laughed again, and despite the growing unease within B over Bulliard's apparent arrival, it was a good enough laugh that he laughed along a little, too.

"This is for you." Viscarro placed a gift-wrapped box on Marla's desk.

Marla prodded the box with a dagger. It had a bow. A *pink* bow. "Huh," she said.

"It is a gift, to thank you for agreeing to see me on such short notice."

"What, is it full of poison gas? That wouldn't bother you, since walking corpses don't breathe. But you wouldn't be stupid enough to assassinate me after making an appointment to see me. So, what? Some slow-acting poison?" If this was an attempt on her life, she'd be annoyed—B had sensed no traitorous intent from

Viscarro, but his powers had been haywire at the time, so maybe he'd missed something.

"It's not gas, or poison, or mind control, or anything else." Viscarro perched himself on the edge of one of her guest chairs. "It is nothing but a gift, I assure you."

Marla severed the ribbon with her dagger, levered up the lid, and tipped the box over on its side. A necklace, silver with a shimmery black stone in the center, slid out onto her blotter. "Am I suppose to wear this? What, is it cursed?"

"It is merely a beautiful necklace. Wear it, pawn it, throw it out the window, it's your choice. It's yours."

"Okay. Well. Thanks? This better not be an attempt at courtship."

Viscarro shuddered. "Such things are of no interest to me, anymore. This is strictly a business meeting."

Marla leaned back in her chair, still keeping an eye on the necklace. Viscarro didn't give gifts. He was a taker, a hoarder, and wouldn't part with one of his treasures, even a gaudy trifle like this, without reason. And if it wasn't meant to hurt her in some way, that meant . . . "So what can I do for you?"

"I have heard . . . certain rumors . . . about a valuable item that may be in Felport."

"Why come to me? You chase down antiques all the time by yourself."

"Considering the nature of the item, I thought it best to come to you," Viscarro said.

"Gods, just spill, would you? What are you talking about?"

"The Borrichius spores. If they're here, and for sale, I would like the opportunity to bid on them."

Marla laughed. "You're kidding, right? Do you want me to bring you Santa Claus's sleigh and the Easter Bunny's magical never-ending egg basket while I'm at it?"

"I have always believed the spores were imaginary as well," he said stiffly. "But I have recently received . . . actionable intelligence . . . to suggest they exist, and are in the city, or will be soon."

"You took some bullshit rumor seriously enough to come up out of your dank dark hole in person? I'm surprised at you. Look, I can tell you with one hundred percent honesty that I have no reason to believe the spores are in Felport, or ever will be."

"Very well," Viscarro said. "I apologize for wasting your time. I simply felt *compelled* to come and ask." He stared at her fixedly when he said "compelled," and Marla rolled her eyes. What, he thought she was an idiot? The completely out-of-character gift and his earlier unprompted mention of mind control were plenty to clue her in.

"Fine, whatever, get lost, would you? I've got work to do." As Viscarro rose, Marla said, "Oh, by the way, where'd you hear this rumor about the spores? I don't like people throwing my name around so carelessly."

"It was an anonymous source," Viscarro said. "But one I had reason to take seriously."

"Helpful as always. I'll see you at the next council meeting. Don't let the door hit your bony ass on the way out."

Viscarro departed, and Marla picked up her phone

and called Hamil. "Hey, big guy, I just had a meeting with Viscarro, and somebody's got their hooks into him. I don't think it's a straight-up puppet-master mind control thing, because he was dropping hints to tip me off, but somebody's got heavy leverage over him."

"I see. What would you like me to do?"

"Maybe you could drop by his lair, casual-like on some pretense or another, and see if you can suss out what's going on?"

"I certainly—"

"Wait, wait, the damn phone is beeping at me. Hold on." She hit a button to switch to the other line—Hamil had insisted she get call waiting, "Unless you think there will never be *two* crises happening at once?"—"*What?*"

"Marla, this is B. I just got through meeting with Granger—"

"And I'm sure it was scintillating, but I've got a situation here."

"I think you have *two* situations, then, because Granger told me Bulliard is in town."

"Mr. Mushroom? How the hell would Granger know that?"

"He's a nature magician, and he's got a sense for others of his kind, I guess—he brought it up unprompted, and there's not a lot of doubt."

"Huh." Things tumbled and clicked into place in her mind. Viscarro was under someone's control. Viscarro was asking about her brother's imaginary magical spores. A psychotic mushroom magician might reasonably be interested in magical spores. "You know, maybe I *don't* have two situations. I think it's probably just one.

Listen, head for Langford's lab, I'll meet you there shortly." She stabbed a button again, and said, "Hamil?"

"Here, waiting oh-so-patiently."

"Never mind about going to Viscarro's place. I just heard that crazy mycomancer is in town, and I'd lay dollars against dimes he's the one pulling Viscarro's strings."

"Interesting. Any idea why?"

"I, uh . . . Fuck. I think it probably has something to do with my brother. He's running a scam, selling the Borrichius spores to Campbell Campion. Or anyway, a big empty crate that's purported to hold the Borrichius spores. Viscarro was here asking about the spores, which makes me think Mushroom Man somehow got wind of the scam, took it for truth, and is here to steal something that doesn't even exist."

"I see." Hamil was totally unruffled. That was mostly why he was her consigliere. "You did anticipate that your brother would be trouble."

"I thought he'd be the direct *cause* of the trouble, not an indirect catalyst for it. I'd like to know how a mushroom mage from Oregon heard about my brother's scam, since the only confederates Jason's got who know fuck-all about magic are me and Rondeau, and I really doubt it was either one of *us* who tipped him off."

"There are eyes and ears everywhere, as you well know. Loose lips and Freudian slips may be overheard."

"Truth, but I don't know who'd get any benefit out of siccing a fungus-worshipper on us."

"That is an interesting question."

"And it's one I'll find the answer to, though I think we should wipe out the big bad guy first."

"Would you like me to muster up any troops to help?"

"Nah, if we go in heavy, Bulliard might get spooked, and if he decides he's threatened, he could make Viscarro put his lair in full lockdown, complete with phase-shifting half a step into another dimension. We'd never get inside then. Better if B and I go in quietly."

"Understood. Do you need anything from me?"

"Call Langford for me. I've got a wish list I think he can help with."

"Of course. Oh, I realize this isn't a pressing issue at the moment, but I thought you'd like to know—I found the Giggler."

"So the fortune-telling freak lives on? Where is he?"

Hamil told her, and Marla grinned.

"Now strip naked," Langford said, and B and Marla looked at each other, then back at him.

"Is that really necessary?" B said.

"I'm a *doctor*," Langford admonished. "Or near enough. But, come to mention it, I have no desire to apply this personally. I'll let the two of you work it out between yourselves." He put a large lobster-pot full of something green, sticky, and reeking on the lab table beside them, along with a couple of plastic plate scrapers. "Apply *liberally*. And completely." He left, shutting the door behind him.

B sniffed the pot, which smelled like tincture of stinky feet. "This is gross."

"That's the sorcerous life. You'd rather get shroomed?" Marla began to undress, and after a moment's sigh, B stripped, too. Marla was naked first, and she dipped her hand into the unguent. The goop inside had started life as several tubes of prescription anti-fungal ointment, but Langford had worked his magic to make it rather more potent. "On the bright side, after putting this on, you'll probably never, ever get athlete's foot again." She rubbed the goop in carefully, on her arms, chest, legs, and every other inch of herself she could reach, including her face, and even in her hair. B did the same, and Marla was preoccupied enough that she didn't even leer at him lasciviously.

"All right, apprentice, now you get to do my back. And any other bits I can't reach on my own. Don't worry, I'll return the favor."

"I'm pretty sure this wasn't in my job description." B slathered a double handful onto her back. At least the stuff was still warm from Langford's alterations.

"I know greasing up relatively young women isn't on your list of life goals. Just close your eyes and pretend I'm a burly guy named Bruce."

"Easier said than done."

Once they were both suitably covered, they got dressed again, their clothes sticking to them unpleasantly. "All right. You ready for this? It's apt to be a fight. I'm guessing Bulliard just has gross motor control on Viscarro. I doubt we'll have to contend with Viscarro's magic, and he's not much of a brawler, so concentrate your efforts on the presumably big and ugly guy."

"I'm ready," B said.

"Don't forget those tricks you learned. Some of them might come in handy. But pace yourself, all right?"

"Of course." He paused. "So . . . are we going to kill this guy?"

"No, we're going to explain the error of his ways and ask him nicely to leave. That's step one. If that fails . . . if it's him or us, sure, we'll take him out. But I think a case can be made that he's nuts, and we can reasonably clap him up in the Blackwing Institute. So we'll concentrate on incapacitating."

B looked relieved, and Marla felt a little flash of annoyance. When people threatened her city—as Bulliard was, just by his disruptive presence—she was willing to do whatever it took to remove that threat. B would have to harden his heart a little if he was going to succeed her someday.

"Let's go pluck a toadstool," she said.

12

Cam-Cam came out to meet them, dressed all in black and jingling with amulets, carrying a laptop bag. Rondeau hopped out, took the bag, and stowed it behind the seat. He'd initially expected a big bag of cash, but Jason had explained that ten million bucks, even in hundreds, would weigh over two hundred pounds. Thank goodness for modern technology. "After you." He stepped aside to let Cam-Cam sit in the middle of the battered old pickup truck's seat, next to Jason, then slipped back in. It was close quarters, but Cam-Cam didn't take up a lot of space, so it wasn't too uncomfortable.

"Last chance to back out," Jason said. "This is a dangerous business. Profitable, sure, but it's not like you need the money—"

"It's not about the money," Cam-Cam said. "I will be known as the man who helped destroy the nation's largest colony of vampires, won't I?"

"True, for all the good it will do you."

"I imagine it will open...certain doors to me. Your sister, for example, will be in my debt."

"He's got a point," Rondeau said. "Marla's gratitude is some pretty serious coin of the realm."

"All right, then," Jason said. "Off we go." He put the truck in gear and drove down Cam-Cam's long driveway.

"Not much of a car." Cam-Cam winced as the shitty shocks bounced them down the hill.

"Less conspicuous," Rondeau said. "Like our lovely attire here." Rondeau took his clothes seriously, though Marla said his fashion sense was only appropriate in Bizarro World, so he'd been bummed to dress in the paint-stained T-shirt and corduroy pants provided by Jason, who was wearing much the same. "A Hispanic guy and some white trash—no offense, Jason—in a busted pickup don't get a second glance, even in your neighborhood. People just assume we're gardeners."

"We are gardeners," Jason said. "At least, spores are sort of like plants, right? And these spores grow *money*."

"Where are we headed?" Cam-Cam asked.

"A back road north of the city, basically in the woods." They didn't have to go far. Cam-Cam lived near the beaches, already on the outskirts of Felport proper. They fell into silence, each with his own thoughts—Jason doubtless figuring additional angles, Cam-Cam probably fantasizing about becoming a sorcerer, and Rondeau just riding a wave of pleasure at what a big scam they were getting away with.

Jason took the truck down a dirt road lined closely on both sides with sagging trees, pulling into a lot that held the foundation and other blackened remnants of a burned-down house. He put the truck in park, honked the horn—two shorts, one long—and then lit a cigarette. "Now we wait." He blew a stream of smoke out the window. "The seller should be along shortly."

After about five minutes a four-wheeled ATV with a trailer attached came trundling into the lot from a dirt trail. The driver wore an opaque black motorcycle helmet and camouflage fatigues.

"All right." Jason got out of the truck, followed by Rondeau and Cam-Cam.

"Who the fuck is that?" The man in the helmet's voice was muffled. He pointed at Cam-Cam. "I don't know him."

"He's the man with the money," Jason said. "You really don't want to object to his presence, believe me."

The driver cursed. "You should've brought the money on your own."

"Oh? You send your business partners out alone with access to offshore accounts and trust them to do the right thing? I see you're here in person to accept delivery."

"This payload is too important to trust with my boys," the driver said, still not removing his helmet. "All right. Let's do this."

Jason nodded toward Cam-Cam, who held the laptop bag.

"No," Cam-Cam said. "Let's see the package."

The driver sighed, went to the trailer, and unfastened a gray tarp. He threw it back to reveal the thing they'd come to buy.

The big crate was even more impressive now than it had been when Danny Two Saints first showed it to them. There were chains, in gold and silver as well as dark iron, and the woodcut runes were painted in dark slashes of scarlet and cobalt blue.

"Hmm." Cam-Cam walked around the trailer, examining the crate. "How do I know there's even anything *in* there?"

"You questioning my word?" The driver took a step forward, making it clear he had a couple of inches in height and breadth over Cam-Cam.

Cam-Cam didn't flinch. "Yes, I am."

"It's okay," Jason said. "Easy to find out. You got the device, Rondeau?"

"Yup." Rondeau went to the truck, reached under the seat, and took out a polished wooden box with a lid that latched. Until yesterday, the box had held his best flask, a steel funnel, and a couple of metal shot glasses—the set was a gift from Marla for the date they'd randomly decided to call his birthday—but he'd cleaned the box out at Jason's suggestion. He carried the box over to the trailer, set it carefully on the edge beside the crate, and flipped the latch.

"This," said Rondeau, "is a divination wand made by Marla Mason herself. Sort of a supernatural Geiger counter."

The thing in the box had a handle of forked, gnarled wood, with a silvery metal sphere bound to the end with copper wire. Various dangling chains, ending in silver half-moons, golden stars, and tiny crystals, jingled when Rondeau picked it up.

"You don't mind if we verify the goods, do you?" Jason looked at the driver.

"Fuck you, Mason. I've been doing business with your sister for years. But knock yourself out."

"Okay." Rondeau started to extend the wand—then paused. "Do you want to do the honors, Mr. Campion?"

"How does it work?" Cam-Cam took the wand from Rondeau carefully.

"Just wave it slowly over the crate," Jason said. "If the spores are inside—even as well shielded as they are, for our protection—the wand should react."

"All right." Cam-Cam moved the wand over the crate.

It buzzed and jangled furiously in his hand, and Cam-Cam nearly dropped it. He drew it back, and it stopped moving. Cam-Cam reached out again, and again the wand buzzed to life, like a baby's rattle full of bees. He drew it back, and it stopped again—because Rondeau thumbed the little remote control in his pocket. The sphere on the "wand" was just a tea ball from his kitchen, soldered shut, and inside was a little remote control bullet vibrator he'd purchased from the sex shop three doors down from his club. Rondeau was proud of the wand. He'd made it himself, with some tips from Danny.

"All right?" Jason said.

Cam-Cam nodded. "I'm satisfied." He handed the wand back to Rondeau, who carefully returned it to the case.

Cam-Cam opened his padded bag, drew out a slim laptop, and placed it on the seat of the ATV. He opened it up and logged in to a secure banking site, entering numbers with great rapidity. He turned the screen around, and the driver—who was actually Danny Two Saints in disguise—leaned over and entered an account number. "You can do the honors," he said, stepping back.

Cam-Cam nodded curtly and clicked the touchpad a couple of times. "There, the transfer is done."

The driver held up his finger, took out a cell phone, made a call, rattled off a long number, listened for a moment, then closed the phone. "The funds are all accounted for on my end. Nice doing business with you."

"Give us a hand getting this thing into the truck?" Jason said.

The driver, Jason, Rondeau, and Cam-Cam all took hold of the crate and carried it toward the pickup. "It's not as heavy as it looks," Cam-Cam said.

"The spores are practically weightless, and the metal tube they're in doesn't weigh much more," the driver said. "All the rest of this weight is padding and armor and magic to keep the things inert. There's no telling what the spores were last programmed to do. I don't want to find out. How are you guys planning to open this safely anyway?"

"Don't worry about that." Jason slid the crate into the pickup.

The driver grunted. "I guess you've got Marla's organization at your disposal, so maybe you won't all kill yourselves. I'm going to head for my cabin upstate for a few weeks, though, just in case you do end up murdering everybody in the city."

"Your faith in us is touching." Jason slammed the

truck's tailgate shut. He and Rondeau tied down the crate and covered it with a tarp of their own.

"Take care, gents." The driver drove off in his ATV.

"Okay." Jason reached under the driver's side of the pickup's seat to pull out a pump-action shotgun.

Cam-Cam flinched. "What is this?"

"Caution." Rondeau took a chrome-plated, pearl-handled handgun from his waistband, and reached into the glove box for another pistol. "You know how to shoot?" He handed the gun, a ridiculously huge Desert Eagle, to Cam-Cam.

"I, ah, no—why will we need to shoot?"

"Safety's here." Rondeau showed him. "Trigger's there. Switch off one and pull the other, and get ready for a hell of a fucking kick if you need to use it."

"This is always a delicate moment," Jason said. "Right now, the dealer has your money, and we have his merchandise. A certain unscrupulous type of person might decide they want to take their merchandise back, and keep the money, too. Marla vouches for this guy, but this kind of cash does weird things to people. Makes 'em behave out of character."

Cam-Cam held the pistol awkwardly, one-handed, while Rondeau made a show of scanning the perimeter. "But surely Marla would seek revenge if he attacked us."

Jason shrugged. "He could always say we never showed up. Like I said. It's a delicate moment."

"Why guns?" Cam-Cam said. "Why not defend us with magic?"

"Magic is good for lots of thing," Rondeau said, "but guns are made for killing, and they're a lot more reliable, and deadly even in unschooled hands." Rondeau looked around one last time, then said, "Doesn't look like ambush is imminent."

"Into the truck, then," Jason said. "Rondeau, you ride in back with the crate. Cam-Cam, I'll trade you weapons—you ride shotgun. Keep the window down, and the nose of that gun hanging out." He passed the shotgun to Cam-Cam, who looked at it with alarm, but got into the truck as directed. When Cam-Cam was looking away, Jason shot Rondeau a big grin. *Yeah,* Rondeau thought. *This really is pretty godsdamn fun.*

"Keep an eye out." Jason started up the truck.

Rondeau held on to the sides of the pickup's bed, looking around. They went around a curve on the dirt road . . . and found the way blocked by a black SUV with darkly tinted windows.

Rondeau slid open the little window at the back of the pickup's cab. "Oh, fuck," he said.

"Yep." Jason stopped the truck. "The trees are too close on both sides of the road, so we can't drive around. We should back up—"

Someone burst from the trees on Cam-Cam's side and rushed the truck. He wore a heavy dark cloak with a hood and gloves, despite the heat. "Shoot him!" Rondeau screamed, and for a moment he thought Cam-Cam would freeze and spoil the whole effect.

But there was a cataclysmically loud boom, and the man in the cloak staggered back, fell . . . and then got up again.

"Fuck me," Jason said. "It's not the dealer. It's a vampire. Rondeau—"

"On it." Rondeau jumped down from the truck. Cam-Cam was saying something, babbling, really, but Rondeau concentrated on doing his moves as rehearsed. He whipped out a crucifix damn near the size of a tennis racket—it had belonged to Danny Two Saints's uncle the priest—and brandished it at the hooded figure, who fell back, keening in pain and terror. Rondeau pulled a sharpened wooden stake from his pocket and launched himself at the attacker, knocking him down, and drove the stake . . . into the dirt between the attacker's arm and side. But from Cam-Cam's panicked perspective, it should look like a heart-strike.

Rondeau got up and prodded the supine figure on the ground with his foot. The dead vampire was Danny Two Saints again, providing his adeptness as a quick-change artist, though he'd gotten the SUV into position as soon as Jason honked the horn before their transaction, so all he'd needed to do was pull on the cloak, mask, and gloves. Rondeau tugged at the cloak, and a gout of smoke rose up, along with a stink like rotten eggs, and he stumbled back, gagging. "Shit," he said. "Definitely a vampire, all wrapped up for daylight shenanigans."

"That smoke—" Cam-Cam said.

"They don't do so well with sunlight," Jason said. "They *burn*. Leave him, Rondeau, and move that fucking SUV out of the way."

Rondeau went to the vampire's ride, did a neat three-point turn, and squeezed past the pickup on the narrow road. He came back and hopped into the pickup's bed again, just in time to hear Cam-Cam say, "—thought they, I don't know, dissolved into dust?"

"This isn't a TV show," Jason said. "Vampires aren't much like they look in the movies. Stakes work, crosses work, sunlight works... but they aren't sexy, and their bodies don't just vanish when they die. They rot fast, though. Won't be much left of that guy by morning. I'd strip him and let him burn up, but that stink doesn't come out of your clothes or your hair for *weeks*."

The stink, Rondeau had to admit, was a nice touch. The smoke bomb concealed in the cloak had been Danny's idea, but the stink bomb was all Jason's.

"Let's get back to your place, Mr. Campion," Jason said. "And hope this vampire was just following the dealer, and not specifically looking for *us*."

"We'd better take precautions anyway," Rondeau said.

"Better safe than exsanguinated," Jason agreed.

"Viscarro!" Marla yelled, hitting the buzzer at one of the many doors to the subterranean sorcerer's catacombs. "This is Marla! Tell Bulliard I want to talk to him!"

After a moment, a speaker crackled. "I, ah, that is, I don't know anyone called—"

"Come *on*," Marla said. "Is our visiting country bumpkin *that* dumb? I obviously know he's here, so he may as well talk to me."

Another pause, then a voice that was not Viscarro's: "Come in."

The door swung open, and Marla entered, B following. They went down a few hundred yards of twisting brick-lined hallways before reaching the central vault.

Marla noted with interest that Viscarro had installed a concrete bunker. Possibly he'd been motivated by the same desire for increased security that had led her to beef up the protections at her own apartment. Viscarro stood near the bunker, beside a young disheveled-looking man who seemed vaguely familiar, and . . .

"Bulliard, I presume?" she said.

The mycomancer was a big bastard, with a serious wild-man-of-the-woods vibe, though it was hard to tell where his long beard left off and drooping fronds of hanging moss began. His clothing might have been animal skins, or vegetation, or simply layers and layers and layers of filth. He wore a faded pink plastic pig snout, which should have been funny, but wasn't. "Marla Mason," he said, and flung out his hand.

Something hit Marla's cheeks and sizzled. She laughed, wiping at her face. "Nice try, fungi. But impolite. I came to talk, not fight, but—" She nodded to B, who stepped forward and flung a tiny rock at Bulliard.

The stone hit the sorcerer in the chest, and he staggered back and slammed into the concrete bunker, hard. B had chipped the tiny stone from a much larger rock in Fludd Park and bound them together with sympathetic magic, so the pebble hit Bulliard with the force of a thrown boulder. The boulder in the park had almost certainly flown through the air, too, but it was next to the duck pond, so the only possible casualties were unwary waterbirds.

"Now that the pleasantries are out of the way," Marla said. "How about we talk business? You're here for some spores, yeah?"

Bulliard straightened, wincing and rubbing his chest. "I am."

"Too bad. They aren't real. So sorry. Bye-bye."

"You lie," Bulliard said.

"No, I *don't*. Where did you hear this crap about the spores anyway?"

"Him." Bulliard nodded to the nondescript young man, who was trying to fade into the background.

"Okay, where did *he* hear it?"

"Can't say," the guy said. "Confidentiality. The magical kind."

A light went on in her head. "Oh, hell, you're the courier, I've seen you around. You've done work for me, yeah?"

"Yes, ma'am."

"And now you work for *him*?"

"It's not a job so much as it's slavery," he said. "If you could maybe kill him and get rid of these mushrooms growing into my brain stem, I'd appreciate it."

"You really can't tell me who gave you the message about the spores?"

"Not without my head exploding."

Marla considered. "Would your head explode before you finished telling me, or after?"

"Before. Definitely before."

"Hell. You'd say that either way."

"Enough," Bulliard said. "The Mycelium has authorized me to . . . negotiate." His mouth twisted in distaste.

"Because you know I can squish you like a dung beetle, no doubt. There's nothing to negotiate *for*."

"We can offer hundreds of kilograms of *Tricholoma*

magnivelare," Bulliard said. "The American matsutake. Its value varies, but it often sells for ninety dollars per kilogram in Japan."

Marla snorted. "You're talking about less than a hundred grand. For the *Borrichius* spores? That's not even close to a reasonable offer."

"You misunderstand. The Mycelium offers this as an annuity, in perpetuity. The mushrooms are rare and valuable, but it is trivial for us to produce them. Will you accept this offer?"

Jason probably would, she thought—but while it was possible to trick someone like Cam-Cam, she couldn't deceive Bulliard, not when it came to spores. He practically *was* spores. She sighed. "Look, Bulliard, you've been had. There are no spores. It's a lie. A trick. A scam."

"I don't believe you," Bulliard said. "The Mycelium doesn't believe you. The spores are valuable. Of course you would lie to protect them."

"Sure. I'm *not,* but I *would,* you've got me there. But, either way, you're not leaving here with them. You can pack up your shit and leave town, right now—after you release Viscarro and the courier here from whatever nasty control you've got—or you can stay and get turned into mulch. Totally your choice."

"There is a third option," Bulliard said. "I could make you into fertilizer for the Mycelium."

"All right, then." Marla unsheathed her dagger of office. "Let's dance."

Bulliard rushed them, and so, improbably, did Viscarro, moving with spidery speed. Marla planted one foot and whirled for a roundhouse kick at Bulliard's face—aiming for that stupid pig-nose—but he dodged aside with surprising dexterity. Viscarro was tangling with B, and Marla felt for him—fighting that guy must be like fighting a mass of living coat hangers, and Viscarro couldn't feel pain—but he appeared to be holding his own okay. B was armed with a length of pipe wrapped in gaffer's tape to make a grip, and Marla had laid some inertial magics on it, so the pipe hit *hard*. Marla slashed out at Bulliard with her knife and sliced into something, though whether it was flesh or fungus or clothing she couldn't tell. Her hands were sticky from the fungicide, but it didn't hurt her grip on the knife, and even though Bulliard was big and fast, she knew she could take him. Kicking ass was what she did, while the mycomancer probably depended a lot more on shoving mushrooms into people's brain stems. She darted forward to make another strike—

Something exploded against the back of her head, and everything went black.

B saw Marla go down. The courier simply walked up behind her and smacked her in the back of the head with a heavy ceramic pot. B cursed, swung his pipe at Viscarro's knee, and heard a satisfying crunch. Viscarro went down, and tried to stand up again, but the knee wouldn't support him, and he gave up—or, rather, Bulliard gave up on puppeting his body around. "Damn it, Bowman," Viscarro complained. "I'm *dead*, I can't *heal* from that kind of injury, I'll have to take the leg off and get a prosthesis."

"Sorry," B said automatically, and backed away. Bulliard and the courier were approaching him, trying to flank him, and Marla wasn't moving. Was she dead? She *couldn't* be dead. He'd seen her take much harder hits... but only when wearing her magical purple-and-white cloak, which could heal nearly any injury. She didn't wear the cloak anymore, fearing the cost of its magic, and he didn't know how much of a beating she could soak up on her own.

At the moment, though, B had to worry about his own skin. "Bye-bye, birdie," he said, and turned into a pigeon just as Bulliard dove for him.

As he spun and flew toward the high domed ceiling, he saw Bulliard stumble, and the messenger looked around in confusion. The change had been quick enough that B wasn't sure they'd even seen him become a bird—they might think he'd disappeared. He flapped over the courier and cooed, wishing he could crap on cue, but apparently birds didn't have sphincter control. The courier looked up, cursing, and B changed back into human form, dropping all his weight onto the man's head and knocking him to the ground, where his crumpling body conveniently broke B's fall. B rolled off him just in time to see Bulliard looming over him, reaching out with hands the size of cast-iron skillets—

B took a breath. *Focus, Focus, Focus,* he thought, and time slowed. He carved up space-time, opening a hole in the inches between Bulliard and himself, a gulf, a chasm, a tiger pit... a portal. Real time reasserted itself, and the mycomancer lunged...and vanished, disappearing into the floor. B didn't have the skill with manipulating space to create a pocket-dimension to hold him, though such a pinched-off prison would have been wonderful at the moment—but he could do something almost as good.

Bulliard had fallen into the floor, but he fell *out* of the ceiling, tumbling from vaulted space above, bouncing off the bunker, and landing in an ungainly and unmoving heap on the floor.

B stumbled toward Marla. He'd tired himself out before they even came here by making a sympathetic connection between the little rock and the boulder in the park, and now, in addition to that, he was disoriented from being a bird, and his head pounded from cutting up space-time. He knelt by Marla, nearly pitching forward on his face in the process, and shook her.

Marla's eyes opened, and she groaned. "Anybody get the street address of that *building* that hit me?"

"Thought. You. Dead." B's vision was blurring a little at the edges.

"My head's harder than that." She sat up and looked around. "Damn, B. You did this?"

"Yes." He slumped over, yawned mightily, and closed his eyes. *I'll just rest for a minute. Just for a minute.*

After easing B down to the ground, Marla went to Bulliard, knelt, and checked for a pulse. There was none. She rolled his body over—he was lighter than she'd expected, much of his bulk made up of layered clothes and caked-on grime—and pried open his eyelids. Pupils were nonreactive. No sign of breath from his nostrils. No rise and fall of his chest. She poked the point of a dagger into the fleshy part of the sorcerer's thigh, and not only did he remain unmoving, the wound didn't bleed much—barely even oozed.

She went over to Viscarro, who was sighing long-sufferingly on the floor. "All right, corpsy, let's get those shrooms out of you." Hold still." Marla cut at Viscarro's neck with her dagger of office. "This knife is sharp, it'll decapitate you if you aren't careful. That wouldn't kill you, but I bet you'd hate being a head on a shelf somewhere. You never struck me as the Orpheus type."

"Just hurry, before Bulliard awakens!"

"I wouldn't worry about that. There." She held the tiny mushrooms, caps and stems, in the palm of her hand, where they sizzled and withered on contact with her fungicide. "You sure this is all of them? I could..." She shuddered. "I could strip your carcass and check the rest of you, see if you've got mushrooms hidden in more delicate places."

"That won't be necessary," he snapped. "I'm *keenly* aware of my own body and all the parasites attached thereto." Viscarro rubbed the back of his neck, which was nicked and gouged. "Damn it. I need a new leg, and there are holes in my neck."

"You're welcome. I didn't sever any nerves, so quit your bitching." Marla was no surgeon, but Viscarro didn't feel pain or bleed, so cutting out the mushrooms was easy. She looked at the unconscious courier. She didn't dare try to cut the mushrooms out of him—he was living flesh, not a lich, so he would bleed, and she'd kill him, likely as not. She'd have to get Langford to work on him under anesthesia. "You got a prison cell for these two?"

"Oh, yes. A torture chamber as well."

"Eh, Bulliard looks dead, so I'm guessing torture is probably moot."

Viscarro cursed. "Your apprentice made Bulliard fall from the ceiling. Drat. I'd planned on paying him back for his rudeness."

Marla looked up. That was a good thirty-foot drop. He'd probably snapped his neck on impact. B would feel guilty for killing the man, probably, but she'd make sure he got over it. If the mycomancer really *was* dead. "I'd rather be safe, though. I've known a few sorcerers who were quick even though they *looked* awfully damn dead, present company included. Put Bulliard's body somewhere secure, would you? Just in case he's playing possum. I'd hate for him to open his eyes and come at me like the end of a cheap horror movie."

"I'll find a nice deep hole for him, don't worry."

"Even if he's really dead, I want Langford to check him out, make sure he's not carrying some kind of biohazard on his skin or anything. And *don't* steal the pig nose. I know magic when I see it, but I want to get it checked out before we do anything with it."

"Can I have it when you're done?" Viscarro said.

"If it's not anything I need. Can't you show a little gratitude for us saving you and ending your enslavement?"

"I'm one of the city's sorcerers," Viscarro snapped. "Saving me is your *job*. I don't thank garbagemen or dogcatchers, either. I'll have my apprentices put these two away."

"Okay. No torturing the courier. He's no more responsible for his actions than you are." Which didn't stop her from harboring just a little bit of resentment toward the guy herself. He'd hit her hard, and she was a little worried she had a concussion.

She went over to B and nudged him with her foot, but he only snored. Poor kid had tried to do six impossible things at once, and that would take a lot out of even a seasoned pro. "You mind if B keeps snoozing here? He pushed himself hard, without enough training, and he's going to have to sleep it off. He's apt to wake up ravenous, too. Can you feed him?"

"I suppose my apprentices eat, so there's likely food somewhere. I'll make sure they see to his needs. You're paying for my new prosthetic leg, by the way."

"Take it out of next month's tribute. And give me a receipt." She looked around, making sure she didn't have any double vision, and decided she was probably capable of soldiering on.

"Where are *you* going?"

"Couple errands." She sighed. "I was going to have B call up an oracle for me, so I could find out who told Bulliard the Borrichius spores were in Felport. But B's down for the count." She chewed her lip thoughtfully. "Still, he's not the only source of otherworldly information in town, is he? I've got other options. Shit, I need to call my brother, too, tell him to finish up his business with the spores tout suite, just in case there are any other out-of-towners coming—"

"So the spores *are* real?" Viscarro said.

"No, never mind, it's complicated. Take care, Viscarro. I'll come back in a couple hours to see how B's doing, and send someone to work on saving the courier and autopsying Bulliard."

"Oh, good," Viscarro said sourly. "More visitors."

The messenger woke in a dim place, and sat up, groaning. His head hurt, his back hurt, his shoulders hurt, his teeth ached, and at some point he'd bitten his tongue. Now he was in a dim cinder-block cell with a metal door, and Bulliard was beside him, sprawled inelegantly on the floor. The messenger crawled, wincing, to Bulliard, and prodded him. "Hey, mossface, look at the fine mess you've gotten us into now." Bulliard didn't move, and the messenger grinned. "Are you dead, Bulliard? Gone to the great honey mushroom colony in the sky? Well, if you're *not,* let me take this opportunity to make sure you *are.*" He reached out for Bulliard's throat, intending to squeeze until he felt the windpipe collapse—but he couldn't even make himself touch the mycomancer's skin. "Oh, *fuck,*" he said. The mushrooms in his brain stem were still controlling his movements. Was it just really good magic? Or was Bulliard less dead than he appeared?

"The Mycelium will not be pleased." Bulliard opened his dirt-colored eyes. "Hmm. A cell. I had hoped they would simply bury me, or place me in a less secure room, upon finding me dead."

"You don't sound dead. I know how dead sounds, and it doesn't sound like you."

"Fly agaric," Bulliard said. "A beautiful mushroom. *Amanita muscaria,* beloved of shamans, bringer of visions. The Norse used it to incite berserker rages—I have used it for that myself. But it can also cause unconsciousness, and symptoms that mimic death." He sat up. "I was not sure I could win the fight directly. So I chose to deceive our attackers and bide my time."

"Great plan. Now we're locked in a cell."

"Yes. But I was not dead. I was still, but I was *listening.* Marla Mason said that she wished to warn her brother. She was afraid he might be in danger, if others came looking for the spores."

"Oh, shit. You think her brother has the spores? I didn't even know she *had* a brother."

"I have no doubt he is a great magician," Bulliard said. "But he will not expect me to come for him. People seldom expect attacks from the dead."

"Great. But how do we get out of here?"

"Like this." Viscarro opened the door. He leaned on an old-fashioned wooden crutch. "There's an escape tunnel here to the right, it will lead you to the surface."

The messenger blinked. "Why aren't you locked up in a cell with us?"

"Marla believed she cut all the mushrooms out of me, that I was free from Bulliard's influence. And she did cut them all out . . . at least, the ones in my neck. The ones at the base of my spine, however, she was unaware of, and I found myself inexplicably unable to *tell* her."

"The Mycelium believes you gave a message to Marla

Mason, warning her of our presence," Bulliard said. "The Mycelium advocated tighter control of your words after that. I did as my god bade me."

"Fine. I trust this fulfills my obligations to you? Can I be free now?"

"I prefer to keep you in reserve, though I don't care how you occupy yourself, as long as you remain here, and do not attempt to hinder me."

"So noted. How do you intend to find Marla Mason's brother? I didn't even know he existed until recently. His haunts are unknown to me."

Bulliard tapped the side of his pig's snout. "When I know what I am looking for, I can always root it out."

13

Rondeau's phone rang. Marla, calling from her office. "I gotta take this, guys, it's the boss."

"Give her my regards," Cam-Cam said, cool as you please, and Jason said, "Send my love." They went back to their discussion of the next day's plan, a road trip to meet with the Aeromancer's representatives. In reality, Danny Two Saints would be lying in wait to ambush them again on the way, spoiling the deal and freaking out Cam-Cam, who would be led to believe his life was in danger, and that they needed to lay low for a while to keep the heat off and so forth. But if Cam-Cam could put up the capital to hire some particularly vicious mercenary vampire hunters as protection—actually other confederates of Jason and Danny's—they might be able to try again in a week or two... It was all part of the plan to keep stringing Cam-Cam along and bleeding him for more money. Rondeau was sort of dizzied by the scale of the operation, which was really only beginning, but like Jason said, this was no three-minute pop song of a con they were writing here—it was more like an opera on the scale of Wagner's Ring Cycle. Before it was over, they'd have Cam-Cam terrified he'd been turned into a vampire, paying serious money for a miracle cure; they'd send him on a trip to South America to meet with a legendary (and entirely invented) vampire king-in-exile, who would demand tribute before discussing the weaknesses of his brethren; they'd have him paying a rogue priest to turn his whole estate into sanctified ground, and the water in his pipes to holy water. Jason said it could go on indefinitely. Jason had *ideas*.

"Hey, Marla." Rondeau walked into the formal dining room, well out of earshot of Jason and their mark. "We're over at Cam-Cam's."

"I figured. Look, tell Jason he's got to wrap this up quick, and do the blow-off."

Rondeau blinked. "What? We're just getting started!"

"Take what you've got now and *end* it. I know that's not what Jason has planned, but my brother can improvise with the best of them."

"Okay." Rondeau pinched the bridge of his nose and squeezed his eyes shut. "Okay, boss." He knew she had a good reason. She wouldn't ask him to do this otherwise. But . . . "Mind if I ask why?"

"B and I—mostly B—just killed a sorcerer named Bulliard who came to town looking for the spores, that's why. Somehow word got out, and serious people are taking my brother's bullshit *seriously*. There could be more bad guys coming, and I don't want Jason to get hurt—I kind of like having the guy around."

"Hell. I like him, too. I didn't say a word to anybody, Marla, I swear. Maybe it was Cam-Cam, I don't know—"

"No, it wasn't Cam-Cam, or Jason or his crew, either. Whoever sent Bulliard the message used a special courier, the kind only sorcerers use. It wasn't me, and it wasn't you—I'm not even asking, I *know* it wasn't you—so I don't know who the fuck it was. Jason and I talked about it a couple of times in public, so somebody must have overheard. I'm going to find out who it was and have a talk with them, too. The kind of talk you do by *punching*."

"Do you need my help?" Rondeau said. "With anything?" Working with Jason to scam Cam-Cam was a hoot and a half, but it looked like that fun-time train was pulling into the last station anyway, and Marla had just reminded him he had *real* responsibilities. "I should've been there with you and B, fighting this guy. I'm sorry. Shit."

"Hey, I gave you permission to moonlight. I'm not pissed at you—if we'd needed you, you better believe I'd have called. Right now what I need you to do is keep my brother from getting *killed*. Tell him to blow Cam-Cam off. You got a big chunk of money already, right?"

"We did."

"Tell Jason that'll have to do for now. We'll find him another pigeon."

"I'll do my best." Marla hung up on him. Only after she was off the line did he realize he had no idea what to say to Jason. He couldn't say, "Sorry, there are bad magic-wielding murderers coming for us," because

Jason didn't believe in magic. Which meant Rondeau was going to have to come up with a lie that *Jason* would believe.

He put his phone away, took a deep breath, and went into the living room. "Hey, Jason? Can we talk in private?"

Marla caught a bus to the financial district and went into the lobby of a skyscraper with darkly mirrored glass walls. The security guard at the front desk saw her coming and immediately picked up a phone and whispered into it. He rose, smiling, and extended his hand to Marla. "Ms. Mason, such a pleasure to see you, can I get you anything to—"

"I'm going up to see Nicolette." Marla went around him toward the elevator.

He sidestepped into her way. "Ah, Ms. Jordan is otherwise engaged at the moment, but if you'd be willing to—"

"Move or lose a foot." She was still wearing the green gecko boots, not her nasty enchanted steel-toed boots, but she could shatter an instep without magic. She stomped forward, and he danced back.

"You can go right up," he said quickly, and hurried back to his phone as she stepped into the elevator.

Marla eyed the mirrored walls as she rose. Turning an elevator into a deathtrap would be a pretty good way to assassinate her, she supposed. She'd better think about some contingency plans against that eventuality. Nicolette was a chaos magician, drawing power from uncertainty and disorder, and as such, she couldn't be trusted to do *anything*—not even to act in her own best interest. Marla never dropped her guard around the woman, and did her best to avoid her, but she had need of her assets now.

The top floor of the skyscraper was a penthouse apartment, and the elevator doors slid open onto a locked door. Marla hit the intercom button and said, "It's Marla. I need you."

Nicolette's voice, without a hint of static on the intercom, said, "I thought you were bringing your apprentice the day after tomorrow?"

"No apprentice, just me. I need your services. Or the services of someone in your service."

"Is this one of those 'for the good of the city' things again? It's been a bad year for that."

"Just open the fucking door, Nicolette, or I'll have to open it myself, and then you'll have to buy a replacement."

"Come on in, I'm in my office."

The door clicked open, and Marla stepped through, into a jumbled disaster of a living room. This apartment had once belonged to Nicolette's old mentor, a diviner named Gregor, who'd been executed for his crimes against Felport a few months previous. Nicolette had inherited his estate, and it had been a very tidy estate indeed, since Gregor was a notorious minimalist perfectionist control freak. His apartment had been spare to the point of Spartan, but Nicolette had . . . done some redecorating. The place was wrecked. Marla couldn't even identify any furniture, though there were certain lumps suggestive of couches and armchairs. The place was full of stuffed animal heads, dusty empty picture frames, hideous kitschy lamps, bolts of mildewed fabric, and what appeared to be the engine block from a bus. The beautiful floor-to-ceiling windows, which looked out on the city and the bay beyond—one just lighting up and the other becoming a void of rumbling darkness as night fell—were defaced with spray-painted markings that looked like graffiti tags merged with runes. Marla's apartment was no showpiece, but it was just messy with neglect, not actively trashed.

Oh, well. Necromancers tended to include skulls in their décor, and pyromancers were partial to flambeaux, so it made sense that a chaos magician would decorate with wreckage. Too bad the place smelled like fish sauce and burned wiring and industrial astringents.

Marla carefully navigated the trash heaps, wary of tetanus, down the hallway to what had been Gregor's office. This room was relatively neat—just an armless dressmaker's dummy lying in the middle of the floor, and ragged strips of wallpaper dangling from the walls—and Nicolette was inside, sitting at her computer, blue light reflecting on her narrow birdlike face. "Be with you in a minute," she said. "I'm transferring cash from one of my offshore casinos. This online gambling stuff is the *shit*. Suckers roll in from all over the world, and you don't even have to cheat them, just trust in their basic inability to do *math*."

Marla grunted. She wondered if Jason would like running a site like that, and seeing money run in like water rushing downhill, or if he needed the element of the grift to keep himself interested. "Don't see how it helps the local economy so much."

"You get your cut, boss lady, and I trust you roll it back into the community and all that." She leaned back and cocked her head. "What can I do for you?"

"Monster came to town. I killed him. But I have some follow-up questions, and he's in no state to answer them."

Nicolette hmmed. "Monster, huh? Those are usually 'its,' not 'hims.'"

"One of those fiend-in-human-flesh type situations." She shrugged. "It's not important—he's been contained. But I need some extra-sensory perception to clear up a few nagging little questions."

Nicolette shook her head, the charms woven into her bleached-white dreadlocks bouncing and jiggling. "I may be living in a seer's tower, but you know I'm not a seer myself. Hell, I get my buzz from uncertainty. Not sure why you came here. Isn't Bradley Bowman supposed to be a psychic?"

"B overexerted himself today. He's resting. But my errand can't wait. You have something I need, Nicolette."

"What, did you hear about my divining spiders? I'm working on them, getting them into shape, but they're more for pattern-matching than actually answering questions, and they're a long way from being ready to—"

"I need to see the Giggler, Nicolette." Marla watched the chaos magician's face closely. She was a student of faces, and knew the truth of a person's feelings often flashed, involuntarily, across their expressions, for as little as a fraction of a second. There were forty-four facial muscles related to fear, uncertainty, anger, and mistrust, and Nicolette moved a large percentage of them in very telling configurations, for just an instant. Then all was smooth again.

"The Giggler? I don't—"

"Sure you do." Marla unsheathed her dagger of office and cut a loose thread dangling from the hem of her shirt. She didn't put the knife away when she was done. "The Giggler. Crazy motherfucker with a gift for telling the future. Went on a rampage years ago, cut the guts out of a bunch of sorcerers to read his fate in their entrails. People called him the Belly Killer. This ringing a bell? I *knew* Sauvage kept the guy alive to use as a little pet oracle. Your late and unlamented boss stole him away after Sauvage died—didn't think I knew that, did you?—and you, my dear, inherited him."

Nicolette didn't bother to hide her expression now. Her eyes were flat slits of hate.

"I know." Marla tried to put the semblance of genuine commiseration into her voice, though she was loving this. "It's a bitch to find out one of your secrets isn't so secret after all. What good is a hole card when everybody knows what you're holding? Don't worry, I'm not enacting any eminent-domain bullshit, you're welcome to keep the Giggler. I don't want responsibility for his upkeep anyway, the guy eats like a legion of pigs. I just need access to him right now."

"You won't tell anyone else I've got him here?"

"Nah, we're good."

"All right." Nicolette rose, beckoning Marla. "Guess I don't have a lot of options." They went back to the elevator. "Not much good having a fucking oracle if he can't tell me stuff like *this* is coming," she complained.

"That's the problem with oracles. You have to know what questions to ask, and how to ask them, and how to interpret the answers. My new apprentice is a hell of a seer, but it's still no good if you don't know exactly what you're trying to find out. Vague questions get vague responses. So what do you use the Giggler for?"

She shrugged. "I don't consult him as much as Gregor used to—you know I like surfing the uncertainties. But he's good for alerting me to upcoming stock market fluctuations."

"Oh? Is that all?" Marla was amused. The elevator arrived and they boarded.

Nicolette inserted her penthouse key, turned it, then pressed the basement button twice. "Well, he also gets me blackmail material for people I need to lean on."

"That's more like it." Marla grinned.

"What do you need to ask him anyway?"

"I'm not a big fan of repeating myself. You can hang out while I question him if you don't have anything better to do; you'll hear it then."

They rode to one of the building's secret subbasements in silence. The elevator doors opened onto a dim concrete hallway festooned with graffiti that seemed to squirm and writhe away from the eye.

Nicolette preceded Marla down the hall, and Marla wrinkled her nose. She had a high tolerance for stench, but it was pretty rank down here. "Giggler!" Nicolette said. "We've got a visitor!" They went through an open door into the Giggler's chamber.

"Wow, he's got the same interior decorator you do." Marla looked around at the concrete cell, which looked like a collision between a garbage truck and a white elephant sale.

"He finds patterns in trash—he started out reading entrails, after all, so this is a step up in the hygiene department. Gregor used to try to keep the place cleaner, but I just go with the flow." She leaned against the doorjamb. "He's in there...somewhere. Go ask your question."

"Did you bring presents?" The Giggler emerged from beneath a pile of cheap Mexican blankets smeared with peanut butter and—Marla hoped—chocolate. The seer had greasy black hair, snot caked on his upper lip, and eyes like a couple of holes punched in nothing.

"No presents." Marla crouched to look him in the eye, from a judicious distance. "Just my presence. You remember me?"

"You saved my life." The Giggler tittered, a high-pitched, irritating noise that made Marla's back-brain shudder.

"Insofar as I didn't kill you when I had the chance, I guess I did. Want to return the favor?"

"*Your* life doesn't need saving." The Giggler had a sly look on his face.

"That's good to know. I need some questions answered."

"Yes, you do." The Giggler slithered the rest of the way out of the covers and onto a chair-sized heap of garbage bags and Bubble Wrap, which popped and squeaked under his weight. He settled into it like a king on his throne, his pink bathrobe rumpling around him. "Personal first, or business? Your brother, or the beast?"

Marla blinked. "Ah. You're such a good seer you saw what my *questions* were going to be?"

The Giggler tittered again. "Which, which, which?" he said. Or maybe "Which, which, witch?" It was hard to tell.

"Felport comes first." She *did* want to ask about her brother, though she'd just about decided to trust him, at least as far as she could throw him. She wouldn't mind a little outside confirmation of her instincts, but finding out who had brought Bulliard to town—and if there were likely to be more outside intrusions—was the more pressing issue.

"Your brother is no danger to the city," the Giggler said.

"Also good to know. A sorcerer named Bulliard came to my city, late last night or early this morning, looking for something—but you know that."

The Giggler nodded sagely—or as sagely as possible, given the dried booger dangling from his chin. "I know everything, but you still need to *ask*."

"Right. Someone told Bulliard to come here, sent him an anonymous message. I need to know—who did it?"

"She's right behind you," the Giggler said. "She has a hammer."

Marla didn't think, just dove and rolled, scattering empty cracker boxes and old shoes as she did. She popped back up as Nicolette's sledgehammer struck the concrete floor where Marla had been.

"See? *Your* life isn't in danger." The Giggler giggled.

"*You* sent the message to Bulliard?" Marla drew her dagger again, with rather more purpose this time. She should have been gratified to know her suspicions about another traitor in her midst had been correct, but it was cold comfort. Maybe if she'd brought Bradley to Nicolette *first,* he would have sensed something, and this could have been avoided. Just bad luck. "What the fuck? How did you even hear about the spores?"

"Spies everywhere, boss. Eyes everywhere. You know how it is." She glanced at the Giggler. "Ingrate. After all I've done for you."

The Giggler showed his stubby yellow teeth. "I will always have a pot to piss in and a seat to sit on, for so long as I live, so help me gods."

"Didn't see this coming, did you?" Nicolette snatched a charm from her hair and tossed it toward the Giggler.

Before the charm—it looked like a tiny yellow glass pineapple—hit him, the Giggler let loose a deep and weary sigh. "Of course I did," he said.

Then the pineapple expanded and exploded into a thousand needle-thin spines, piercing the Giggler's face, chest, arms, and hands, and deflating the Bubble-Wrap throne. As he sagged and sank, the Giggler said, "Took you long enough," and closed his otherworldly eyes.

"Now, that's just wasteful. He was a good seer." Marla kept her eye on Nicolette's hands. The charms in the chaos magician's hair represented hours of dedicated enchanting, each one a nasty spell, though it was hard to tell what any of them did—porcelain skulls, a glass eye in a wire cage, a jade frog, a wisdom tooth trailing roots.

"He betrayed me." Nicolette shrugged. "It's no good having someone that untrustworthy in your organization. I've got you outgunned here, Marla. You didn't come expecting a fight, and this is my turf. Let's try to reach an understanding."

"The only thing I'm interested in understanding is *why*? What's the angle? You wanted Bulliard to steal the spores for you? But he didn't even know who you *were*."

"Giving that kind of weapon to a nutcase like Bulliard is bound to increase the net chaos in the world, Marla, and that's only good for me. Plus, having him come to town, stomping around, fucking things up for you, that makes things messier in Felport, and that's definitely to my advantage. The more things tumble down here, the higher I rise. You're way too *orderly* for my taste. You make the trains run on time, when I'd rather have a few of them derail every now and then. It's not so complicated. I am what I am, and what I've always been."

"How can I tolerate somebody like you in my organization, Nicolette?"

"Point. But I'm opposed to organizations in principle anyway. And imagine the chaos around here if you were to suddenly disappear." She snatched a charm from her hair.

"Urizen Protocol," Marla said loudly, and Nicolette froze like a statue, one hand tangled in her hair, the only sign of life a high thin scream—like the sound of a teakettle just starting to boil—issuing from between her clenched teeth. Marla went to her and gently pried the faceted blue charm out of the chaos magician's hand.

Then she drew her dagger and sawed off all Nicolette's dreadlocks, one by one, depositing them carefully in a plastic grocery bag she found near the Giggler's corpse, padding the charms with bloodstained shreds of Bubble Wrap. "Sorry for the Samson-and-Delilah thing, hon, but the paralysis won't last for long, and I need to get you neutralized."

Nicolette's throat worked, and her lips parted enough for her to say, "What have you done?"

"You murdered your last boss, Nicolette—on orders from me, but *still*. I never trusted you. So I had my friend Mr. Beadle—you know him, obsessive-compulsive little guy, has an affinity for straight lines and right angles and law and order and everything you *aren't*?—do me a favor. He posed as a window washer and put some nice gold-inlaid binding spirals all over the outside of the building for me, very subtle, and all keyed to my code phrase. You're bound up right now in a cage of orderly forces; it won't hold out against you for long, but, well, long enough. You didn't seriously think I'd let you into the highest councils of the city without some kind of insurance, did you? An attack dog is useful, but you gotta have a shotgun near to hand in case the thing turns on you someday. One question—is Bulliard the only bull you set loose in my china shop, or are there others coming?" Nicolette didn't answer. "Come on, now. You need all the leniency you can get. Speak up. Are there other nasty surprises coming?"

Nicolette said "No." She couldn't technically hiss a word with no esses in it, but she did her best.

"That's a comfort." Marla fished around in the many

pockets of her black cloak until she found a little sachet of sandalwood and chamomile. "I'm tempted to just hit you in the back of the head with that sledgehammer you aimed at me until you go unconscious, but Dr. Husch gets mad when I bring her brain-damaged patients—"

"Husch?" Nicolette hissed—she might have been alarmed or appalled, but since she couldn't move most of her facial muscles, Marla couldn't be sure.

"I'm having you hauled off to the Blackwing Institute. If Dr. Husch decides you're crazy, we'll lock you up there. But if she decides you're competent, well . . . either banishment or execution." She sighed. "I'll have to hold a fucking *meeting* with the other leading sorcerers to determine your fate, since you're one of us. I hate meetings. I'm much more a rule-by-fiat type, but you gotta make allowances."

"You can't—"

"Night-night." Marla threw the sachet at Nicolette's face. It bounced off her nose, and Nicolette glared, grunted, and then dropped into a deep and magical sleep. Marla took her under the armpits and said "Arioch Protocol" to disable the order spells. Nicolette's weight came slumping down, and Marla lowered her to the floor. The chaos magician should sleep for a few hours, so deep she wouldn't even dream.

Marla patted Nicolette down and found a cell phone—her own phone was charged, for once, but only because it was plugged in and sitting on the desk in her office. She couldn't get reception in the basement, but the sleeping and the dead would keep, so she carried the sackful of charms to the elevator and rode back up to

Nicolette's apartment, then called Hamil and told him what had happened. "Better send some guys over to bundle her out of here, and make sure Mr. Beadle comes along, too. I took her charms away, but Nicolette's dangerous just by herself, especially in a situation this disorderly. Oh, there's a corpse to clean up, too. Good job finding the Giggler, but he's not going to do anybody any good anymore." She called Rondeau, and went straight to voicemail, and then tried B, but got the same—Rondeau was, she hoped, busy convincing her brother to drop his scam, and B was probably just sleeping.

It was all over but the cleanup. She'd get Nicolette squared away, then deal with Bulliard's corpse. She could be in bed by midnight without even hustling much, if she wanted.

Marla sighed, sat down cross-legged on the stained concrete floor, and began sorting through Nicolette's charms to see if there was anything worth commandeering.

As night began to fall, Bulliard paused in his snuffling down some random alley and said, "We require transportation. Marla's brother is too far to reach quickly on foot."

"How about a motorcycle with a sidecar?" the courier said. "That would be sweet. Or, I know, a hot air balloon!"

Bulliard went to the end of the alley and pointed to a battered old truck parked beside a sagging wooden fence. "Hotwire that for me."

"Sorry, big guy, I was never a car thief. I wouldn't know where to begin."

"You are *useless*. I can't understand why the Mycelium won't let me kill you."

The courier flashed back to his glimpse of Bulliard's god, that terrible, knowing face that wasn't really a face. He still wasn't sure if the thing he'd seen was real, or a mere hallucination—whether Bulliard was deluded, or truly in service to something terrible and inhuman. It wasn't a question he liked to dwell on. The courier was a fan of pizza, weed, beer, and watching sports on television. This crap was way outside his mental comfort zone. "If I got a vote, I'd vote for *releasing* me, but whatever. Find us a car, and I'll drive you. What, you want me to do *all* the work?"

Bulliard stomped out of the alley, onto a street. The courier had no idea where they were—he'd never spent a ton of time in Felport, just coming in and out on a few deliveries—but it didn't look like a nice part of town. A low-rider vintage Chevy Impala convertible with four guys inside came cruising down the street, music thumping brutal bass, and Bulliard stepped in front of the car and held up his hand in a stop-right-there gesture.

The car slowed and stopped, and a couple of Hispanic teens jumped out of the backseat and sauntered over. "Check this motherfucker out," one said. "A mountain man."

"I require your vehicle."

"I require your wallet," the guy said, and the others laughed.

Bulliard hit him so hard he flew back and landed on the hood of the car, groaning.

The other two bounced out of the car, one with a knife and the other with a tire tool, and the driver glanced at the courier, who held up his hands. "Don't worry about me, bro. He's the one with the anger management problem. But you're better off just tossing him the keys and taking off, trust me."

"Fuck that," the driver said, but nervously, glancing at his friend, who was no more sure than he was. They took a few steps closer.

Bulliard simply walked around them to the car—they backed away warily at his approach—and opened the driver's door. "Come." He gestured to the courier. "You will drive."

"Get the fuck away from my car!" The driver went at him swinging his tire iron, and Bulliard disarmed him and chucked him bodily toward the gutter. He gestured again, impatiently, and the courier darted around the last two guys, mouthing "Sorry." They backed away, eyes wide.

Bulliard held the door open for him, and the courier slipped in. "Sweet ride," he said. "I'll try to leave it somewhere relatively intact, all right?"

"We will drive this back to the forest, once we've acquired the spores," Bulliard said, climbing into the backseat.

The courier snorted. "Right. Because this car sure isn't conspicuous. It's got *flames* painted on the side, mossface. They'll report it stolen, and the cops will stop us, and you'll kill the cops, which will in turn bring *more* cops. Even you can't withstand a blizzard of bullets, am I right?"

Bulliard grunted. "Very well. We will acquire more subtle transport when our business is done."

"Cool. Hey, guys, you want to get your friend off the hood? Otherwise he'll fall off when I start moving."

The two came forward and lifted their friend away. "We'll fucking kill you, man," one of them said, but not very confidently.

"Promises, promises." The courier put the car in gear.

14

Rondeau had no idea what he was going to say to Jason. Bullshitting a professional bullshitter was going to be tough. "It'll just take a minute."

"No," Cam-Cam said. "No more private conversations that don't include me. Is that understood? I've put up the money, we've acquired the spores, and I am a *full* partner now." The chain-wrapped crate was in the middle of his living room, and he stared at it as he spoke, like a religious fanatic gazing upon a holy relic.

"The man's right," Jason said. "We're in this together. What's up?"

"Ah, but it was a call from Marla, and it's, you know . . . sorcerer stuff."

Cam-Cam lifted his calm, serious eyes to Rondeau. "Then I definitely insist on being included."

Rondeau sighed. "Well, okay. A sorcerer from out of town heard about the spores somehow, and came to steal them." Cam-Cam sat up straighter, and a look of an-

noyance flashed across Jason's face—he thought
Rondeau was *improvising,* and Jason had made it clear
that improvising was strictly a no-no at this point.
"Don't worry, Marla took care of him. But unfortunately, this means word got out about the spores being in
town, so we'd better be on our guard." He glanced at
Jason. "Your sister wants us to speed up the transaction
with the Aeromancer, and get the spores out of town
ASAP."

"If you could give me just a second to discuss this
with my associate." Jason's voice was pleasant enough,
and if Rondeau hadn't *known,* he never would have
guessed the grifter was furious.

"No," Cam-Cam said. "I told you, no more shutting
me out. That's the whole point, I'm *in* now."

Rondeau looked Jason in the eye, wishing for telepa-
thy. *"Marla says* we need to wrap this up, Jason. It's not
my call, it's *hers.* I'm sure she has a good reason."

Jason appeared to get it—at least, he frowned, and
looked thoughtful. "This is a delicate operation. She
should know we can't rush things. There are lots of arrangements left to be made."

"Nevertheless, she wants us to make those arrangements with all due haste."

Jason pondered, then shook his head. "No. Can't do
it. Not without risking the whole mission, and I'm not
comfortable letting a bunch of vampires run loose just
because Marla got spooked. We'll proceed as planned."

"But Marla said—"

"Marla isn't running this op," Jason snapped. "She

runs the city, but she doesn't run *me*. I'll talk to her about it later, all right? You can call and tell her that."

Well, he'd given it his best shot. Marla would have to play the heavy and make Jason drop this … but what if bad shit happened in the meantime? He opened his phone and called Marla's office, but there was no answer, and when he tried her cell, he got nothing but voicemail. He talked as if she were on the line. "Marla, Jason says things are too delicate to—I *told* him. But you said you neutralized—oh. Shit. Shit shit shit. Okay. Yes, okay, you got it." He shut the phone. "Marla says she has reason to believe we're in *imminent* danger, and we need to get us, and the spores, to a safe location." There were safehouses all over the city, but he was thinking of his nice cozy club, particularly the secret conference room hidden in a broom closet in the back. That room had magic-deadening capabilities, rendering the spells of most sorcerers useless, and if some big bad out-of-towner did manage to track them there, they wouldn't be able to do a lot of damage.

"This is dreadful," Cam-Cam said, but he looked more excited than anything else.

"This is … unexpected," Jason said. "I don't think—" His phone rang, and he answered, then frowned. "Cam-Cam, do you know anybody who drives a low-rider Chevy Impala convertible?"

Rondeau thought it must be Danny on the phone—he was supposed to lurk around the grounds and fake another vampire attack later on.

"No, I don't think so," Cam-Cam said. "Who are you talking to?"

"We've got eyes everywhere." Rondeau was trying to keep up his end of the scam, but he had the feeling things were about to crater, and fast. Something was happening, and it couldn't be good.

"Fuck!" Jason said, eyes widening. "They just— somebody just took out the guard at your gatehouse, and they're coming up the driveway now."

"Panic room," Cam-Cam said, in a distinctly unpanicky voice. "Help me with the spores."

Rondeau and Jason both looked at the box. If something *was* attacking them, they didn't have much interest in carrying an empty crate, but the show must go on. "You go ahead and get the room open," Jason said. "We'll bring the box."

"It's just down this hall, to the right." Cam-Cam hurried away.

Jason and Rondeau crouched and lifted the box. "What the *fuck* is going on?" Jason grunted as they rose with their burden.

"Somebody heard about the spores," Rondeau said. "A big bad someone. They're coming to steal them. Marla took one guy out, so this must be another. And there might be more. That's why she wanted us to wrap this up, before we got hurt."

"The things aren't even fucking *real*." Jason's whisper was harsh and disbelieving. "Sure, Cam-Cam buys it, but people with *weight* believe this magic shit?"

"You'd be surprised."

"So where's my sister now? Shouldn't her organization be protecting us?"

"She's dealing with her own issues," Rondeau said.

"But I can call her consigliere...when I get my hands free."

"This is ridiculous," Jason said. "A beautiful play like this, blown because some morons can't tell fantasy from—"

"Come *on,*" Cam-Cam called from the end of the hall, and they followed. The room held a few bookshelves, but one wall was solid steel, with an imposing door standing open. Inside was a well-appointed, if small, room, with a cot, a shelf of rations, and a bank of surveillance screens.

"Sweet," Rondeau said. Jason grunted and backed into the panic room, Rondeau following, and Cam-Cam pulled the door shut behind them. As they set down the box—which didn't leave a lot of room inside the panic room for them—Cam-Cam turned on the screens.

One showed a convertible parked in the driveway, empty. "They're in the house." Cam-Cam pushed buttons and flipped through views. Abruptly, the screen showing the living room went dark, but it was just the lights going out, not a camera malfunction. "They cut the power," Cam-Cam said. "But the cameras are on a separate circuit, and this room has its own generator."

"Call your man," Jason said, and Rondeau nodded.

His cell phone didn't work. "Uh, I'm not getting any reception—"

"These are three-inch-thick steel walls. Of course you aren't getting reception," Cam-Cam said.

Rondeau swore. Why couldn't he have a sweet magical cell phone like Marla's, which got reception practically anywhere? Probably because he used to have one, and lost it, and Langford had refused to waste time building him another.

"Here, use the landline." Cam-Cam gestured, and Rondeau picked up the handset.

"It's dead."

"That's impossible. It's secure, the line is heavily armored." Cam-Cam picked up the phone, stabbed at the buttons a few times, then shook his head. "It must be . . . sorcery."

"Right, because that's more plausible than a technical difficulty," Jason said. "Fuck. So we're trapped in here. Okay. But at least whatever's out there can't get in *here,* right?"

"Right." Cam-Cam nodded. "It's impregnable. I had an acquaintance who suffered a home invasion a few years ago, and after that happened, I had this room installed. Besides, I hit the alarm when we closed the door, so the police should be coming soon." He frowned. "But, you know, it's not a *silent* alarm, and it should be making quite a racket."

"It seems not." Rondeau started to say that sorcerers were really good at neutralizing things like phones and alarms, but didn't like to contemplate the nasty look Jason would probably give him. "I think we should assume we're on our own." Rondeau also doubted this room would keep out a determined sorcerer. Sure, it was tough, and it would probably slow the bad guys down, but wielders of magic had a way of making openings where they were needed.

"Where are they?" Jason said, leaning over the screens.

A young man dressed in black ambled into sight of the camera trained just outside the panic room's reinforced door. The room was dim, lit only by moonlight through the windows, but he looked to be in his twenties, with messy hair—not a particularly imposing sight. "Can, uh, you guys hear me?"

Cam-Cam pressed a button beside a microphone. "We can. What do you want?"

"Me? The sweet release of death, at this point. But my, uh, let's say 'employer' wants the whatchamacallit spores. You probably oughta hand them over."

"Go to hell!" Jason shouted, and the guy winced.

"Okay. Nice knowing you. Not that I know you... never mind." The guy stepped back, and someone—or something—else entered the room. It was shambling, bearlike, and hardly looked human.

The thing—the sorcerer—drew close to the door. "There are no magical wards here," it rasped. "Only steel. Not even silver or iron, but steel. This will be but the work of a moment."

A horrible squealing sound came from the door, which visibly shivered in its frame. Cam-Cam opened a cabinet and took out a pistol, and Jason drew a gun from his own waistband. "What the *hell,*" he said.

"Sorcery," Rondeau said simply. He didn't have a gun, but he had other weapons, and he wasn't thinking of his butterfly knife—which, against whatever *this* guy was, would be as useless as Jason's and Cam-Cam's guns.

Jason looked at him and frowned, and then the door tore loose with a horrible wrench and the stink of burning metal. Jason raised his gun and squeezed off a couple of shots, shockingly loud in the enclosed space, but they didn't appear to make much of an impression on the thing in the doorway. Rondeau figured it was a person, somewhere under the matted vegetable matter and fungal reek—like something from under a rotten log—but it was hard to be sure.

"Where are the spores?" it said.

"In the box," Cam-Cam said promptly. "Take it, with our compliments."

The sorcerer shoved his way in, and they all pressed back as far as possible to make room. Jason was staring at the sorcerer, then at his gun, and then back again. The sorcerer—was it Bulliard, not quite as dead as Marla thought?—grabbed the box by one of its chains and dragged it out into the wider space outside the panic room. "This must be very well warded," he said, bending down and snuffling. "I sense nothing inside it at all."

Rondeau and Jason exchanged glances.

"These chains are not magical. These runes are meaningless." Bulliard tore apart the chains like they were rotten twine. He began tugging on the well-bolted lid.

"Don't open that!" Cam-Cam shrieked. "The spores, there's no telling what they're programmed to do, they'll kill us all!"

"All of you, perhaps." Bulliard paused in his efforts and looked at them. "But I have nothing to fear from any spore." Brown mushrooms popped up under his hands, along the seams of the crate, and the wood rotted and burst. Bulliard tore open the crate like a man ripping apart a dinner roll, and pulled out the welded metal box inside. Evidently frustrated, Bulliard slammed the box against the exterior wall of the panic room once or twice, and one of the welded seams popped open. The sorcerer slipped a finger under the crack and pulled, ripping open the box and spilling the contents onto the floor.

"A lead pipe," he said, looking at the items at his feet. "A bucket." He kicked the five-gallon bucket, knocking off the tightly sealed plastic lid, and sand and water poured out.

"Also some packing peanuts and Bubble Wrap," the sorcerer's associate—apprentice? slave? herald?—said cheerfully. "Hell of a haul, boss."

"There are no spores here." Bulliard kicked through the ruins of the crate Danny had so carefully fabricated, and loomed in the doorway of the panic room. "You have *wasted my time*. You have wasted the *Mycelium's* time." He extended his filthy hands, mushrooms sprouting from his palms and fingertips, and advanced into the panic room.

"You guys are fucked," Bulliard's assistant said.

B was having a dream.

He was a bodiless floating entity, unable to control his movements, looking down on the world. Below was a forest of mushrooms towering high as buildings, their caps as broad as the decks of aircraft carriers and curved like domes, red and white and green and orange, sending up a collective stink of rot and sweetness and meaty scents, mingled into a disgusting aromatic mélange. As B swooped down past the caps, in among the high stems, nodes of bluish and greenish bioluminescence sparked to pale brightness, illuminating the ground below.

Rondeau wandered in the forest beneath, lost, clothes torn, blood running from wounds in his chest, stumbling and calling out. B tried to go to him, to help his friend, but he may as well have been a bit of dandelion fluff in the wind, floating without volition. Rondeau stumbled and fell, sinking into a thick peaty mass that closed over him like tar in a pit. Suddenly B was *there,* inches from Rondeau's sinking form, trying to reach out for him, but with no hands, he couldn't. Rondeau sank into the reeking mulchy earth, and was lost to—

"Darkness," whispered a voice, but it was a whisper in timbre and not in volume; in volume it was the voice of a god, perhaps the voice of Bulliard's god, the Mycelium. "Oblivion. Darkness. Oblivion. Darkness. Darkness. Darkness."

B sat up in a dark place the size of a closet, trembling, hungry, exhausted. But that dream, it was one of *those* dreams, a message from wherever his messages came from, and he didn't need an oracle to interpret it, at least not the broad outlines—Rondeau was in danger, and B needed to save him.

He stood up, eyes adjusting to the gloom, and found himself in what seemed to be a closet...or a cell. Where was he? What had happened? Hadn't they *won?* He went to the door, where there was no knob, only a window blocked with a metal grate, and he pounded, shouting, "Hey! Let me out of here!"

"Ah, young master Bowman," rasped Viscarro from outside the door. "You're awake." The door creaked open. Viscarro was in the hall, leaning on a crutch—except it wasn't a crutch, but a long-barreled rifle.

"Why did you lock me up?"

"I remain under Bulliard's influence, though he is not exerting direct control, and I find myself temporarily at liberty. Marla cut out the mushrooms at my neck, but there are others, at the base of my spine." Viscarro held out a hunting knife, hilt toward B, and B took it. "Cut them out of me before Bulliard decides I'm still useful."

"How did Bulliard even get *away*?"

"I told Marla I would lock him up. Then, when Marla was gone, I let him go. I haven't been myself today. Now, please, the mushrooms?" Viscarro hop-turned around, lifting up his shirt to reveal a cluster of pale pink mushrooms sprouting at the base of his knobby spine.

"Do I, ah . . ."

"Take as much of the flesh as you must, and try to pull the mushrooms out carefully—the roots are wormed into my spinal column, tapped into my nervous system."

B knelt, cutting. "I don't have time for this. My friend—"

"Is in danger, yes, of course, I'm sure, but if you *don't* do this, and Bulliard reasserts his control over me, you'll never make it out of my lair alive, Mr. Bowman."

B worked intently, ending up with a few shreds of dead flesh and four intact mushrooms with trailing roots.

"Toss them on the floor, please." Viscarro held a can of lighter fluid—where had he gotten *that* from? B complied, and Viscarro squirted the mushrooms, then muttered some phrase under his breath, and the flesh and fungi caught merry fire, shriveling to blackness. "Very nice. That's all. You can run along."

"Where am I? How do I get out?"

"That depends on where you need to go."

"I—" He paused. "Fuck. I don't know."

"That is a snag."

"I need an oracle."

"I gather they come when you call."

"Yes, but—" He turned, and turned about, and went down the grimy hallway, shoving open the door to another cell, where iron shackles dangled from the wall. The shackles were empty...but there was a scatter of old yellow bones on the floor. "There's something here," B said, that dreamy feeling stealing over him. He drifted into the cell, staring at the bones. "Hey there."

"Hey," said the dead man in the cell, fragments of bone rising up to float in his otherwise ghostly form—a couple of fingers, a few fragments of spine, the orbit of an eye socket. He was haggard, a portrait of a starved man drawn in pale blue smoke.

"Fascinating," murmured Viscarro from the hallway behind him, but B hardly noticed.

"I had one of *those* dreams," B said.

"I know. Your friend is in danger, from an unexpected source."

"What can I do?"

"Rondeau will die, if you don't go to him."

"But if I go, I can save him? He'll live?"

"That's right." The dead oracle lifted a ghostly cigarette to his mouth and drew deep of the smoke, which was exactly the same color as his body. "If you go fast enough."

"Where?"

"A mansion, on a hill, with a view of the bay and the city. You can get there quickly, as the pigeon flies—down this hall, up through the first drain in the ceiling, then fly north by northeast for five minutes, look for the big estate with the Spanish tile roof." The ghost paused, bones bobbing, then said, "And the convertible Impala parked out front."

"Got it. Can I—"

"Keep asking questions, and it won't be fast enough. Just so you know."

B nodded. "Okay. What kind of payment do you require?"

"That son of a bitch behind you. He locked me up here. Left me to die slowly."

"Dirty thief tried to steal my treasures," Viscarro said. "The apprentices know the rules. Don't feel bad for *him*."

"The payment," B said. "Come on, you said time is short, what do you need?"

"Stab Viscarro in the throat for me," the ghost said.

B spun and drove the hunting knife hilt-deep into Viscarro's throat. The force of the blow knocked the subterranean sorcerer back, and he dropped his crutch and hit the floor of the hallway.

The ghost laughed, and then the bones clattered back to the floor with a sound like tumbling dice.

Viscarro moaned and sat up, pulling the knife out of his throat. "You grazed my voice box." His voice was wreckage and sandpaper.

"Sorry," B said. "Call us even for the false imprisonment." He became a bird and flew away.

Bulliard came at them, Jason fired his useless gun again, and Cam-Cam started shaking his fake amulets and chanting some nonsense he probably thought was a charm of protection or banishment. Rondeau realized he was going to have to step in. Marla didn't want Jason to know about the existence of magic, but a sorcerer with the charm of Charles Manson and the personal hygiene of Peter the Hermit had pretty much blown *that*.

Rondeau Cursed. It was his ability of last resort, a power of unclear origin—some sorcerers believed he was mispronouncing the words of creation, or had tapped into the primal language of incantations, or was insulting natural order in the fundamental language of the universe. However it worked, the Curses had unpredictably destructive results, which generally didn't damage the speaker—but might harm anyone or anything else in the vicinity.

The results of this Curse were particularly disastrous, perhaps because Rondeau was in extremis. The house shook as if in an earthquake, and Bulliard stumbled, falling back and tripping on the remains of the crate, landing on his ass . . . just in time for a large chunk of the ceiling to come crashing down on him.

"Damn," Bulliard's assistant said. "You know, he got dropped *from* the ceiling earlier today, and now you dropped the ceiling *itself* on him. No wonder this dude lives in the woods."

"Who the fuck are you?" Jason brandished his weapon.

"I'm a young man who's eager to meet your bullet," the courier said. "Because, due to the fact that I'm not running away and whooping with joy, I can confirm that Bulliard isn't dead. Bullets didn't kill him—did you think a hunk of ceiling would?"

Bulliard sat up, groaning, showering plaster as he rose. "I will kill you all."

"Whoa, now," his assistant said. "You're pretty beat up, mossface. That skinny dude has some kind of good mojo, too—when he said whatever he said, I felt the heat way back here. And what, exactly, are we fighting for?"

"The spores." He shook his head. "But...Marla spoke truth? The spores do not exist?"

"What is he talking about?" Cam-Cam said. "Why was the crate empty? Were we—did the dealer trick us?"

"That must be it, the dealer—" Jason began.

"It's over, Jason," Rondeau said. "Don't you understand? This guy will kill us to get the spores, or torture us to find out what we know. Shit. There *are* no spores. It was a scam, Bulliard. We were running a game on this guy." He gestured to Cam-Cam. "You got some bad intel, is all."

"I see." Bulliard brushed himself off. "That is... troubling."

"Give us your keys, dude," the assistant said.

"What?" Jason held his gun half up, half down, unsure what to do.

"The keys to that pickup—come on, toss 'em over. I'd

hate for things to get ugly when our, ah, negotiations are going so well."

"Better do it, Jason," Rondeau said.

Jason dug out his keys and flung them to the assistant, who caught them adroitly. "Much obliged. Sorry for the mess."

Bulliard started away, then stopped and turned back. "The Mycelium does not apologize to mortals, but... give Ms. Mason my own regrets. She told me the truth, and I did not believe her. Tell her, if she finds out who gave me this false information—who wasted my time, and the Mycelium's time—and she wishes my assistance in meting out appropriate retribution, I will be *happy* to oblige."

"Consider the message delivered," Rondeau said.

Bulliard withdrew, along with his assistant, who gave them a little wave on the way out.

"That was bracing," Rondeau said.

"You piece of shit," Cam-Cam said. "You lying piece of *shit*, how dare you do this to me?"

Jason ignored him. "All this... magic... It's all *real*?"

"It's not *all* real," Rondeau said. "The spores are total fucking bullshit." He paused. "Likewise vampires."

"You and Marla... you scammed *me*?" Rondeau couldn't tell if Jason was amused or furious.

"Not sure you'd call it a scam, since we didn't *want* anything from you. Marla just wanted to protect you, keep you from getting hurt."

"You don't protect someone by giving them *less* information." Jason's eyes were hard, dead things—definitely not amused, then. "If I'd known the real lay of the land, I could have worked this differently. I could have—"

"Taken me for *more*?" Cam-Cam grabbed Jason's shoulder and tried to spin him around. Cam-Cam was smaller than Jason, though, so it didn't have much effect. "Ripped me off *more efficiently*? You aren't even an initiate in the mysteries? *Nothing* you told me was true?"

"Sorry," Jason said. "You were just a pigeon. I'd hoped to pluck you a lot more thoroughly, but I'll settle for those tail feathers I took off you today."

"You guys all right?" Danny Two Saints was in the doorway, dressed all in black, face streaked with dark facepaint, a walking shadow. "Sorry I didn't step in before, but I had the feeling I was outgunned."

"You believe this shit, Danny?" Jason said. "Sorcerers, all that, it's *real*."

"Hey, if you believe in God and his angels like I do, it only makes sense to believe in the devil and his minions. There are people with powers. I told you about my grandmother with the evil eye. I didn't take Ronnie for, whatever, a black magic kind of guy, but who knows?"

"Fucking *magic*," Jason said, affronted.

"Anyway," Danny said, with the air of someone broaching a difficult subject. "Looks like we've played out this string. We got a nice sack of cash out of it. I say we blow this guy off." He nodded toward Cam-Cam.

"You won't get away with this," Campion said. "I'm a rich man. I have *resources*. I'll hunt you down, and see that you suffer."

"I know you would," Jason said, almost kindly. "But we won't let you."

Jason lifted his pistol and shot Cam-Cam twice in the chest.

"That's done, then," Danny said.

Rondeau stared at Cam-Cam, who only gasped once or twice after he fell, blood welling up from his chest like water from a spring, then slowing as he went still. "You—you *killed* him."

"Not our preferred form of the blow-off," Jason said. "But an acceptable method that's served us well in the past." He looked meditatively at Cam-Cam's corpse, then sighed. "I guess you'll have to tell Marla about this."

"Um," Rondeau said. He occasionally did stupid things—trusting Jason was apparently one of them—but he wasn't a stupid man. "No way. I'm standing here, I'm an accessory to the crime, I can't tell anyone without incriminating myself, right? It's our secret. Marla never has to know."

"That's right," Danny said. "He's right, isn't he, Jason?"

"When you're right, you're right," Jason said.

"Still," Danny said. "Even so."

"Even so." Jason pointed his gun at Rondeau, and pulled the trigger.

Rondeau had never been shot before. Being hit in the chest with a sledgehammer might have been comparable—or perhaps swallowing a bomb. All sensation in his legs instantly vanished, and he fell, an agony of ripping and tearing filling the upper half of his body. His heart was like a terrified animal in his chest, backed into a corner and fighting for its life. Staring at the ceiling, his vision began to go white at the edges, and there was a strange heat on his skin. The blood running out of him, he supposed. Someone seemed to be turning a knife in his lungs, too. A hot knife. After a few eternal seconds, though, the pain began to recede and everything became strangely distant.

I will take Jason's body when I die, Rondeau thought, calmly. Knowing the immortality of his mind—or soul, or psyche, or whatever—had always been a comfort to him, and made him cocksure and reckless. He hadn't anticipated the *pain* of dying, but he knew, for him, dying was not an ending, but simply a doorway. He would pass through that door, climb into Jason's head, and shove out the man's poisonous soul. Then he would raise Jason's gun and kill Danny Two Saints. Having a plan made him feel better. Almost serene.

"He's bleeding out," Danny said. Rondeau was surprised he could hear so clearly, that conversations could go on in the wake of the gunshot's tremendous noise. "But he's not dead. Want me to put one in his head?"

"Nah," Jason said. "It would spoil the scene. We need to stage the bodies, make it look like Cam-Cam shot Rondeau, and Rondeau shot Cam-Cam. Provide a good convincer for the CSI types. You got that covered?"

"Yeah, yeah," Danny said. Rondeau felt a gun shoved into his hand, and his arm lifted, and his finger mashed against the trigger until the gun went off. "One shot in the wall, powder on the hands," Danny said, half to himself. Rondeau tried to hold on to the gun, to use it on Danny, but it fell from his loose fingers. He heard himself moan, distantly.

"Now for Cam-Cam. Give me your gun, Jason. You know, Cam-Cam *had* a gun, probably registered in his name and everything, you should've shot Rondeau with that."

"These weren't laboratory conditions, Danny. You play the hand you're dealt."

"Truer words."

"Sorry about that, Ronnie." Jason nudged Rondeau with his toe. "But if word got back to Marla that I offed Cam-Cam, she'd...think ill of me. And that would spoil things. I need her to trust me, at least for one more move."

"Speaking of which, since things are fucked all to hell here, how fast do you want to move on Part Two?" Danny said.

"Tonight works for me."

"You aren't worried about, you know...she's a witch? Sorceress? Whatever the fuck? She might be hard to bump off."

"Not really. I'm her brother. She won't expect an attack from me. Ronnie here can do some spooky shit—or he could, before his lung started collapsing—but I got the drop on him just fine. It's all about the element of surprise. I'll call Marla, break the bad news to her about her friend dying at Cam-Cam's hands, she'll be consumed by grief, etc."

"Gotcha," Danny said. "She's sad, you can make it look like a suicide. We'll put out the word she was fucking Rondeau here, they were closer than anybody thought, she couldn't live without him, yadda yadda."

"Not...hurt...Marla," Rondeau said.

"Sorry for that, too," Jason said. "But her being alive stands in the way of me inheriting her fortune, so something has to be done."

"It's not often a mark sets herself up that way," Danny said from somewhere off to the right. There was another gunshot. "Putting you in her *will*? She's asking to get her ticket punched."

"I was as surprised as you were, but she just has faith in brotherly love, Danny. She's in my will, too, as far as that goes. If she was still dirt poor and didn't have anything worth inheriting, she wouldn't have a thing to worry about. But since she's rich, well..."

"Guess that's the downside of success," Danny said. "Okay, we're all set here. You were careful about prints?"

"You know I was."

"Then we should be all right, I think. We should blow before the cops get here. Even way up here in a house on a hill, somebody must've heard that commotion. Careful going around Ronnie—don't step in that blood puddle. Footprints, we don't need."

"You don't think he'll survive for the paramedics, do you?" Jason said.

"Unless he's got a couple more gallons of blood than the average guy, he won't last another ten minutes."

"Why?" Rondeau mouthed, hoping to keep them here until he died, and was free to steal Jason's body.

But Jason only said, "For the money, stupid," and then they were gone.

15

Bradley flew, and even in his anxiety and worry for Rondeau, there was a joy in flying and being a bird, even a humble pigeon. He flapped and rode currents until he saw a likely mansion below, a sprawling estate ringed by a high wall, and there, a circular drive with a convertible parked by the front door. B landed on the hood of the car—it was still warm, the engine running—and transformed into himself. The sudden return of his full weight staggered him, and he slid from the hood and sat on the asphalt drive. He was very tired. He'd done too much today, pushed reality around more than was good for him, and his mind and body were crying out for rest. But before he could fall down and sleep, he needed to help Rondeau. It wasn't fair, but there it was. You ate what the world brought to your table.

B got to his feet unsteadily and lurched toward the open front door of the mansion. Inside was darkness, and he almost whispered a charm to step up his night-vision, but he might have more pressing needs for magic soon, and he didn't dare waste any of his feeble reserves of energy. His eyes would adjust.

There were many rooms in the mansion, but he followed the terrible smell of gunpowder, the terrible sound of silence. In a small room, scattered with wrecked bits of wood and metal, lit mainly by the moonlight through the windows, he found two bodies, and one of them was Rondeau, his face slack, blood all over his chest.

B went to his knees beside Rondeau and touched his throat, where a pulse staggered along like a drunk on the edge of collapse. "Rondeau, can you hear me?"

Rondeau's eyes didn't flutter open; they snapped. "B," he said, voice thready as his pulse.

"It's okay, I'll get Marla, I'll get help. You'll be okay." B was no doctor—he'd never even played one in a movie. Rondeau looked bad, but sometimes even minor wounds looked bad, didn't they? People bounced back from all sorts of things, and with the attention not just of doctors but also of magicians, Rondeau would have a better chance than most.

"Dying," Rondeau said.

"No way." B tried to sound upbeat. "I consulted an oracle, and it said I would save you. So don't sweat it. The universe has spoken." B wadded up his jacket and pressed it against the wound in Rondeau's chest, where blood was still leaking out. He fumbled one-handed with his phone, trying to think who to call—Marla, Hamil, 911? He'd never felt so helpless, watching his friend breathe shallow and ragged, clearly close to breathing his last.

B had learned to turn into a bird, to live without breathing, to drag the past into the present, to bend space itself—but why hadn't he learned anything *useful*? To heal wounds. To turn back time. To keep the people he cared about safe.

Before B could dial his phone, Rondeau grabbed his wrist with surprising strength.

"*Listen*," he said. "I'm *dying*. Run."

"What? I—"

"*RUN!*" Rondeau shouted, an effort that clearly took almost everything he had left, and suddenly Bradley understood. He'd come to save Rondeau...and now Rondeau was trying to save him.

Bradley stood, tried to turn into a bird, didn't have the strength, and settled for running away.

He tripped on a piece of chain and sprawled face-first on the floor, just in time to hear Rondeau's last long exhalation. He pushed himself up, wondering how long he had, if it was seconds or minutes or—

But he didn't have any time, of course. The oracle had told him Rondeau wouldn't die. Bradley just hadn't asked the right follow-up questions. It was all about knowing what to ask. He'd received hints, but hadn't understood them. The voice of his own doom had been overwhelming, so strong he'd been unable to bear it, so strong he'd banished it from his own mind.

Bradley's world dissolved. He'd suffered from migraine headaches when his psychic powers first manifested, marathons of agony complete with hallucinatory lights and thought-destroying pulsations of pain. This was far worse. Pain, light, something alien in his head turning and gnawing and clawing and biting, and then the light receded. He couldn't fight. There was no fighting this. He was lost. He wondered if the thing in his head—the thing that had been his friend, once—could hear his thoughts. He thought, *It's not your fault*. He thought, *You can't help your nature*. He thought, *I did save you*.

Then he thought nothing.

Darkness. Oblivion. As promised.

After the Giggler's corpse was taken away to Langford's lab and Nicolette's snoring form was hauled off to Blackwing, Marla left Nicolette's building—scratch that, the currently untenanted building—and pondered her next move. She hadn't eaten yet. Dinner would be good. She wondered if Rondeau and Jason were done gaining their ill-gotten gains. She figured she might need to talk Jason down from being really pissed off at having his scam unceremoniously ended, and she might as well get fed while she got yelled at. Nicolette's phone was still in her pocket, so she called Rondeau, and Jason, but neither answered, and neither did B. He might still be sleeping, but ... she called Viscarro's direct line to check.

"Marla," he said, his voice strange and labored. "I've been trying to reach you. I have information."

"So spit it out."

"Bulliard is not dead. He was merely pretending."

"Oh, fuck. Did he escape?"

"Not escape exactly. I opened the door to his cell for him."

"You did *what*?"

"I was still in his thrall. There were mushrooms left, in the base of my spine, that you did not cut out. Fortunately, some time after Bulliard left, Bradley Bowman regained consciousness, and cut the last mushrooms out of me."

"Shit on a *biscuit*. Where's B now?"

"I gather he had a vision of some kind. He summoned an oracle, which told him only he could save Rondeau's life, and then...flit. He turned into a bird and fluttered away."

"Where did he go?"

"Out a sewer grate and north by northeast, though beyond that, I couldn't say. Someplace within a few minutes of flying for a pigeon, apparently."

Cam-Cam's mansion. If B was going to save Rondeau, that was the likeliest place—Rondeau didn't spend much time in the northeast part of the city otherwise, being more a south-of-the-river kind of guy. "Goddamn you, Viscarro, you're more trouble than you're worth."

"*You're* supposed to defend the city from insane interlopers, Marla. It's not my fault you fell down on the job. In fact, I understand Bulliard's presence is rather *because* of you."

"Tou-fucking-ché, you walking corpse." She snapped the phone shut, then immediately called Hamil. "Shit has impacted fan at Mach 1. Bulliard—"

"Was just spotted leaving the city crouched in the back of a pickup truck," Hamil interrupted, "driven by his enslaved courier associate. Do you want us to give chase?"

Marla, rarely indecisive, had to think for a moment. "Send someone to follow him at a discreet distance. Someone expendable. If Bulliard's done something bad, we might need to get our hands on him, but if he's just tearing out of town because we kicked his ass so bad, I say let him go."

"All right. Hold on, Marla, I have a call on the other line—"

"Damn it, Hamil, don't you put me on hold!"

"It's a call on my *private* line, Marla, and since I'm already talking to *you*, that means there are only a handful of people it could be, all certainly worth anwering."

"Okay, take it."

The phone clicked, and Marla paced back and forth on a corner, black cloak flapping, torn between hauling ass to Cam-Cam's mansion and waiting to see what Hamil's mystery caller had to say first.

He clicked back over. "It was Bradley. He sounded . . . jumbled. Apparently he just came from Campbell Campion's mansion. I don't know what went on there, but B said you should meet him at the club, that it's vitally important he speak to you right away. He's there now. He said it's a matter of death."

"Life and death?"

"He only said 'death,'" Hamil said, and Marla felt something in her heart go cold.

"Okay. Send some guys up to Cam-Cam's and see what's happening. I'd better go see B."

"I hope it's nothing too serious," Hamil said.

"A matter of death? How could that be serious?" Marla closed the phone.

* * *

When Marla arrived at the club, B was in her office, sitting in one of the mismatched chairs on the visitor's side of her desk, holding his head and weeping. Marla, mentally preparing herself for the worst, put her hands on his shoulders. If anything, that made him sob harder. "B. It's Marla. I need you to tell me what's happened." She paused, not wanting to say it aloud, but forced herself: "Did something happen to my brother? Or to Rondeau?"

"Oh, no." His voice hitched with restrained sobs as he lifted his face to hers. "Rondeau's just *dandy*. And Jason, Jason's fine, Jason's just exactly how he's always been."

Marla moved the other chair so she could face him and sat down. She'd never seen B like this—his tropical blue eyes seemed to look over some inner wasteland. "Then what's wrong? What happened?"

"I always thought it would be like taking a stroll," B said dully, looking at something far away. "I thought, when my mind left my body behind—my *host* behind— I would look around, pick a new body, walk around the place, kick the tires, saunter in, and take up residence. But Marla, ah, Marla, it was so much worse. It was like *drowning*. When my body died, I was forced out, and suddenly I had no lungs, no heart, no flesh, no bones— but I was so afraid. How is that possible? I thought fear was about the body, that's what you always say, fear's just the glands and hormones talking, you can control it. But I couldn't control it. I floated up, I saw my corpse, and then ... and then ..."

He broke down again. Marla stared at him. "B. I

don't understand. Was this a vision you had? One of *those* dreams?"

"I grabbed on to him," B whispered. "I saw him there, the only warm body close by, and I just grabbed on. When people are drowning, they panic, don't they? Sometimes they even drown the people trying to rescue them, they grab on and pull them under. That's what I did. He came to rescue me, and I pulled him under. I lost him in the depths."

Marla reached out and took his hands. "B, what do you—"

"I'm not *B*!" he shouted, jerking away his hands. "I'm not B—don't you understand, B's dead, I killed him, I stole his *life*." He stood up, walked to the wall, and punched it, hard.

Marla stood up, her dagger in her hand, tears welling in her eyes. "No. No, no, no. You aren't telling me this."

He turned to face her. "I am. I did. Marla…I'm Rondeau. I'm in B's body, but I'm *Rondeau*."

Marla crossed the room, slammed him against the wall, and pressed her forearm against his throat. The knife in her other hand waited, ready for whatever she chose to do with it.

"Marla," B—or Rondeau, the monster she'd always called Rondeau, wearing her apprentice's body like a *suit*—gasped around the weight against his throat. "I wish you could kill me. But then I'd only take your body, and I'd go insane from the guilt of it, Marla, I would, so please don't."

Marla stepped back, and B—no, Rondeau, she had to remember he was Rondeau—slid down the wall, sitting.

She had to get herself under control. She took a deep breath, exhaled, took another, and said, "Tell me what happened. And if you lie to me, I'll know, and I'll *hurt* you."

"I wouldn't lie to you." He stared at the air before his face. "Though you might not believe me. And you can hurt me if you want. I deserve to be hurt. B had a vision that I was in danger. He was right. I was shot. I was dying. He came to help me, but I knew I didn't have long to live. I told him to run, but he didn't understand at first. By the time he did understand, it was too late. My body died, and whatever I *am* floated up out of me and looked for a new host. I didn't have a *mind* then, exactly, Marla. Or, I did, but it was lost under the fear. You know how people become when their lives are in danger, when the veneer cracks and the animal takes over, and they do whatever they must to survive, no matter how horrible. That's what I did. There was no one around, no potential hosts, no one except B. And he . . ." He shook his head. "B is lost."

"You're a monster," Marla said. "I always knew, in the back of my head, what you were. You stole the body of some starving street kid, you stole his *life,* but I never knew that kid, so I didn't have to think about it. Maybe I even thought you did the kid a favor, saved him from a life of misery and violence, gave him release from his pain. But this . . . You didn't do Bradley any favors. You murdered him."

"If I could commit suicide without killing someone else, I would," Rondeau said, and she'd never heard him sound more serious.

Marla didn't want to believe him. She wanted to believe he was a calculating monster, a psychic parasite who used and took without regard for the human cost...because then she could give in to her rage, she could kill him, and it would be a righteous thing.

But she'd known him for too long. And he'd known B. Rondeau and Bradley had been friends. Hell, they'd even been lovers, briefly, on a prior trip to California. She believed Rondeau regretted taking B's life.

But just because Marla believed him didn't mean she could forgive him, any more than she could if he'd accidentally run B over with a car.

She sat down in a chair. "You need to get out of my sight, Rondeau. Take a long vacation. Come back when...Don't come back. Not until I call you."

"I can take a boat out, by myself onto the bay," he said. "Onto the ocean. If I go far enough out, and jump in, maybe I'll drown, and if there are no people around, maybe..."

"Don't risk it. There could be a scuba diver. Guy in a shark cage. Somebody passing overhead in an airplane. You could never be sure. And who knows. You might just float, blow on the wind, until you find a new host. You're probably unkillable." She laughed, harshly. "We used to think that was a feature, not a bug."

"I'll go, Marla...but I need to tell you more first. About how I died. About who killed me."

"I assume the scam went bad," Marla said. "I assume Cam-Cam realized he was being played, and got violent. Guys like him always have guns in the house—they think they have so much to protect. Am I right?"

"Close. But wrong. Marla . . . You won't like this."

"That's good. I'd hate to change the tone of the evening."

"That sorcerer, Bulliard, wasn't really dead."

"I heard."

"He tracked us somehow. He busted in on us—Jason, Cam-Cam, and me. He tore open the crate, the big crate that was supposed to have the Borrichius spores inside, and when he found out it was empty . . ."

Marla looked up. "He killed you? Did he hurt Jason? He must have, you didn't take *his* body. Shit, Rondeau—"

"No, I said Jason's fine. When Bulliard found out there were no spores, he was pissed, but I Cursed him and drove him away. I guess he didn't see anything worth fighting for at that point, so he just left. But when Cam-Cam realized he'd been scammed, that we'd been playing him all along. . . . Marla, Jason shot him."

"In self-defense." She didn't phrase it as a question.

"No. Cam-Cam was pissed, but not violent. Jason gunned him down. Cold blood. He said it wasn't an elegant blow-off, but one that had served him well in the past."

"Fuck."

"Then Jason shot me, Marla. The old me, my old *body*. He and his friend Danny Two Saints staged the bodies, made it look like Cam-Cam and I killed each other. They left, and a couple of minutes later B showed up, and, well, you know what happened from there."

Marla rubbed her temples. "Okay. Damn it. Jason said he was done with that heavy shit, but I should have known better."

"He's your brother, Marla. Of course you wanted to believe your brother."

"Don't you try to comfort *me*, you body-snatching piece of shit." She stared at him, trying to burn a hole through him with her gaze alone, and he looked away.

"Jason also said he wasn't really in it for the money, that he just grifted because he loves the game, but that's bullshit, Marla. It's all about the money. He and Danny talked, while I was lying there bleeding. They're planning on killing you."

"That doesn't make any sense. What's the angle? They think you're *dead*, there's no reason for them to worry about me finding out the truth."

"You told Jason he was the sole beneficiary of your will. He wants to collect."

Marla scowled. "That's just *stupid*. I don't *have* anything. What, he wants my heaps of dirty laundry? I don't even have a savings account! Everything I have belongs to the office of chief sorcerer, not to me—" She stopped.

"Jason doesn't know that," Rondeau said, which was, of course, just what she'd been thinking. "He didn't even know magic existed until earlier tonight, when a sorcerer attacked us. And just because he believes in magic now doesn't mean he understands the socio-political structure of the council of sorcerers here. He knows you're a rich crime boss, probably figures even if you're hiding some of your ill-gotten gains in secret accounts and false names and front companies, your legitimate assets are still worth plenty."

"He's my *brother*," she said.

"Your brother is a murdering shit."

"Takes one to know one."

"No argument here, boss." Rondeau—gods, but he *looked* like B, her B, who was supposed to be her successor, who was supposed to help keep her temper in check, who was supposed to bring some softness and diplomacy to the operation—stood up. "I'll go now. I've got my—I've got B's cell. Call when you want me. Or don't call at all."

"Maybe I'll ask Langford to find a way to kill you for real," she said.

"Maybe you will," he replied, and went away into the night.

"I'm so sorry, Marla." Hamil poured her a brandy, which she accepted. She wasn't much of a drinker, but there was a time and a place, and this was both. They sat in overstuffed armchairs in Hamil's beautifully appointed library, and Marla wondered if she could still cry, or if that capacity had dried up out of her. "Bradley was a very promising prospect, and I know how you felt about him." He paused. "I do wonder how you're feeling about Rondeau now."

"That's one of the questions, isn't it? I always knew what Rondeau was capable of, but I never really thought through the implications. He was just my unkillable sidekick. If someone got the drop on us and put a bullet in him, why, he could just steal the shooter's body and turn the tables. I used to think he was my ace in the hole, but now he feels more like a stick of old dynamite sweating nitroglycerin—he could go off at any time. What if we're together somewhere and he chokes on a chicken bone? Has a sudden heart attack and, pop, lights out? If I'm the person standing next to him, what's to stop him from stealing *my* body, and shoving me... wherever he shoved B?"

"We made certain assumptions," Hamil admitted. "We thought he could choose which body he would take over next. None of us realized the experience would be so... primal for him, so driven by panic. He only possessed one body before this one, and apparently the circumstances of that possession were different—Rondeau has few memories before taking over that little boy in the alley, just of drifting in the air. Perhaps that time he had just been born, however he was born... or he'd just arrived from whatever place or plane he came from. We were drawing conclusions from insufficient information. Rondeau is a deep mystery, even to himself, but our day-to-day familiarity with him served to obscure that fact."

"A deep mystery with the potential to kill anybody unlucky enough to be near him. I don't know if I can work with him anymore, Hamil. Even when I get over just flat-out being pissed, and the fear that I might be his next unintended victim... he looks like *B*. How can I work with the guy when every time I look at him, I'm reminded of how he killed one of my best friends in the world?" She finished the brandy and set down the glass, gently, so she wouldn't break it. "In a way, I lost two friends tonight. And my brother. I feel responsible for the death of Cam-Cam, too, since I helped set up Jason's godsdamn scam. When it comes right down to it, everything that happened tonight is my fault." She sighed. "I think I'm so pissed at Rondeau because I'm pissed at *myself*. It's been a bad day."

"Speaking of your brother . . . what are your plans?"

She shrugged. "I wait. He'll call. You better believe he'll call. I'll see what he says, I'll meet him, and . . . I'll ask him some questions. What I do after that depends on his answers."

"Let me know if I can do anything, Marla."

She abruptly rose. "Nope. This is personal, obviously. Not city business. I'll deal with it."

"If not as your consigliere, then I'm here for you as a friend."

"You might want to reconsider that. Being my friend doesn't work out so well. The only thing worse is being my family." She gathered her black cloak about her and went to wait for her brother's call.

The door to the bedroom opened, and Rondeau tensed, but it was only Hamil. "Marla just left."

"Oh." Rondeau put down the monograph he'd been reading—there wasn't a lot of literature by sorcerers on the subject of body-stealing, and nobody did it the way he did, but Hamil had dug up what info he could. "Is she still . . . ?"

"Yes. She is."

"Thanks for taking me in. I didn't know where else to turn."

"You know I've always had a fascination with your true nature, Rondeau. The chance to interview you about your experience was useful."

Rondeau grunted. Hamil was the one who'd arranged the magical surgery for Rondeau to get a new jaw all those years ago, after Marla ripped off his original jaw to use as an oracle. Hamil hadn't done it out of the kindness of his heart, but in exchange for the chance to study Rondeau for a while. They hadn't found out much about his true nature or origins, though. "Glad to be of service." Rondeau couldn't get used to his voice—it didn't sound like his own, but it also didn't sound like his memory of B's voice; he was hearing B the way B sounded to *himself.* He tapped the monograph. "This thing says I might retain aspects of the old body's personality. Is that right?"

"It's a theory. So many things are glandular, hormonal, driven by the flesh, by muscle memory."

"I'm shit with a knife now—I tried. B didn't know how to handle a blade, and I know *intellectually,* but in execution, I'm clumsy. I haven't tried Cursing, because I don't want to wreck up the place, but I bet I lost that, too. Also... I'm pretty sure I'm gay now. I've been thinking about boobs, you know, and about my girl Lorelei, and nada. Could be I'm just depressed, but I don't think so."

"It's certainly possible. You may also have Bradley's... other abilities."

"The visions, you mean?"

"Among other things."

Rondeau sighed. "I guess I could still be of some use to Marla, if that's true. If she'll have me. Do you think she will?"

"I'm unsure," Hamil said. "But I begin to think your

plan might have some merit. That it might ease the transition."

"Yeah?"

"Yes. I can give you the name of a skilled illusionist. He can make you look like—well, like Rondeau again, permanently. So that when Marla sees you, she won't be reminded of Bradley."

"You think I can just pick up my old life where I left off?"

"We've exerted our influence with the police. Your body has been removed from the crime scene, and officially, Campbell Campion was the victim of unknown assailants in a home invasion. If you go through with the illusion, no one needs to know that Rondeau is dead, though Bradley will, unaccountably, have vanished."

"Gods. Where're my, ah, mortal remains?"

"In Langford's freezer. He'd like to dissect it, and see if the brain shows any anomalies, due to its long occupation by . . . whatever you are."

"Guess I don't get a say in the matter."

"I think you should pick your battles."

"Right."

"The illusion will not be easy on you. Your old body was taller than Bradley's, more thin, and the illusory body you see in the mirror won't match your new physical reality—you'll bump your shins and hit your head and misjudge spaces for quite a while, I'd imagine, before you adjust."

"A few bumps and bruises are a small price to pay. Set it up."

"All right. About that . . . other thing."

"Yeah," Rondeau said. "Work on that, too. Find a way to bind me to this body forever, so this never happens again."

"It may not even be possible, but if it is . . . You would give up immortality? You're sure?"

"If this is immortality," Rondeau said, "then give me death."

16

Marla sat in her office, waiting by her phone. The club was quiet—she'd shut off the music, shooed out the customers, and sent the DJ and bartenders home before hanging a "Closed Until Further Notice" sign on the door, scrawled in black Magic Marker on a piece of cardboard and secured with duct tape. Marla didn't read, or pace, or chew her nails, or organize her desk. She just sat, and looked at the triple-locked bottom drawer of her desk, and tried not to think.

The phone rang a couple of hours after midnight.

She picked it up. "Hello, bro."

"Hello, sis." Jason sounded tired. "I'm sorry I didn't call sooner. Things...got ugly. I guess you must have heard."

"I heard."

"I'm sorry. I'm so sorry. It's my fault Rondeau...That Rondeau died."

She considered. "How do you figure?"

"I brought him into this. I wanted to teach him the grift. I didn't expect things to get heavy. This guy came out of nowhere, Marla. Like a wild mountain man, impossibly strong, bullet-proof. I've never seen anything like it."

"His name is Bulliard. He's gone now. Left town."

"That's good, I guess. When he found out there weren't any spores, I thought he was going to kill us. Rondeau's the one who drove him off, I don't know how—I guess maybe *you* know how." A moment, a silence he probably expected her to fill, but she didn't. "Rondeau was really brave, Marla. He saved our lives. And then Cam-Cam, fucking Cam-Cam... once he realized he was being conned..."

"He pulled a gun. Rondeau shot him, he shot Rondeau. That's what the cops say."

"Well... He pulled a gun, he shot Rondeau, and *I* shot Cam-Cam. But my buddy Danny helped me stage it to look the other way, so things wouldn't get... you know, any more complicated. I know it was a shitty thing to do, and I'm sorry. I hope you understand."

Clever boy. If she'd thought the scenario was a little fishy, Jason would have just gone a long way toward assuaging her doubts. If she hadn't heard the truth from the corpse's mouth. "No, I understand, I'm not upset."

"So... Magic, huh? You might've told me."

"I was just trying to protect you, Jason. The way you always protected me."

"I get that. But still... It's a lot to wrap my head around. If I hadn't seen some of that shit with my own eyes, I wouldn't have believed it."

"I guess you know what I am now."

"I guess I do."

No, she thought. *No, you really don't.*

"Want to come have a drink with me? Talk things out? Raise a glass to Rondeau? You and me were just getting close again, and I don't want this bad stuff to drive a wedge between us. Plus, I should give you Ronnie's share of the take, so you can make sure it goes to... whoever should get it."

"That sounds right. Where?"

"You know that bar where we all had dinner, the Foxfire Tavern? I rented it out tonight for a private after-hours party, was planning to celebrate our success. I know it's no time for celebrations, but come over, we'll get a drink."

"When?"

"I'm at my hotel, give me twenty minutes?"

"Sure. See you then."

"I love you, Marlita. I'm sorry again."

"I love you, too, Jason," she said, unsure herself whether or not she was telling the truth.

She looked at the locked bottom drawer of her desk, and decided against opening it. Not yet.

Marla couldn't risk walking through the front door, or even sneaking in through the back, so she teleported to the bar. Teleportation was dangerous, and could trigger migraines, and there was a good chance of dying every time you tried it—there were things lurking in the interstices between universes, and they were hungry, and they had claws. Marla considered the possibility of dying to be a plus rather than a minus. Being eaten by things from the in-between would spare her a lot of pain and heart-sickness.

Unfortunately, she made it there alive, appearing beside a potted plant near the ladies' bathroom. There was a single long tear in the back of her black and silver cloak, where something in the sparkling darkness had reached out and snagged her, but no other damage.

There were a few lights on in the bar, dim, and she heard voices. Jason was there already, of course, sitting in a booth, talking to his accomplice, presumably Danny Two Saints.

"Do you want, you know, a heartfelt greeting or anything?" Danny said. "Last words, like that?"

"Nope. Easier if you just bushwhack her as soon as she comes in."

"Not going to try to fake a suicide? I kind of liked that idea. Elegant."

"Sure, but it's a lot more trouble, and anyway, she's a crime boss. If she pops up floating in the river, nobody will think twice about it. Just a gang thing."

"True." Pint glasses clinked. "Here's to the path of least resistance."

Marla hadn't really doubted Rondeau, but she'd hoped, somehow, he was lying, trying to throw guilt off himself and onto her brother. But it was true. It was all true. She quietly removed her cloak—she couldn't have it flapping—and walked up a wall using the gecko boots, padding silently against gravity, and worked her way spiderlike along the dark, beamed ceiling until she clung over their booth, directly above Danny Two Saints. He was starting to go bald on top. She reached into her pocket for another sleep sachet…and then, instead, reached into another pocket for one of Nicolette's charms. She had several in that pocket, wrapped individually in bits of tissue, and wasn't even sure which one she'd grabbed. Maybe Danny would be lucky. Or maybe whatever charm she chose would be so bad it would kill Jason, too. Then she could tell herself it had been an accident, mere chance—maybe even fate, though she didn't believe in fate any more tonight than she ever had before.

She unwrapped the charm without looking and dropped it onto Danny's head.

The resulting splash was fairly hideous—*Must have been the red paintball*—but did Jason no harm beyond splashing him with blood and other things. He didn't scream, just shouted a curse and jumped out of the booth, looking around wildly, but not looking up. From his point of view, Danny had simply exploded.

Marla had hoped overkill violence would cheer her up, but the hole she was in was far too deep for that.

She fished out the sleep sachet and tossed it at Jason, who dropped like a narcoleptic drunk. Marla spoke the word to make her boots unstick and dropped, turning in the air to land in a crouch. Marla checked Jason's waistband and took away his gun, and the knife in his jacket pocket, and the knife in his other pocket, and the gun in his ankle holster, and sighed. The whole thing depressed her. She went back for her cloak—no reason to cause trouble by leaving her clothing at the scene of a messy death—then picked her brother up in an over-the-shoulder carry. She contemplated the walk back to the club, and thought, *Fuck it*. She teleported again.

Her cloak was pretty much entirely ripped off her back by the entities in-between, leaving just a few ragged shreds dangling from her neck like the cape of a post-modern comic book anti-hero, but she was unscathed, and, amazingly, Jason was, too. She wasn't having any luck tempting the uncaring universe into killing her tonight.

She carried her brother to the room that had belonged to B, dumped him on the bed, and locked the door behind her—not manually, but with a spell. A battering ram couldn't have opened it. Marla pulled over a chair, sat down near the foot of the bed, and watched her bloody brother sleep for a while.

Marla took another sachet from a pocket in the remnants of her cloak, a pungent mix of bergamot and geranium, and hurled it at his head. The wakefulness spell jolted Jason upright as if he'd taken a shot of adrenaline to the heart, and he fell off the side of the bed and went sprawling on the floor in his shocked first movements.

"Hey, bro," Marla said.

"Hey, Marlita," he said, rising slowly from the floor. "What's happening?"

"I know what you did, Jason. You know I can do magic, but you don't *get* it. I know things. I can—" Her mouth went a little dry. "I can speak with the dead."

"You can't trust the dead," he said promptly. "The dead are jealous fucking *liars*."

"I know what happened. How you shot Cam-Cam.

How you shot Rondeau. How you planned to kill me, to inherit my fortune." She shook her head. "There's no point in trying to bullshit me. We're past that."

"Okay. So we're past it. What now? You do to me whatever you did to Danny?"

"That depends entirely on the outcome of this conversation."

"Oh, so there's something I can say to make you spare me? Just tell me my line, sis, and I'll say it with gusto."

"I just want to know—"

Jason went for something in his jacket. Marla was across the room in a flash, pulling his fingers back, tearing away the knife he'd had concealed inside. Marla bounced him off the wall and returned to her chair, holding the knife, which was wickedly serrated. Jason leaned against the door across the room, not even looking sulky, rubbing his hand.

"How many goddamn knives do you carry?" she asked.

"When I'm planning to kill my sister, the wicked witch of the East Coast? As many as I can. What's that line from the Bible? 'Thou shalt not suffer a witch to live'?"

"Now you've got religion?"

"My friend Danny, the one you just murdered? He figured you must be in league with the devil to do the things you do. Seems plausible to me."

"It's a theory. Since when do you have anything against deals with the devil?"

"Why didn't you *tell* me?" His eyes were wide and beseeching, and Marla was stunned by the sudden openness of his expression, by the pain in his voice. "You found out something like this, you found magic, and you let me keep going along as I always had, grubbing and grifting, when there was . . . when there was *wonder* out there in the world?"

Marla shook her head. "Won't play. You were planning to kill me before you knew magic was real. Try again."

He relaxed, all that naked pain vanishing in an instant. "Ah, well. Worth a try. You really want to know why, Marlita? Why I planned to kill you, my own sister, my by-God flesh and blood?"

"I really do."

"Because you're *nobody* to me," he said, with relish, as if he'd been waiting a long time to say it. "Once we were family, and we looked out for each other, but that was a lifetime ago. My sister was a little girl with steel in her spine and venom in her tongue, and she was loyal. But that night you left me to my own devices, stuck with a dead body and nobody to help me out, abandoned me after all I'd done for you, that was the night you stopped being my sister. You gave it up, you washed your hands of me, and I returned the favor. In the years since then— not too far off from twenty years, Marla, and that's a lot of years—you've only gone farther away. You aren't my family. Danny, he was my *brother*, he proved himself again and again. But you? You're a stranger who happens to bear a passing resemblance to my little sister, but as far as I'm concerned, my sister is dead and gone. What's more, you're a *rich* stranger. And what I do to rich strangers is, I take their money. I pick a mark, and I use whatever I can against them—if they like gambling,

I become a gambler. If they like art, I become an artist. If they like real estate, I become a developer. If they want their long-lost brother back . . . I become their long-lost brother. And if, when it comes down to the blow-off, I have to kill them, *c'est la* fucking *vie*."

"Guess that explains it, then." She could remember times in her life when she'd felt hollow, and tired, and wretched, but never quite so completely as she did now.

Jason wasn't done. "Fuck, Marlita, you're a *sorcer-ess*."

"Sorcerer," she said absently. "It's like actors, it's sexist to say 'actress.' Same with us."

"Rondeau mentioned that. Before I killed him. You might as well be an alien, as far as I'm concerned. Are you even human anymore?"

"I think inhumanity runs in our family. Why did you kill Rondeau?"

"Because if I hadn't, he would have told you I killed Cam-Cam, and you would have stopped trusting me, and then I would have had a tougher time making you *dead*. That's all. Nothing personal. He was a nice kid."

"He was. He was *my* brother." She was thinking of B, instead of Rondeau, but that was too much to explain, and she was in no mood for explaining.

"Then we're each short a fucking sibling after tonight's events, aren't we?" His eyes were narrowed, and she saw hate looking out at her. She thought it was the first genuine expression she'd seen from Jason since he came to town. "Want to call it a draw?"

"No, I don't." She teleported out of the room, back to her office, and once more, was disappointed when she didn't die along the way. Nothing even scraped her with a claw this time.

She'd made her decision, so she began the laborious process of unlocking the bottom drawer of her desk. It was essentially a magical bank vault in miniature. Viscarro had made it for her, and nothing short of a nuclear strike could have opened it without her say-so. She kept two things inside it. One was the jewel that contained Viscarro's life.

The other, she thought, *is the thing that contains my brother's death.*

Marla didn't teleport back into the room. After three times already, she was going to have a teleportation hangover tomorrow so bad she'd wish for death—just like now, but for new and different reasons. She didn't want to risk becoming lost in the in-between. She'd made a decision, and now she had to follow through.

She opened the door. Jason was lounging on the chair Marla had been using.

"Nice cloak," Jason said. "Very . . . virginal."

"Thanks." Marla drew the white cloak around her. It was only white on the outside. Inside, the lining was the purple of an ugly bruise, or of dyes made from poisonous flowers. Technically, it wasn't actually a cloak. It just looked like one. What it *was,* she couldn't have said, exactly, except that it was old, and malevolent, and sly, and had plans for her. Things like that—objects with minds of their own and powers untold—were usually called artifacts by sorcerers. Other sorcerers were jealous she owned such an artifact, and many coveted it. In that respect, Marla thought they were idiots. "I have to kill you, Jason."

"The feeling's mutual, dear."

She shook her head. "But I don't think I can do it. You're my brother. You're one of the big reasons I am . . . the way I am."

"To my everlasting shame."

"Don't be cruel," she said softly.

"Don't betray me. Oh, wait. That's almost twenty years too late. Oh, well. Life is full of disappointments."

Marla took a breath. With a mental command, she could reverse her cloak, and the purple lining would switch places with the white exterior. Clothed in the purple, she would lose her conscience, her morals, her regrets; she would become a murderous thing, and would not hesitate to rip Jason apart. She'd promised herself she would never use the cloak again, because the toll it took on her mind was too great, and because it was too dangerous, but there was no other way she could bring herself to murder her own brother. "I'm sorry, Jason."

"Oh, moment of truth? Can I have some last words?"

"Of course."

"Just one last word, then: 'bang.' "

Jason suddenly had a little gun, and he shot her in the stomach. She went down, blinded by pain. Gut shots were the worst. She curled up on her side, drawing her knees to her chest, trying to protect the part of her that had already been pierced. Jason had pulled the knife from the lining of his coat, but she wasn't sure where the gun came from—maybe some apparatus up his sleeve?

It'd popped into his hand like a magician's bouquet of silk flowers. He'd played her. Jason had never expected to stab her with the knife—he'd just wanted her to think she'd discovered his last secret weapon, thwarted his final trick. *Got me again, bro.*

"Say hi to Danny when you get to hell," Jason said. "He was a religious man, but let's be honest, guys like us don't get into heaven." He looked at her with cold disinterest, and she knew there was nothing she could say to stir the stone of his heart. He raised the pistol again.

She closed her eyes. She didn't want to watch her own brother shoot her in the head.

Marla woke almost two hours later, weak, with blurred vision, and a headache that was probably equal parts teleportation and head-shot related. She breathed a sigh of relief anyway—she'd had some fear Jason would dump her body somewhere, and that she might lose the cloak in the process, which would have been the end of her.

She sat up, trembling, and unhooked the silver stag beetle pin that held her cloak to her throat. The cloak had healed her—the white side could repair almost any injury, given time, apparently even skull-and-brain-shattering gunshots—but she didn't want the thing on her shoulders anymore. Two lumps of misshapen lead lay on the floor where she'd been left for dead. Keepsakes.

Jason knew she was a sorcerer now, but he still didn't understand what that *meant*. Marla's kind were hard to kill. Apparently Jason's kind were hard to kill, too. She had to admire him. She was also beginning to think she might be able to hate him—which meant, next time they met, she might not need the cloak in order to finish him off.

She dragged the cloak back to her office and stuffed it into the bottom drawer of her desk. After falling heavily into the chair, she reached for the phone—but there was no one she wanted to call. Clawing open the top drawer of the desk, she opened a bottle of powerful painkillers, dry-swallowed three pills, and crawled back to Rondeau's spare room, into the bed.

The mussed covers still smelled like B. They still smelled like Jason. They were smeared with bits of Danny Two Saints' blood. It seemed a fitting bower.

"Will you go after Jason?" Hamil said. "I daresay we could divine his location. You're related by blood, so I could create a sympathetic link—"

"He'll turn up." She sipped a cup of the strong Turkish coffee Hamil favored. After two days, her headache was mostly gone. They were in the front room of the Wolf Bay Café, sitting at a window, watching summer fade outside. "Or he won't."

"If you'd like, I can have someone . . . take care of him. So you won't have to deal with it."

"Jason's my problem. He was never a threat to Felport itself, so it's not right to bring the city's resources into it. It's a personal matter."

"Fair enough."

Without looking up from her coffee, she said, "Is Rondeau okay?"

"He's . . . as well as can be expected. I heard from him yesterday. I check in. Would you like me to give him a message from—"

"No. I don't have anything to say to him." *Yet*.

"I know it doesn't seem like it now, Marla, but things will get better."

"I know they will. I'll *make* them get better."

"What do you mean?"

"I'm going to bring B back to life."

Hamil set his cup down gently. "Marla. Necromancy doesn't bring people back—not really. Even if you can conjure his spirit, it won't be the same. Death changes you. You of all people know that."

"I'm not talking about necromancy."

"Then what?"

"I know people, Hamil. And things that aren't really people. And they owe me favors. I'm going to call them in."

"Do you think that's wise?"

"Wise? No. But necessary."

"Home again." Bulliard sat down in a clearing that looked much like every other clearing they'd passed, plucked what appeared to be a poisonous toadstool, and munched it with relish.

"What the fuck am *I* still doing here?" the courier demanded.

"I have no idea." Bulliard talked with his mouth full. It was disgusting. "The Mycelium desires your presence."

"That's just great." The courier, filthy and exhausted after the long drive—across the fucking country *twice* in less than a week, that was no way to live, even for a slave—sat down in the underbrush.

I am vast, whispered a voice in the courier's head, and the fungal magician sat up—he could hear it, too. *If one part of me is destroyed, I live on. But I have no such redundancy among my followers. I begin to think this is a mistake. Bulliard has...limitations...I had not expected, and needs assistance.*

"No, master." Bulliard rose to his feet. "I need no help, especially not from *this*—"

"Thpt," the courier interrupted. "You couldn't even drive. You couldn't even, like, order a *sandwich*. You're hopeless." He paused. "Not that I'm making a case for my indispensability, here."

You failed. Both of you failed. The spores are not here.

"I was deceived, master." Bulliard put his hand over his heart. "I could not bring you the spores, because they do not exist."

Nevertheless, I am displeased. You will be reprimanded.

"Master, please, don't—" Bulliard didn't get any further before he started to gag and claw at his throat. He fell to the ground and convulsed.

"What the fuck?" The courier scrambled back.

He will not die. I have only allowed the poison in the mushrooms to touch him lightly. But as for you ...

"Strike me down," the courier said, closing his eyes.

So the Mycelium was real. It wasn't just old Bully talking to himself. The discovery was not comforting.

You failed, the Mycelium said. *Why then should I reward you? No, you will remain here, and serve me in those matters where Bulliard cannot. I may occasionally need an ambassador into human lands. You will serve that purpose, and others. In the meantime, your presence will be an ongoing punishment for Bulliard . . . and for yourself. . . .*

"You've got to be shitting—"

Silence, the Mycelium said, and the courier didn't hesitate to obey—not because of any magical compulsion, but because he'd found a whole new field of despair beyond what he'd assumed were his own absolute limits.

This is what I propose, the voice of the Mycelium, the largest organism on Earth, whispered. *Serve me willingly, and gain my strength and exalt me, and be exalted.*

The courier considered. "Do I have a choice?"

Serve unwillingly, and in misery.

The courier sighed, and looked at Bulliard's still-twitching form. "If I say yes, can I give this fucker a kick?"

The Mycelium's answer was, perhaps, coolly amused, or maybe the courier was just projecting. *You may.*

The courier stood, drew back his boot, and planted a kick in the fungal sorcerer's ribs, grunting at the impact. "Fuck." He limped away. "Stubbed my toe." He sat on a log and considered his options. "Same shit, different day." He plucked a poisonous mushroom. "So how do these taste anyway?"

Marla opened one of her unsecured desk drawers and picked up a little silver bell. It was precious, and deep magic, in its way, but it wouldn't work in anyone else's hand, so there was no reason to keep it locked up. She rang the bell.

A pale, beautiful man with long hair and rings on all his fingers came in from a door that ceased to exist as soon as he passed through it. He smiled, a bit distractedly—he'd probably been busy. He usually was. "Marla, dearest, what can I do for you?"

"I have a friend. I *had* a friend. He died a few days ago."

Death's expression became more focused, and concerned. "I'm so sorry. Would you like me to arrange a meeting?"

"No. I want you to restore him to life."

Death whistled. "Marla...There are precedents, of course, one can go into the underworld and retrieve a loved one, but the costs are more than you can afford to pay."

"Even for me? Don't I get...special privileges? Given our history?"

"You're asking this from me as a—a favor? In light of our personal relationship?"

Marla didn't want to make presumptions on this man, who wasn't a man, but who was very important to her, and especially important to her future. But this was for *B,* and she knew that if she was the one who'd died instead of him, B never would have stopped trying to bring her back. "That's right."

"What's his name?"

"Bradley Bowman."

Death's eyes widened. "Ah, yes, him. He went to the underworld, once, when he was alive—years ago." He frowned. "But . . . he's not there, Marla. Nowhere in my realms. You're certain he died?"

Marla closed her eyes. "There were . . . special circumstances. His body is still walking around, but there's a different mind inside it."

"I don't know where his spirit went, Marla, but I'm afraid I didn't claim it. If his body still lives, but his mind is lost . . ." He shook his head. "He is beyond my reach."

"He might just be gone," Marla said. She began to cry. She couldn't help it. Rondeau had shoved Bradley out of the circle of life and death entirely, consigned him to darkness and oblivion. B didn't even get to go to *hell*—he'd just ceased to be.

"I should go," Death murmured. "Call me, anytime, and I'll come."

"I'm sure I'll be seeing you soon enough." She waved him away.

She went to Genevieve next, peeling two dozen oranges and piling the peels in a heap and breathing deep the scent of citrus, her eyes closed. When she opened her eyes, she was in the courtyard of Genevieve's palace in the sky—though it wasn't the sky of any world Marla or anyone else on Earth could look up and see.

"Marla." Genevieve stepped into the courtyard, her caramel-colored hair wild, her violet eyes concerned. She was a psychic, and more—a reweaver, capable of altering existence itself to suit her wishes, capable of dreaming new realities into being. Genevieve's powers were so vast and dangerous that she'd voluntarily absented herself from Earth, to a pocket universe of her own creation . . . but she and Marla kept in touch.

"I need your help, Gen." Marla extended her hand, and Genevieve touched it briefly. She wasn't much for physical affection, which suited Marla. She didn't have to explain herself, either, because Genevieve could read her mind, and that suited Marla, too. "You've brought people back from the dead before—Mr. Zealand, and St. John Austen."

Genevieve widened her remarkable eyes. "Not *really*, Marla. People I know very well—people whose *minds* I know well—I can create constructs of them. But it's not really them, you know. Not exactly."

"They can think, they believe themselves to be real, and that's good enough for me," Marla said stubbornly.

"They can't even leave my palace, Marla. They don't have enough reality to survive in the world outside."

"Better that B live here, where I can visit him, than live nowhere."

Genevieve shook her head. "I never even met him. I couldn't possibly—"

"He lives in *my* mind, Genevieve. Can't you get into my mind and find all you need? You can have full access, with my blessing, ransack my memories, drag it out of me, do whatever you have to—"

"Marla, I *can't*. It would be like making a photocopy of a photocopy, don't you see? He might *look* like B, but inside he would…all wrong. Full of blank spaces, and worse yet, places I'd filled in with my best guesses. He wouldn't be your friend. He wouldn't even be a…a *picture* of your friend. He would be a shadow puppet. An abomination."

Marla crossed her arms. "You won't do it?"

"If you ask me to, I will." She shuddered. "Are you asking me to?"

Marla remained tense for a moment, then slumped. "It really wouldn't be any good?"

"No. It would be bad. I'm so sorry, Marla. I wish—"

"Don't worry about it. Give Zealand and St. John Austen my love. Could you send me home now?"

Marla spent the next day curled up on the futon in her living room, staring at the ceiling, and thinking. She'd killed a god, once. She'd successfully invaded the underworld. She'd bested the creature who claimed to be the king of the elves, in a duel. She'd saved her city more times than she could count on her fingers. Surely, surely, she could do something about *this*.

* * *

She thought of a way. *It might destroy me,* she thought. *It might even destroy the* universe. *But what the hell. Nothing ventured, right?*

Rondeau opened the door, expecting an orderly with a lunch tray. He was staying in a musty little cottage on the grounds of the Blackwing Institute. The cottage had belonged to the groundskeeper, back when the Institute was a mansion, and Dr. Husch was letting him stay there for as long as he needed.

Marla was on the doorstep. "Shit," she said. "You look like *you* again."

He couldn't look her in the eyes. That was no surprise. He couldn't even stand to look at himself in the mirror. Staring at her green boots, he said, "It seemed like the thing to do."

"But you're still in B's body, under that glamour. And Hamil says you probably have his powers."

"I...think I do. I can see things, things I couldn't before—ghosts, I think...and weirder stuff."

"You can summon oracles? Open paths where there are no paths?"

"I don't know, Marla. If you need me to, of course, I'll try."

"Great. Get your shit. We're catching a plane out west."

Rondeau blinked. "Where are we going?"

She looked at him with scorn and contempt. "To fix what you *did,* if we can." Her expression softened. "To fix what *we* did." She turned and started walking across the vast green grounds, then called back, over her shoulder: "To bring B back to life."

Rondeau took a step outside the door. "You found a way? You really found a way?"

But Marla didn't answer. *She doesn't need to,* Rondeau thought. Marla always found a way. No matter what it cost.

ACKNOWLEDGMENTS

Thanks go first to my loving spouse, H. L. Shaw, for infinite quantities of support, for acting as a sounding board, and for being my biggest fan. I received invaluable feedback, friendship, moral support, and/or all of the above from Greg van Eekhout, Susan Marie Groppi, Michael Jasper, Jay Lake, David Moles, Cameron Panee, Lynne Raschke, Jenn Reese, Anne Rodman, and Scott Seagroves.

My editor, Juliet Ulman, supported the crazy ideas I had for this book, and wouldn't let me get away with being lazy or taking the easy way out. As always, my agent, Ginger Clark, made sure everything ran smoothly; film rights agent extraordinaire Holly Frederick made some wonderfully unexpected things happen; my copy editor, Pam Feinstein, saved me from the tiger pits of continuity errors and logical gaffes; and my cover artist, Daniel Dos Santos, wrapped it all up in a gorgeous package.

As a longtime fan of caper movies and books about

grifters, I can't possibly mention everything that influenced this book, but I'll hit a few of the major works I discovered or revisited in the course of my research. In film and TV, the con artist movies of David Mamet, *The Sting,* and *Hustle* all loom large; in print, I leaned heavily on *The Big Con* by David W. Maurer and *How to Cheat at Everything* by Simon Lovell. I found Toni Howard's account of the *Bonbonne D'Uranium!*—which inspired Jason's long con—in *Grand Deception,* edited by Alexander Klein.

Finally, I'd like to thank my son, River Alexander Pratt Shaw. I wrote this book during the first six months of his life—and the best six months, so far, of my own.

ABOUT THE AUTHOR

T. A. Pratt lives in Oakland, California, with partner H. L. Shaw and their son, and works as a senior editor for a trade publishing magazine. Learn more about your favorite slightly wicked sorcerer at www.MarlaMason.net.